WELCOME BACK, JACK

WELCOME BACK, JACK

LIAM SWEENY

Published By

American
Apocrypha Press

WELCOME BACK, JACK

Book and cover design by Cory Freeman

Printed in the United States of America

The Troy Book Makers • Troy, New York • thetroybookmakers.com

Published by American Apocrypha Press

To order additional copies of this title, contact your favorite local bookstore or visit www.tbmbooks.com

ISBN: 978-0-9897014-0-2

Library of Congress Control Number: 2013948242

For Dad, who needed something good to read.

CHAPTER ONE

'Black earth crunched beneath his feet as he walked down the husk of the once vibrant street. He stared around at the void and swore it was staring back at him. Clinging low to the ground, black vapors twisted to and fro, inky tendrils crawling over his sneakers. He saw the house, pristine in the middle of ruin; his stolen-childhood home.

'He was six years old back then. It was three in the morning and his parents were two doors down. He hid under the bed when he heard the sounds of his mom and dad screaming, wood splintering, glass shattering.

He pissed the floor and shit his pajamas, didn't move until the big cop with the big gun called out to him the next morning. Had he been the cop, carrying him out wrapped up in a blanket, he would have known that there was too much blood smeared all over the walls for his parents to still be alive.

That day, he became the man of the house of horrors.'

'And here he was again, in this hell-home. And standing at the gate was the man on the porch, arms folded, streaked in blood ...'

It was three a.m. Jack Taggart fumbled for a match as his fingers trembled in the frigid late November air. He had a Zippo that Mary had given him, but he never had the time to get fluid for it.

The smell of a burnt match replaced the smell of hot coffee he'd had to sacrifice that morning. He took a whiff of the matchstick, grunted and tossed it to the curb.

Third nightmare he had in a week. For once, he was glad to get the wake-up call.

Gamble was late, as usual these days. His wife wasn't like Mary. When Jack's phone rang in the middle of the night, Mary'd push him off the bed if she had to. She always had fresh clothes laid out for him on the chair in the bedroom before she turned in for the night.

Gamble's wife was in love with a man in a uniform (not that Gamble wore one,) but she wasn't in love with being on-call herself. Plus, He became a new dad six months ago. Jack had a kid too, but Paul was fourteen.

"It's a mess in there, Jack," said Jeff Mitchell, the responding officer who secured the crime scene.

"The evidence techs were already in processing the house. You guys are okay to go in. The M.E.'s still in there, plus a couple techs vacuuming for fibers."

Jack took a deep drag of his smoke, feeling the kick of cold carcinogens tickle the depths of his lungs; he trailed his exhale with a cough. 'Gotta quit these fucking things'.

"Whatta we got in there? I barely got anything in the call."

Mitchell scratched his neck and folded his arms. "9-1-1 got the call about an hour ago," he said. "I heard he knew the dispatcher's name; just like the other two."

Mitchell flipped out his notepad. "Three victims, a whole family; father, mother and daughter, it looks like. The father took one in the head; the other two … not so lucky."

"Thanks, Mitch" Jack said as he started up the stairs.

"You might want Vicks for your nose. Everyone's been asking for it. It's bad, Jack."

Jack poked his head in the doorway. It was rank with decomposition.

"Nah," Jack said as he walked back down. "Don't think it'll help."

"Suit yourself."

Just then he saw Gamble walking toward him, the patrol lights catching his tight, curly hair and his wrinkled, disheveled clothes. Jack stifled a laugh with a grunt, ever thankful for Mary.

"Sorry," Gamble said, "Sarah was up with the baby. And get this; she's rockin' the baby, the kids screamin' so she brings him into our room and slams into the bed each time she hits the swing!"

Jack finally could chuckle. "How's it feel being double-on-call?"

"Shoot me,"

Jack grabbed Gamble around the neck by the arm.

"Hold off on that till we get done with this." He said jokingly as he flipped his cigarette down into the storm drain. "It's probably you-know-who … I haven't been in yet. Techs gave us the go-ahead."

"Let's get to work, then." Gamble started up the steps to the aged brownstone like he was wearing concrete shoes. Jack was right behind him. A crowd had gathered around Fourth Street, busybodies wearing pajamas and overstuffed jackets. Even the kids were out. Jack wondered if any of them would bring in a lead.

Jack scanned the crowd, tried to catalog each face, but the light wasn't good. Maybe the killer was watching the response, and Jack would see a face come up in the investigation he'd recognize.

The floodlights poured out the open door, revealing tape, empty body-bags, and the vacuum running across the edges of the living room carpet.

A portly man, near bald except for the sides, wearing a dirt-streaked cardigan, was sitting in a recliner, calm-looking. Serene; more like posed. He was staring blankly ahead, eyes glazed over and frozen by the hole in his forehead. Maybe a .38 Caliber, by the look of the entrance wound.

Jack donned a pair of gloves and picked up a framed picture from the stand by the chair. They were in the mountains, the Adirondacks, maybe.

They had back-packs and walking sticks, and they must have been high up, judging by the view in the background. The father had them bunched up in his arms, and they were all smiling.

The youngest, the daughter, had an exhilarated look on her face; her eyes lit up and her cheeks flushed. Jack flipped the picture over, popped out the back. On the bottom, *Kyla's B-Day!* written in blue pen.

"They looked happy. Man, this guy's an asshole..." Gamble said. Jack didn't notice him looking over his shoulder.

"She's about Paul's age in this pic." Jack said.

"It's a damn shame. Come over here, check this out."

Gamble led him to an office area in the living room, just a desk with a laptop and papers at odd angles covering every surface.

Gamble picked up a stack of papers and rifled through them. "What the hell did these people do to deserve this?" he said. "There's receipts from Second Chance, Helping Hands of New Rhodes, the Red Cross, Salvation Army... this was a decent family."

Jack scanned through pages, receipts and placed them back on the desk gently.

"Yeah, how did *they* end up like *this*?" Jack said. "What's the victimology here?"

"I don't know, but we'd best get into the kitchen. They want to bag the father."

"Don Mason."

"What?"

"That's his name. Don Mason. His wife is Sheila, and the daughter's Kyla."

"Yeah, sorry…" Gamble said, "I knew that. This past day's been a nightmare."

As they soon discovered, the real nightmare was in the kitchen.

The two women; he'd have to say "women" because of their hair length and bone structure – that's what little could be discerned from what he saw. There were no clothes, no *skin* below the hair-lines … it was like the anatomy pictures of the muscular system he'd seen in science class.

Precise, clinical … and damn near sterile; no pools of blood. There *had* to be pools of blood, but there weren't, just muscle fibers, milky-white tendons and sinew, crisscrossed with faded blue veins and a cloudy patina of something slick coating the bodies. Gamble groaned in disgust.

"He had time, twisted fuck …" Jack nodded.

"Go check the living room again; check the back wall behind the recliner, see if he was even shot here."

Gamble went into the living room. Jack grabbed one of the techs.

"Did you spray in here for fluids?"

"Our first stop," the tech told him. "Found just a little pooling underneath the bodies, on the table from where they were … umm …"

"Posed,"

"Yeah, but other than that, there should be more blood. A lot more."

"Is the M.E. still out there?"

The tech pointed toward the living room. "Your partner's talking to him now. He's been in here already to get time of death."

"Thanks." Jack looked at the scene, closely examining everything. The bodies were sitting upright at the table; they must have been posed and held until rigor set in. In another few hours, the bodies would have lost rigidity and collapsed, sliding off the chairs.

The smell was overpowering; he regretted not getting some Vick's. There was a dinner-plate in front of each body, with silverware laid out. Their elbows were on the table, hands cupping the edges of the plates like a macabre suppertime scene.

Jack couldn't pin it to the other murders by the crime scenes, but the call to 9-1-1 linked these cases, and he knew what that meant.

The South End Killer, as the neighborhood was calling him by then, had killed three people before this, in two separate incidents. His M.O. was erratic; his only calling card was the fact that he knew the name of every dispatcher he talked to when he phoned in.

They'd limited the suspect pool to thirty possible people who would know names. None of them seemed a likely monster. And the Feds were knocking on the door.

"The M.E. said they've been dead for more than twenty-four hours," Gamble said. "I also talked to the upstairs neighbor. She told me the daughter was a loudmouth, her words, but she hadn't heard her over the weekend.

"She said she didn't hear any other voices or anything. And the wall behind the husband's head was clean. He wasn't shot here."

"They're in rigor in the kitchen," Jack said, "Rigor peaks at twelve. They should be out of rigor by now."

"This has got to be him."

"I'd bet on it," Jack replied, "but the other murders he could've done by himself. Not this one.

"How would he get all three bodies in here, assuming he did his ... *carving* ... elsewhere, without anyone noticing anything?"

"Yeah, this is a nosy neighborhood," Gamble said. "I worked Patrol in the South Substation part-time. Before I got this cozy gig.

"So what do we want to tell the Captain?"

Jack walked outside, tapped a fresh cigarette on his pack and got the match to light the first time. He lit up more to kill the smell still in his nose.

"I don't think we'll have to tell him much. Harken said if he struck again, we'd have a task force. So my bet is to head back to the station."

"Sarah's gonna kill me,"

"Better her than him," Jack joked as he walked toward his car. "See ya there, Eddie."

Jack took off on Fourth Street. Ginny's Diner was open, with a full complement of endless coffee. But as much as he'd have liked to stop in, get some breakfast and chat with the old-timers, he wouldn't know what to say.

The sun was coming up, casting long shadows across the South End. It was originally a neighborhood separated by two groups; the Italians who live in northern South End, and the Irish, who lived in the southern part. The canal split the two.

Back in the city's hey-day, they all worked factory jobs and lived factory lives in brick row-houses with rooms barely the size of a walk-in closet.

They were the expendable ones, and, though the nationalities had changed, the stink of desperation clung to the garbage strewn streets like mold.

The hill mercifully kept the rays out of his eyes. They were bloodshot, though he got sleep. He figured seeing the South End Killer's handiwork had taken the dial back on a few of those hours. Plus, the nightmare...

He hoped they had endless coffee and at least something digestible at the station.

Jack and Gamble walked into the briefing room, which by that time had already become the *de facto* headquarters of the task force. The room would fill quickly, with the County Sheriff's Office, State Police and, by the look of the three suits in the corner, the FBI.

On a normal day, the briefing room could fit thirty people; it had a slide out cabinet full of folding chairs. But today they had a big table in the center of it, with organized stacks of paper, like a chow line for information and flow charts.

Jack patted Gamble's shoulder. They each grabbed a muffin and coffee from the collapsible table on the side wall, underneath the whiteboard.

Hanging from the opposite wall was a tapestry of the victims, and Captain Harken was just pinning up crime scene photos from the Masons' apartment. They'd be adding more once the evidence (or lack thereof) was processed.

Harken was their boss. He was a bear of a man; bushy brows, salt-and-pepper moustache sporting perpetual stubble on his chin. He was the kind of guy to blow off steam by spending a weekend in the deep woods with nothing but a sub-zero tent, a twenty-gauge shotgun, knife, WWII can opener and if he felt indulgent, a couple packs of cigars. He glanced at the two of them and motioned them over.

"Sorry to start without you boys," he said, "I assume you know everybody from the Sheriff's department, and that big black guy over there is Commander Teague from the State Police." He tipped his head in their direction. Jack and Gamble nodded.

"The suits are Special Agents Haskell and Decker from the field office in Albany. Right now, it's a joint command. We hope to keep it that way."

Harken gathered everyone around the table and made formal introductions. Then he started the brief.

"Okay, so last night … we can definitively call this a serial murder case. The neighborhood's calling him the 'South End Killer,' so for now, we'll go with that. Is everyone in agreement?" Grunts and nods.

Harken moved to the victim-board with a speed Jack hadn't seen during his time on the force. The coffee must've been open-tap earlier.

"What do we know?" Harken said. He pulled out a pointer and aimed it at the tapestry on the first victim.

"Leiah Marcusen." He swept the pointer along her autopsy picture. "Chase, Malloy … you caught this one. You walk us through it."

"Sure thing," Malloy said. He fished his notepad from his inside coat pocket. "Dispatch got the call at nine-thirty-two on Friday, October twenty-sixth. Caller greeted the dispatcher by name, and quickly gave the location and admitted to killing the victim."

"Her throat was slashed; her carotid was cut clean across. The M.E. stated that exsanguination would've occurred within a minute,"

Chase picked up where Malloy left off. "The body was sexually mutilated," he said, "her breasts were removed with a surgical instrument, but that appears to have been done post-mortem.

"Victim was tied to the bed in four point restraints, the type used in hospitals and psychiatric units. Rose petals were placed over her breast area to cover the mutilation, or perhaps for another purpose."

Malloy walked over to the table. "No discernible trace evidence was left at the scene, but there was blood. As far as we know right now, all of the blood was the victim's," he said.

"We didn't get any reports of suspicious activity, no leads from our canvass that panned out. But it's early yet."

Harken nodded to one of the suits. "Special Agent Decker has been assisting with the calls we've received at dispatch. Special Agent?"

Special Agent Decker, a gaunt, stark man, spoke up. "We've analyzed the calls to dispatch," he said.

"First, we looked at where they came from, but it was a dead end. Internet call, routed all over the world, probably. We're limited in the fact that this isn't national security.

"We also determined that the caller was using a voice synthesizer. We can crack it, but we need a voice to compare it to."

"Okay," Harken said, "let's move on to victim number two. Taggart and Gamble, you caught that one, and the one this morning. Can you give us a brief on what you found from the second case?"

Jack looked over to Gamble, who'd done most of the leg-work on that case.

"There were two victims on the second case," Gamble said. "John Ramos, twenty-nine, shot in the chest, point-blank with a medium-caliber bullet, not recovered. The second victim, Maria Ramos, thirty-two, was found in the kitchen, burnt alive, as established by the M.E., no evidence of a fire, no trace evidence, no blood, no strange prints, nothing. Nada."

"We received the same call to dispatch, same system, nothing different from the first victim," Special Agent Decker added.

Harken planted his hands on the table, shuffled some papers about.

"Okay," he said, "before we look at last night's crime scene, Special Agent Haskell would like to develop a preliminary profile of the suspect and see, based on last night's incident, whether it needs to be adjusted."

Special Agent Haskell was in his mid-sixties, with grey hair lining the sides of his head and wispy, darker hair up top. He was dressed in FBI black, but his suit fit him poorly.

His clothes reminded Jack of Gamble after a night of diaper-duty.

"For starters," Haskell said, "we're in a position where we can't rule anything out, especially the possibility that the killer isn't acting alone."

"Each crime, just looking at the first two, look for all intents and purposes like they were separate incidents. The linking element was the phone calls to dispatch, which were unnecessary calls to make.

"And that's a clue," Haskell said. "He, or they, are playing with us. They're tying their crimes together, they're putting themselves on our radar. But if that's the only connection we can find. All they have to do is stop calling.

"We need to find other commonalities, and the killer, or killers, don't seem to leave any." Haskell cleared his throat.

"We're looking for someone, at least one of them, that's intelligent, probably has some medical or forensic training. He is meticulous, and is someone who doesn't attract attention in the neighborhood."

Haskell continued. "He has no specific M.O. other than the calls, which aren't an M.O, but a signature. Assuming he's one killer, he's confident. He's likely killed before, here or elsewhere. Aside from living in the South End, the victims had no noticeable connection.

"He does appear to do more work on the women; Mr. Ramos was shot quickly in the chest, while Maria Ramos was likely tortured. Yet with the first victim, Leiah Marcusen – her death was quick, and mutilation occurred post-mortem.

"This guy could change tactics, stop calling dispatch, move from the South End. If he's killing where he's comfortable, or if the South End has a meaning to him, we have a better shot at stopping him."

Harken thanked Haskell as he sat down.

"Before we move on to what happened last night, I just want to say …" Harken looked back at the victim board, "we need something, because right now, we're chasing a ghost."

Larry Hershey, the county Medical Examiner, was the last person you'd expect to see squirreled away in a sterile white crypt. He reminded Jack of a picture of Ernest Hemingway he'd seen at a bar with James Cagney. The kind of guy with a superhero chin you'd expect to find looking out over the top of Mount Kilimanjaro with the ridge of his hand over his eyes to block the sun. Instead, he peered over Kyla's corpse with a headband magnifier.

"This is, by far, the worst thing I've ever seen, Jack." He said. "Kinda' wish I worked in Albany County."

"It was worse when they were in rigor."

"I know... I was there, remember?"

"Long day, Larry..." Jack said. "So do we have a cause of death that's *not* obvious?"

Larry took his gloves off, walked over to the side cabinet and slapped on a new pair.

"It's very hard to say." He said. "I've taken a liver sample for tox, but I won't know anything until that gets back. And without the skin... No surface indicators."

Gamble walked over to Don Mason's table.

"They weren't killed in the house." Gamble said. "I mean, if they were, it would've been poison, right? Would something like chloroform show up on the tox screen?"

"I had them test for phosgene; that's what chloroform breaks down to. But I doubt it was chloroform. Enough to knock someone out is usually enough to kill them, and that much – we would have smelled it."

"I don't know what it smells like." Jack said.

"I do." Larry replied. "And I didn't smell it."

"Larry, how come there wasn't any blood? Did the killer drain them or something?"

Larry walked down to Kyla's legs.

"Actually, yes." He aimed the magnifier at the inside of her thigh, using a pair of tongs to separate the muscle tissue.

"Whoever did this split the femoral artery..." He said. "Lengthwise. They would've drained out in a minute. Mr. Mason had the incision too; that's how I noticed it. So I just looked for it with these two."

"You're looking for something like ether as your 'knock out juice'; they wouldn't have drained if they were already dead."

Jack paced the floor, arms folded. Gamble was by Larry's side, looking through the magnifying glass as Larry threw words around like 'perimortem' and 'hemorrhage' but Jack just kept staring at the skinned bodies, still slick with that glossy patina.

"Larry, what's that... *film*... coating the bodies?"

"That's blood plasma." Larry said. "It's mostly clear, and what little red bloods cells are in it blend with the muscle tissue."

"What kind of person can *do* this?"

"A sick individual." Larry said. "But I'm guessing more than one sick individuals."

No, I mean, what kind of person can pull this," he pointed to Kyla's body, "off?"

"Not an amateur." Larry said. "This person has medical training. They're not squeamish; a lot of work went into this. They knew to split the femoral artery, and I've scanned every area of these bodies." He shrugged. "It's perfect. No dermis left behind, no gouges into the muscle fibers..."

"So we're looking for a doctor, or a paramedic?"

"Not a paramedic." Larry said. "They don't have experience cutting up bodies. And most doctors don't have that experience either. Not that removing a person's skin is a procedure *anybody* has experience with. Maybe a plastic surgeon, but that's a stretch..."

"This person's worked with bodies before. I'd look for a surgeon, or a butcher, even."

"Whoever did this," Larry added, "*Whomever* did this; it isn't their first time to the rodeo."

After a long day examining the third case – the pattern, the differences, the adjustments to the profile – and the depressing knowledge that such a monster was prowling the city, Jack and Gamble decided to top off the night at Emerald's, a cop bar in Irish-Town.

Harken had given them both the next day off. Jack agreed to meet Eddie there after he dropped off some groceries.

He walked in and threw his coat on the back rack. Walter poured him a Jameson's and gave a nod. Most days, Jack would have a bit of chat with him; the weather, politics, the usual bullshit.

Walter was retired from the force, and knew Jack like a son. Jack could see the worry in his wrinkles as he slid the glass over. He fished in his pocket, but Walter waved him off. Always did.

"Eddie's on the Grotto, Jack," he said.

"Thanks, Walt." Jack picked up the glass and walked out onto the Grotto through a stucco walkway that spilled out into a deck. The deck hung from the side wall of the building. It was open air; the wall of the building had a D.B. Hardware sign painted up top; an ad from the turn of the century that had barely weathered; the deck had a wrought iron railing and a row of glass tables overlooking the canal below. A ring of ice crept along the edges of the flowing water.

"Hey, Jack ..." Gamble was sipping on a *Pride of Eire*, an ale Walter special-ordered for him.

"Does that swill get better in the cold?" Jack pulled out a chair and set his whiskey down. Gamble laughed.

"I like it at any temp," Gamble said, "Even piss warm."

"So, all go well with Sarah?"

Gamble shrugged. "I don't know what the fuck crawled up her ass this past month, man." He said. "She just told me Pantheon called back about my resume!"

"Pantheon? The data-mining company?"

"Yeah, that's the one."

"I didn't know you were looking for work." Jack said.

"Me neither."

"So, wait; you mean..."

"She sent it to them!"

"Why on earth would she do that?"

"'Cause, and I quote, 'A cop's salary can't give my baby what he needs.'"

Jack laughed. Eddie jabbed him in the arm.

"I'm serious, dickhead! What the hell am I supposed to do with that?"

Jack took sip of his whiskey to regain his composure.

"Ed, you have a kid with her; you're married." He said. "You just gotta' work through it. I mean, she needs a reality check, no doubt, but you got to be the one to give it to her."

"I was hoping you could ask Mary to do it..."

Jack backed away from the table. "Oh hell no! Mary wouldn't touch that with gloves on."

"You guys seem fine, though."

Jack leaned forward.

"Mary comes from a cop family." He said. "Her dad's a cop, Tony's a cop and so is her other brother Mark. She knew what to expect when she married me."

Gamble stretched and cracked his knuckles. "Sorry, man. Today's just been a train wreck. I'm glad we've got tomorrow off."

He looked at Jack. "So how are you holdin up?"

"You know why Harken gave us a day off, right?"

"No, don't even go there ..."

"You don't think he'd want us on this twenty-four-seven?"

"We told them everything we knew," Gamble said. "The big-wigs need at least a day to make graphs and charts and bureaucratic dinner invitations. *That* could take all day tomorrow!"

"I don't know, man ..." Jack sipped his whiskey, and the numbness waltzed by his tonsils before doing the tango in his gut.

"We should be canvassing, getting leads..."

"I know you want to get this guy, and fast, but ..." Gamble looked around, "...nothin' to say we can't spitball some theories here, right?"

"Thought you came here to avoid talking shop?"

"Yeah, normally, but I'm not too keen on being benched, either."

"Thought you said you were glad to have tomorrow off?"

"Just realized I'll have to spend it with Sarah."

The cold winter breeze blew through the hollow of the Grotto, spinning a leaf across the table in a whirlwind.

"How?" Jack said. "How did he do it?"

"Which one?"

"Last night's 'one'," Jack reached in his shirt pocket for his half-kicked pack.

"Okay, we know two things ..." He said. "One thing; he had to abduct them all, so how? What kind of drug? How could it be administered to all three of them?"

"We'll know that when tox' comes back," Gamble replied.

"So there's the father, who had to be subdued, because he wasn't shot there. Could he have been a hostage to get the mother and daughter to comply?"

"Possible," Gamble tilted his bottle skyward and took a big gulp. "But how could he subdue the other two if he's holding onto Dad?"

"He could've tied him up."

"I looked at his body," Gamble said. "There would've been restraint marks."

"Okay, so that's one unanswered question. But however he got them to leave; willingly, unwillingly, knocked out – he had to get all three out of the house." Jack said, his eyes fixed on the water below. "He'd need a van or a truck to hide what he was doing, and nobody we interviewed mentioned any cars there. There's a Handicapped Parking sign right in the space in front of the house; the neighbors would've noticed that."

"Think he could have brought them out back?" asked Gamble. "That backyard empties out into Saint Mike's. Maybe he's got a mausoleum that he popped the lock on."

Jack took out his Zippo and started flipping it open and shut. "Leiah Marcusen lived on First Street, and there's no back alley between Front street and First." He said. "So he had to kill her there. So that kind of makes sense. But even if he can kill Marcusen, get out, and then kill the Ramos's and the Mason's, he had to bring those bodies back in himself."

"Maybe not," Gamble said. "If we're looking at two suspects; C'mon, Jack – everyone's thinking it's a team here."

"That's the only thing that make much sense in light of last night. But the mechanics of all this is … something's wrong, you know? Something's missing"

"Yeah, it doesn't make much sense …" Gamble said. "So okay, then…we take the mutilation angle." He killed his beer. "So many fuckin' angles …"

"Maybe we should look at the two things that tie the cases," Jack said. "The South End, and the dispatch calls."

Walter came out to refresh the drinks.

"Any food?" he asked. "I got Ralphie in the kitchen."

"No thanks, Walt,"

"Am I interrupting?"

"Nah," Jack replied, "We're just going over the cases."

"You were born and raised in this neighborhood, Walt," Gamble said. "Got a minute?"

Walter sat down. He looked over his shoulder. "Yeah, sure... bar's dead; Ralphie can handle it."

"I didn't want to pitch my two pennies in on this one un-asked, but I can't stand it. It's my turf," Walter lit up a cigarette. "Jack ... do you mind the intrusion?"

"No, Walt. I'll never mind. So what's your take?"

"Boone Park," he said.

"Boone Park? That's barely even a park," Jack replied.

"You're right," Walter took a drag, "but everyone in South End has to walk by it at some point or another.

"If you were trying to find a vantage point to select victims, you'd go to Boone Park. And you wouldn't be the kind of person to stand out."

Walter continued. "I heard they can't find a link between the victims, and I'm not saying that Boone Park is it, but two of the buildings were on Fourth Street, with back yards bordering on the eastern slope of Boone."

"Isn't that St. Mike's cemetery right there?" Jack asked.

"Nah; well, yes it is, but it used to be Boone." Walter said. "There's supposedly; and I say *supposedly*... an old tunnel that went under Fourth, an old railroad tunnel from back in the days when Miller's Creek actually had water-wheels on it."

"Tunnel?" asked Jack. "I never knew there was a tunnel there … where is it, exactly?"

"It's buried, I guess," Walter said. "Been that way since the mid-eighteen-hundreds. I heard it went from an old meat-packing plant on the river to midway up St. Mike's … where it used to be Boone.

"And it supposedly had a south-jet off under Fourth to the old port because the roads were shit back then. I don't know much more."

"How did you find out about it?" asked Gamble. "I never heard of it…"

"We used to live on Fourth, just by Grant Street, when I was a little spit" Walt said. "She'd tell us as kids that if we didn't quit whatever it was we weren't supposed to be doing, the tunnel monster would get us."

"It was the boogey-man, and in the day time, when we were brave, we'd take sharpened sticks around the nooks and crannies of the South End, trying to find the gate to the monster's lair. Of course, it was all silliness back then…"

"But if it did exist, the plans would be in the City Planner's office," Gamble said.

"Maybe … if they weren't destroyed. There was the fire in 1921. City Hall got leveled."

"I got a patron, comes in here sometimes, works at the Historical Society," Walter said. "He may be able to narrow it down; he's been looking for it for some time now.

"Name's Ed Mansfield. He should be there tomorrow. Just tell him I sent you." Walter turned his head as the sound of a small crowd in the bar reached his ears.

"Thanks, Walt," Jack said.

Walter smiled as he grabbed the towel from his shoulder and tugged at his apron.

"Happy hunting."

Back home, Jack stared at himself in the mirror after chasing two aspirins with a Dixie cup of tepid water. He had bags, dark and foreboding. He needed sleep, and bad.

Maybe his day off was good after all.

He hadn't shaved in a few days. He ran his hands through his hair, spun the faucet and cupped some water in his palm to splash on his face.

He hated the migraines. Mary snuck up behind him, slid her arm across his chest, her other hand picking at tufts of upright hair.

"Are you okay, Jack?" she said.

"Yeah, it's just another migraine ..." Jack started, but Mary cut him off.

"I mean about this case."

Jack spun around to give her a tight hug. "I'm okay about this, Mary," he said, "I'm just tired, that's all."

"You know you can talk to me, right?"

"Yeah, Mary ... I know ..."

"I'm serious, Jack," she said. "I'm not just a cop's wife ..."

"I know," Jack said. "I'm glad I'm not Gamble, believe me ..."

Mary laughed. Her laughs and giggles were mating calls to the butterflies in his gut. "I feel sorry for that man."

"She sent his resume to Pantheon."

"Why didn't you tell me he was looking for another job?"

"I didn't know... Neither did he!"

Mary covered her mouth. "She didn't!"

This time Jack laughed.

"She did! Oh my God! He has to be livid!"

"She says she can't live off a cop's money. I told him he needed to control his woman," Jack cleared his throat, "No offense..."

"None taken. So what did he say?"

Jack snickered. "He asked if you could do it."

"Oh, no... I wouldn't touch that wearing-,"

"...gloves; yeah, I said that to him."

"She didn't know what she was getting into when she married him though, you have to admit that."

"I'll admit to that ... You should've seen him last night; he looked like shit, and I don't mean the wake-up call either."

"I'm sure they fought."

"Probably," Jack said. "Where's Paul? Did you guys eat dinner already?"

"Umm, yeah, Jack. It's eight-thirty. I saved some for you, if you didn't fill up on donuts at the station."

"Ha-ha ... comedian," Jack said. "And it was muffins."

So, kid gloves

Jack lay awake for two hours, running variables in his head, like a reality-chess game. His adoptive-father was a grandmaster, played in international tournaments. Even Jack almost won a tournament in London when he was sixteen.

Papa Taggart once wanted him to follow in his footsteps, but it never went that way. Still, sometimes he played by himself, against himself, when the station was dead, or he was stumped on a case.

So he played with the variables, but he kept running into the possibility of a tunnel.

It was important, it had to be. Someone who could find it would have access to the two crime scenes where they could've brought bodies in through the back.

And short of the man he'd meet tomorrow, the only people who might know where it was would be people who lived in the South End. But did it really exist?

Jack had a growing unease. Even with a possible lead, and going through all of the unknowns, there was still something important missing ... he just couldn't place it. He kept making moves and counter-moves until he fell asleep.

'...Jack was running as the blackened earth slipped out from under him. He was going nowhere, the monster gaining on him. All Jack could do was think its name, as if he could use the words to ward it off:

Clyde Coleman, Clyde Coleman, Clyde Coleman ...

Jack ran, and as he did, he grew up, watching his life move on a reel-to-reel. His childhood, his awkward high-school years, the school full of bullies, and the times he spent alone, the odd kid, the one without his real family.

Then he saw his college years, the blur of them anyway, and Mary and marriage and the police academy. It wasn't long before he had a gun in his holster, and he pulled it and spun around to face his pursuer, the man who made his nightmares, who took so much from his waking world ...

But all he saw was his own reflection in a silvery sheen.'

Jack waited in the lobby of the New Rhodes Historical Society. The room was a museum of photographs encased in translucent plastic boxes.

In the mid-to-late eighteen-hundreds, New Rhodes was a center of industry for the whole nation.

It was the first "steel capital" before that distinction went to Pittsburgh. It had thriving steel and textile mills, a flourishing panorama of Victorian architecture, canals, trolleys, and was one of the first cities to have electricity.

Jack got up and walked around, glancing at handlebar mustaches and top hats, flowing dresses, and a city that rose and fell with the American dream.

He had to lament that New Rhodes had been reduced to a new panorama; of baggies, heroin needles and gang signs spray-painted on the walls of time-battered bodegas.

Sure, there was an artistic revival, but … he didn't get called to those neighborhoods much.

Dr. Edward Mansfield was a broad, stout man with a brown felt fedora covering his grey-white hair. He had wire-rimmed glasses that he slid up his nose as he walked over to greet Jack. He extended his hand; strong grasp, not what Jack would've expected from a man who, he guessed, couldn't be younger than seventy.

"Thank you for seeing me, Dr. Mansfield," Jack said, "I appreciate it."

"Not a problem … Jack, right?" Jack nodded. "Call me Ed."

They walked through a hallway with more simply-framed pictures, until Ed opened the door to his office.

The peach walls of his office bore shelves decorated with trinkets; gaskets, gears, rusty pieces of machinery from a long-begotten era.

There were old maps on the wall near the window; one looked like it was a topographical map of New Rhodes before there were any real buildings on it.

"1789," Ed said. "It's a reproduction, of course; the real one is in the gallery."

"Hard to believe ..." Jack commented.

"Indeed, there was a time when this was mostly farmland," Ed said. "Didn't last long, I'm afraid. The soil's poor here. The bedrock is too near the surface. I don't know if you've ever noticed that the city, the flat part, you know, doesn't have many large trees."

"I never noticed," Jack said, "but I never really looked."

"Few people do. But that's another story. Walter told me that you were inquiring about a tunnel?"

Jack took a deep breath.

"Walter said that there may be a tunnel between Boone Park in the South End and Saint Michael's cemetery on the hill. Is there any truth to that?"

"Well," Ed leaned back in his chair, glanced out the window, "Possibly... no; *probably*." He hunched over, propped his elbows on the desk and interlaced his fingers.

"What I said about the bedrock being so close to the surface," He said, "bad for farming, but great for building tunnels."

Ed cleared his throat.

"The boom in New Rhodes during the industrial revolution hinged on two things: the creeks that run down the hill from the mountains, and the Hudson River. The original factories used water-wheels to power them." He said.

"The east side of New Rhodes is residential now, but that's where all the factories were. As you know, there are three creeks that run through New Rhodes, and the roads, back then; I mean, the mid-to-late eighteen hundreds, the roads were made for horses, not cars.

"Getting products from the factories to the river was easier to accomplish by making underground tunnels. Gravity brought the goods to the river on small railroad cars, and then they'd hook the cars to the water-wheels to bring them back up."

"So the tunnel does exist," Jack said.

"I don't doubt it," Ed said. "Many of them. I've been on a hunt to find them for years. I was a city planner from '62 to '82."

"Don't you have, or wouldn't you have had, a map?"

"Sadly, no." Ed replied. "During the fire of 1921, the old City Hall burned, along with the records' storage office. The new electric and gas grids were the primary things to re-map, so they didn't pay much attention to the old tunnels.

"They would've been out of use by that time, anyway. Once every so often a tunnel's discovered, one or two, small sections, you know. They get filled in, barely ever make the news. I've heard stories, tried to track them down …"

Ed chuckled. "I've been known to hunt through the bushes with a hard-hat and a head-lamp, but there's really no record. Even when I was a city planner, they were little more than a rumor."

"But, if, like Walter said, there was a tunnel between an old meat-packing plant on First Street and St. Mike's, where would be a good place to look?"

"The only meat-packing plant in the South End was built in 1920, if it's the one I'm thinking of," he said.

"So the tunnel wouldn't have been in it. But it might be near it if there was an older plant, maybe?" He put his index finger to his lips.

"Back then, most of First Street was a wharf. A tunnel could be anywhere in the South End. Again, the fire took out a lot of records…"

"I understand." Jack said. "But wouldn't a tunnel have to be near one of the creeks?"

"Not necessarily. The factories were large; they could use horses to carry their goods across the face of the hill, so those tunnels would be wherever they put them."

He got up, walked around to the side of his office with all of the trinkets, picked up a gear. "With gears, shafts and pulleys, they could pull the carts up from pretty much anywhere."

"So, you have no direct knowledge of any tunnel running through Boone Park and St. Mike's?"

"No, but I've heard the stories of it … hell, looked for it a couple of times. No luck." Ed said. "But I'd try looking in old city directories and microfiches.

"Find a factory up on top of the hill near there, and you might fare better than I have. I can admit, I haven't had the time I'd have liked to look for it."

"Thanks, Ed. I appreciate the help," Jack said as he got up.

"No problem." Ed opened the door for him. "Do let me know if you find it."

"Will do."

Jack walked out and left the Historical Society. He had one more stop to make that day.

CHAPTER TWO

Jack drove slowly through the wrought-iron gates of Ascension Cemetery, on the top of 105th Street. Despite having been recently expanded when the city reclaimed twenty acres, it wasn't big. Most people were cremated when they died, and the older Albany Rural Cemetery was massive, just across the river, but Jack's parents inherited plots in Ascension.

It was the anniversary of their marriage, not their deaths. On the anniversary of their murders, he buried himself in a bottle of shit whiskey in the study and didn't leave the room. He always took that day off from work, and Mary and Paul knew not to knock. But every year on their wedding anniversary, he'd come up to Ascension and lay a wreath on their tombstones.

Jack was bitter about Clyde Coleman, the man who'd killed them. He tried not to be, tried to focus on the fond memories he had of them. But he was six when Coleman slaughtered them. His memories afforded only fleeting glimpses of their time together.

Then the Taggarts adopted him, so almost all of his childhood memories were of them. Adolescence came, and with it rebelliousness, and he was obsessed with finding out as much about his biological parents as he could.

At first the Taggarts were helpful; they understood.

Though George Taggart was a chess grandmaster, it was a title, not a job. He was a well-respected attorney with Rhodes City's biggest law firm, McCloskey and Solomon.

McCloskey himself dug up as much as he could on Jack's mom and dad and their case. But George wouldn't show it all to him; just the facts about his biological parents. He nearly threw down with George over withholding the details of the crime; eventually they stopped talking.

Once he joined the force, he saw the full case files, and he understood.

Jack remembered the look on George's face when he went to his house that night, after seeing the crime scene photos; the look of years of tension between the two dissolving into the understanding of sad truths.

Snowflakes from a predicted squall were aloft in the air as Jack got the wreath out of the trunk. He was parked on the side of a dirt track. He would've pulled in, but no one visited so late in the year.

The grass was moist, Jack's feet sinking a little into half-frozen turf. He laid the wreath, and pulled out a cigarette. He usually did that; he'd heard his biological dad had smoked a pipe. He reached for the Zippo and tried, failed and cursed himself for being negligent on lighter fluid. He fished for a match.

The names etched in marble burned hot in his mind as they did every year; Jonathan and Louise Myers. Jonathan had been an architect and Louise, a stay-at-home mom. He never thought of them as 'Mom' or 'Dad'; George and Emma Taggart held that distinction. His biological father had been a key developer in the "urban renewal" period in New Rhodes. Not many were happy about his work, but the New Rhodes Agora complex downtown was his crowning achievement prior to his death.

Jack's mind was in a whirl. He always cherished this day, this time, no matter what circumstances preceded it.

So far the South End Killer hadn't left a little boy or girl to survive his handiwork. There hadn't yet been any new Jacks left to face the world like he had.

He had to wonder when that would change.

He got home around nine-thirty. Paul was up watching a B-grade horror flick. Jack and Mary only let him get the cheaper movies on pay-per-view. Jack walked into the kitchen to see Mary and Tony, with a steaming NRPD mug in his beefy hands. Tony worked the graveyard shift. He often stopped over to the house before work.

"Hey, babe …" Jack kissed her on the forehead. "Tony, where's your patrol tonight?"

"South End," he said. "We got double-coverage ever since, you know …"

"Yeah,"

"Honey, you said you were going to the historical society, about the case, but you didn't say why. Is it top secret?"

"Nah, just a wild goose chase, I think." Jack said. He told Mary and Tony about the tunnel, and the dead end.

Jack rubbed the back of his head. "I got a history lesson, no doubt about that … said there are tunnels everywhere, but he couldn't tell me anything about them."

"Hey, Mary … You remember the tunnel down the street from us, where we lived before we moved to Albany, when mom and dad split?"

"I was too young; I barely remember living here when I was a little girl," she said. "I just remember moving back."

Jack grabbed a cup from the cabinet. "So you were in one of the tunnels, Tony? What was it like?"

"Big," Tony said. "I'd say a couple of people could walk through it. It had rusty old rails; not like railroad tracks, smaller ... reminded me of those cars you'd see in mines."

"Is it still there?"

"Nah. The city filled it in when I was in the eighth grade." Tony picked up his mug and took a cautious sip of coffee. "You're going back tomorrow, right?"

"Yeah," Jack said, "bright and early."

"They've upgraded to pizza."

"Well, that's a start,"

"I mean, I only get there in the morning to clock out, but I can tell you, it's real tense in there, brother ... *real* tense."

Tony got up to start his night shift, kissed his sister on the cheek and patted Jack on the shoulder.

"Take it easy out there," Jack said. "Doesn't look like this guy's going after cops, but he doesn't seem to be playing by any rule book. Be careful."

"As always. Most likely be responding to D.V. calls and breaking up bar-fights on the South End Row."

"You never know," Jack said as Tony was on his way out, "the guy might be a regular."

The station house was a zoo. But they did have pizza. Captain Harken briefed everyone at 0900.

"Okay, everyone, settle down and find somewhere to light." He said. "As most of you know, the South End Killer is all over the papers now; even made it to the NY Post." Harken picked up a copy of the post with a picture of the Masons' house, the Coroner coming out with body bags. Jack wondered how in the hell they got those pics.

"There's details in here. The fact that Sheila and Kyla was skinned was in here." He tossed the paper on the table hard enough to give it a landing on the floor.

"If you have kids, wives, husbands, would you want somebody telling the rags that they were killed so horribly? No."

"I don't need to tell anybody here to keep your mouths shut. This is an ongoing investigation, and if anyone asks, that's what you tell them."

Jack sipped his coffee, proud of Harken's ability to silence a room. He was right; Jack never told anything to anyone he didn't vet first.

"This is also still a joint investigation," he continued. "As far as we know, the killer hasn't crossed county or state lines, but people are scared. And I'd say rightfully so."

Harken pointed to Jack. "Taggart – I want you and Gamble canvassing the neighborhood where our third victims were found. Talk to everyone, and go through the crime scene again. If we missed anything, we need to find it.

"Tomorrow, we'll be opening up North sub-station as a command post for the task force. It's bigger, and God knows they need to get things back to normal here."

Jack and Gamble left shortly before ten. He didn't bring up the tunnels in the briefing.

He knew at that point, without any corroboration, they'd look at it the way he did; a wild theory and nothing more. He'd need something else, some proof.

They cruised down Fourth Street, enjoying the quiet, punctuated only by the garbage trucks attending to the week's throwaways. They wouldn't start canvassing right then. The people that worked were already gone, and those that didn't wouldn't be functional for another hour.

They grabbed two cups of coffee from the Morgan's on the hill and pulled into a parking area by the South End Haymakers baseball fields. It was an unofficial rendezvous for anyone patrolling the South End.

"So you talked to that guy from the Historical Society?" Gamble blew on his coffee.

"Yeah," Jack replied, "Yesterday. Ya know how some people can be helpful, but not helpful at the same time?"

"My wife," Gamble said through a chuckle. "Did he tell you anything about that tunnel?"

Jack lit up. He wasn't supposed to light up in the car, but he and Gamble were the only ones who used it, and Gamble didn't give a shit.

"He basically said that the city is filled with tunnels, but all the records were lost in a big fire in 1921. So no one knows where they are anymore."

"So he told you the same thing Walt did."

"In an authoritative, history teacher kind of way," Jack said. "Less, actually ..."

"Do you still think he's using a tunnel?"

Jack let out a sigh that turned into a cough. "I don't know ... I mean, it fits the delivery of the victims at the last two crime scenes. I just don't know how he could've done it without some kind of access."

"I'm with ya on chasing this down," Gamble said, "but you go to Harken with this ..."

"Not a word on it unless I have something more to bring to the table. And let's not ignore any other theory. So ..." Jack cleared his throat, "I have a favor to ask of you."

"I have a price." Gamble smiled, sipped his mud.

"I'll pay ya in *Pride of Eires*," Gamble gave a thumbs up.

"Look, we need to hit the internet, do a little search magic that way and look for *any* other connections we can find. Anything.

I know they've been doing that at the task-force, but ya know, the whole *group-think*, I want to use fresh eyes."

"But ...?"

"Harken will have our asses if we don't canvass."

"So, you do the canvass and I bust out the cyber fury?"

"You're better on a computer than I am."

"And if Harken finds out?"

"Harken will take it out on me either way. I don't think he wants me on the case to begin with."

"Why not? You're the best detective we got!"

"He's old enough to remember Clyde Coleman." Jack said. "He thinks I'll make it personal, and then I'll be a liability."

He took a last drag on his cigarette then pitched the butt out of the window. "Basically, he'll chew you out, but he'll blow up on me. If it pans, he might not do either."

Gamble thought about it. "I can't go to the station, so I'll have to grab my laptop from home." He grinned. "And I want beers all night, Friday night."

Jack laughed. "Deal."

After getting Gamble's laptop from his house, they pulled up to the house on Fourth Street. The crime scene tape had been torn down and was strewn along the street, a common happening in New Rhodes, but Jack could see that the seal on the door was still intact.

He walked up to it and fished for his pocketknife to break it.

"Excuse me, young man, that's a crime scene."

Jack turned to look at an elderly gentleman in a wool flannel and jeans, with a wooden cane and the limp of arthritis.

Jack pulled his coat aside to show his shield. "Do you live around here, sir?"

"I live right next door." The man pointed his cane to the next house. "I'm Willard... Willard Handley. Been livin' in the South End most of my life."

"I'm Jack Taggart." He reached out his arm, and they shook hands. Jack could feel the frailty in his bones. "Do you have a minute?"

"Well, I told that dipshit detective what I knew yesterday," he said. "No offense."

"None taken." Jack said. "I won't waste your time. I'm kind of going *off-script* here a little."

"Well, okay then. You wanna come in?" Willard asked. "I can brew up some tea."

"That sounds fine." Jack hated tea, but *when in Rome...*

Willard showed him into the house. The plaid foam sofa was littered with newspapers. He had a black and white TV with rabbit ears and a marble ashtray by the rotary phone on the end table next to a well-worn recliner.

The walls were covered in old pictures, mostly black and whites, from a happier time in the nation. He had a flag-pole in the corner. Old Glory and the POW-MIA flag hung still, capped by a brass eagle.

Willard grunted about the mess and directed Jack to the kitchen. They sat down to Earl Grey, and lemon out of the plastic squeezer. It wasn't actually that bad.

"Willard, I'm going to tell you something the," Jack cleared his throat for effect, "*dipshit*, probably didn't, but you have to promise me you won't tell *anybody* what I tell you. Can you do that?"

"I spent three months in the Hanoi Hilton in Nam. You're probably too young to know what that means."

"I know it means you can keep a secret."

"Well, whattaya got, son?"

Jack took a deep breath. "Okay. How much did you hear about the murders?"

"Not that much. What's in the papers; I had to give more answers than I got, and I didn't have any to give."

"Alright ... well, here's the secret. Your neighbors were murdered, but we don't think it happened in the house. We think, aw hell, *I think*, that they were murdered somewhere else, and brought into the house over the weekend."

"Their bodies, you mean?"

"Yes. Exactly. Now, I'm trying to figure out how that could happen. We have a witness who said they would've noticed someone bringing ... *things* ... in through the front door, so I don't think that's how it happened."

"That's funny, now that I think about it," Willard said. "If they tried to bring them in back through Saint Mike's, my motion sensor would have gone off; plus I have a video camera back there, and there's my dog too.

"I might not have woken up to the motion sensor, but Kibble would've woke me up.

"And I checked through the video camera after you guys left the crime scene; it's motion-activated, like the light, and it didn't come on, exceptin' for a deer over the weekend."

"Wait; so how is that funny?"

"Oh, yeah," Willard said, "that whole weekend, Kibble would go to the basement door and bark. And he doesn't do that; I don't let him down there."

"Do you mind if we go down there?" Jack asked.

"Oh no, I don't mind," Willard said, pressing his palm against his good leg as he reached for his cane, "but it's a dirt floor. Just letting you know, it's not finished."

They descended the stairs; Willard and Jack both had to duck to clear the stairway. It was clean for a dirt-floor basement.

"I come down time and again to check for mold, dust, cobwebs …" Willard said.

Then he slapped his forehead. "Oh wait!" he said, "I gotta' show you this. Help me out, if you will. Not too good on the kneeling."

They walked into the back of the basement. Willard pointed down to a tarp. "Lift that," he said. Jack lifted the tarp, and he could see the faint outline of a square, four feet by three feet, covered in dirt. He traced his hand along the edge. There was an iron plate, from the feel of it, buried into the dirt.

"Do you have a crowbar down here?" Jack asked.

"Yeah, right here." Willard grabbed one off his tool-shelf. "I had to use it when I found that thing. Damned if I know what it is, though … might be nothing."

"It's worth a look." Jack said.

Jack pried the iron out of the floor and slid it aside. He peered into a hole, about four feet deep, but he couldn't see the bottom clearly.

"Do you have a-?"

Willard handed Jack a flashlight. Jack shone it down into the hole and saw metal. It bore a layer of rust, but he might've expected more. He eased himself down onto the iron plate. It was solid, but it had just a little bit of give to it. He ran his hand around the edges, conscious that if it dropped, he was in trouble. He dug in, but couldn't find an edge.

Jack hopped back up to the basement floor and pulled the iron plate back in place.

"Willard, if we have to get a forensic team in here, would you object?"

Willard waved his hand. "Just tell 'em not to track shit on the carpet," he said, "just had it cleaned."

Jack grabbed Gamble from the car and told him what he had just seen. They decided they'd go into the crime scene house and look at its basement later that day.

Jack had Gamble run an overlay of the street map and all known tunnels; storm tunnels, sewer tunnels, and anything else that might have been under Willard's house. Gamble tried every resource, but nothing was supposed to be under there, certainly not a tunnel.

One thing he did find out was that code enforcement had issued all three crime scene properties with notices for various things; one needed to mow their lawn, one needed to paint their door handle, and another needed to replace a small stairwell. There was a big list of notices. It wasn't anything concrete, but it was a lead.

They talked to a few more people, but unlike Willard, they didn't offer anything new. It was about two o'clock, and they parted ways, canvassing independently until three, when they met at the crime scene. Jack broke the seal with his pocket knife and they walked in.

The smell hit them first; that mix of decay and latex. They were used to it, as much as anyone could be, but it tempered their excitement just a bit. They didn't talk much once they were inside; call it solemnity, call it the fact that the former occupants had yet to get justice for their demise.

Jack and Gamble found the door to the basement and, having slipped their hands into latex gloves, descended the stairs.

Jack wondered if the techs had considered the basement a part of the crime scene. He grabbed his camera before coming in, and he took a shot of a sprig of blue nylon fibers caught in the wood of the stairwell.

The basement was lower than the one in Handley's house, and not so clean. Jack took as many shots as he could; Gamble worked out a grid to search with a rake he'd brought.

They stayed quiet. Jack scanned the floor for any area that looked "off," and when he found one, he mentioned it to Gamble, whose reply would be, "I'll get there." Jack contented himself with taking as many pictures as he could, paying close attention to the stairwell, specifically to the steps.

"Got something!" Gamble said, as Jack heard the rake scrape metal. He was close to where he'd started, as Jack had tried to line him up with the hole next door.

Jack had also brought in a crowbar and, after taking multiple pictures of the area, he and Gamble began to move the dirt away. There was barely any dirt on it.

They got to the plate and pried it up. Again, they were faced with a hole, same size as the one in Handley's house, and with an iron bottom.

This time, Jack had Gamble hold his legs as he went down head first. If it opened, he wouldn't be able to do it while standing on it.

Jack moved quickly, running his hands along the edges, between Gamble's groans of protest. Jack did find an edge this time. He pulled on it with everything he had in him. It budged, sliding towards the back of the house, but only a few inches. Then it froze.

He could feel a cold draft and smell a pungent odor that was trying to pull the lunch from his stomach.

"I got it to budge," Jack said, "and there's definitely something down there."

"I gotta get ya up," Gamble said, "I'm about to drop you on your head."

"Alright, bring me up." When Jack got out, he hunched down and took five pictures of the spot he had gotten open.

They went to the only other crime scene on Fourth Street, and, following the same process, found another chute. That one didn't budge.

On the way back to the station, Gamble brought up the inevitable.

"Holy shit, man!" He said. "I thought the idea was cool, but this shit is *real!*"

"Come on, Eddie… all we know is that something's down there."

"Are you kidding!? That's the big time right there!"

Eddie drum-rolled with his palms along the dashboard. "Did you smell that shit?"

Did *you?*" Jack jabbed back.

"C'mon, man… Don't kill my 'high-on-life' right now… You know what I gotta' go home to."

"Okay." Jack said. "Point."

"You know we have to get Harken on board, right?" he said.

Jack took a drag of his cigarette. "I know."

"Well, we have a solid lead."

"We have two sets of leads," Jack said.

"One, the code enforcement citations, which apply to all three crime scenes, and two, what we just found, which are based on 'local legends', as Harken will put it, and which apply to just two of the crime scenes."

"We never even checked the first one, though."

"I'm just making a point," Jack said. "Harken's under-the-gun, and he's not going to want to have to waste time on an unproven theory."

"So what, we just keep it under wraps?"

Jack stared out the window. "No; we can't do that," he said, "a lead is a lead. It's just gonna be a tough sell, that's all."

"I'll be selling it with ya."

"Thanks," Jack said. "And thanks for believing in this."

"Who knows?" Gamble said as they pulled into the station. "It might even be true!"

"What was so important that you had to pull me off the floor?" Harken said when they were all in his office. Jack was sitting in the chair; Gamble was on Harken's computer, uploading the pics from Jack's camera.

"Harken, we got two leads today," Jack said. "One, we found out that all of the victims' residences got notices from code enforcement. Don't know how much of a lead it is; thousands of those went out this year."

"And you need me in here to tell me that?"

"No," Jack said. "The second lead is … *tricky* …"

"Well, spill," Harken said. "We're moving HQ tomorrow, so clock's tickin' …"

"Okay." Jack then explained the talk they'd had with Walter, then the talk he had with Ed Mansfield; the canvass, Willard's revelation, ending with their exploration of, and findings, at the two crime scenes.

"And you expect me to take all of that to the task force?" Harken said. "I'm barely holding on to this as it is!"

"Captain, if we wanted to bury this lead and make you look like you're chasing shadows, we'd have tossed it to the task force ourselves and took our chances. We don't want that," Jack said.

"Look, I know we've all heard about these tunnels, growing up here; I don't doubt they exist. But couldn't those," Harken pointed to his computer screen, "... *things*; couldn't they go to the sewer mains or something?"

"I cross-referenced all known subterranean structures, everything on record from the 1920s up," Gamble said. "Nothing. Whatever these are, there's no record of them."

"But they still could be storm drains from before 1920, right?"

"Captain," Jack said, "there's no way the third victims could have been murdered off-site and brought back in without tripping Handley's motion sensor or camera, or setting his dog off.

"And the front way; there was a whole row of nosy neighbors who would've seen something; at least one of them would have been bound to notice a stranger moving in and out in a van or a truck.

"Cap', you know me." Jack said, picking up a pencil, as if to draw out the words in the air. "I always want to know how someone does a thing. That's where I start when I investigate.

"They're looking at the calls, and how the victims tie to each other, but I want to know how this guy, these guys, whatever; how they're able to move in and out of a house without detection. The tunnels are the closest thing we got right now."

Harken shooed Gamble off his seat and sat down. He stared at the screen, clicking on all the pictures.

"Looks like you got this one open a little bit ..." he said.

"About two-, three inches," Jack said, "There was a cold draft inside the crack. I'd say it was fairly deep. I could hear echoes of me and Gamble talking when I was down in the hole."

"It smelled like shit too, Captain." Gamble added.

Harken paused, scratched his stubbly chin. He took a couple of deep breaths.

"Jack, I'm going to assign you to go over all three crime scenes with an evidence tech. Who do you want?"

Jack waved the pen through the air to follow the list he was compiling in his mind.

"Freddie Benson," Jack said. "He just got back from vacation."

"Fresh eyes," Harken said. "What do you need?"

"Hank Ellis."

"Hank Ellis? I was thinking a shovel or a pick-axe!"

"I'm thinking Jaws of Life," Jack said. "Well, not that, but something that the Fire Department might have. And since Hank just went over to there from retiring here ..."

"Fine, I'll call him."

"What about me, Captain?" asked Gamble. "Jack!?"

"I'll need you here." Harken said.

"Seriously?" He said. "I'm Jack's partner... I 'got his back, Jack'... Why do you need me here? To track down leads or something?"

Harken laughed. "Yeah, sure," he said. "Really, to keep me sane." He thought about it, chuckled. "You, Gamble... keeping *me* sane."

He got up, opened the door and sent them out, telling Jack to get a good night sleep ... and put fresh batteries in his Maglite.

"That sucked, man." Gamble said.

"Is it me, or was that too easy?"

"I think he's too tired to fight," Eddie said. "We'll catch up. I want details, man."

"And beers, man. Tomorrow's Friday; you promised."

"If I'm still alive, it's open tap for ya' Eddie."

With that, Jack and Gamble parted ways.

Jack met Hank and Freddie at Ginny's just as the sun was peeking over the crest of the hill, the blinds slicing the morning light, making the breakfast menu unreadable from where they sat. Not that it was that hard for anyone to figure out the place had eggs, toast and coffee.

Jack and Hank were long-standing customers, and Ginny made it her usual point to get flirty with Hank, chest out, playing with the buttons of her blouse with her right hand as she held her scratch-pad in her left. She didn't need the pad; she could remember five special orders at once, and Freddie was the only new cat.

He was asking a lot of questions about the shit he was ordering. Jack told him to order coffee. Freddie was a whiz kid, but he was a night-owl asking dumb questions to try to wake up.

"Alright guys," Jack said as Ginny brought them their coffees, "I told you as much as I know when I called you last night. I wish I had more."

"That's alright," Hank said, "I'm happy to help."

"Good, 'cause I want you to run point on the tunnel part," Jack said. He blew the steam off his cup. "Freddie and I are gonna be busy trying to find shit, but we all have to be safe."

"That's fine by me," Hank said.

"You said you stood on one of the ... entrances, or whatever, right?"

"Yeah," Jack replied.

"Did it have any give?"

Jack's brow furrowed slightly as he recalled it. "Yeah," he said, "not much, but it had a little..."

"Don't want to interrupt you guys," Freddie cut in, "but what was the surface like? Smooth? Rough?"

"Rough," Jack said, "Iron with some rust on the surface."

"Okay," Freddie said. "Probably won't get prints off it, then."

"Make sure of that, Freddie," Hank said. "Once we start prying the openings, I mean, if they're not that thick ... we'll probably be mangling them."

"Mangle away," Freddie said.

"So Hank, how are you going to get the entrance loose?" asked Jack. "Could you get anything from the Fire Department?"

"Not the Jaws of Life, if that's what you're thinking." Hank shook a packet of sugar. "I got something close: a hydraulic spreader."

"What's the difference?"

"It does the same thing as the Jaws, basically," Hank said. "It'll get us a twelve inch spread, but we're going to need three inches before we can set it in. You said you got that one open two inches?"

"Yeah, maybe a little more."

"If we can get the spreader in there, and if we can get a twelve inch spread, either the locking mechanism will pop, if there is one, or it'll come loose, or ..."

"Or what?"

"I brought a bunch of small two-by-fours," Hank said, "we can just keep spreading until it's open."

Their breakfast arrived. They ate in relative silence, punctuated by occasional pleasantries from Hank to the regulars and the slap of Freddie's hand to his face. Jack wasn't worried about Freddie. When they got on site, he'd have laser focus. A crime scene was like a hit of crack to the kid.

"What do you think we'll find down there, Jack?" Hank wiped his face with a napkin.

"Don't know," Jack replied. "I just don't know." Jack leaned back for a second, folded his arms and leaned forward, propping his frame on the table with his elbows.

"I did clean my gun three times last night, though."

They arrived at the second crime scene and, as Jack knew it would, the pipe lit up in Freddie's brain. He pored through the first floor *and* the second, inspecting the work of his colleagues, commenting here and there about what they'd missed, like a drill sergeant checking the bed-making of a bunch of weary recruits. He got out his kit and dusted the rod that controlled the front blinds.

"People always forget to dust here," he said.

"He didn't leave prints, Freddie," Jack said, "not there, not anywhere. C'mon, we're going downstairs."

Freddie headed down the stairs, not minding the rebuke. Jack liked him because at least he *knew* he was anal retentive. Hank led, yanked the cord for the light with his free hand, the spreader in the other.

"Freddie, what did you bring as far as lighting goes?"

"I got the best forensic light source we have," he said. "It's powerful, and it has UV and infrared detection."

"Can you go grab that?" Jack asked. "Sorry for calling you down here so quick ..."

"No prob." Freddie jumped back up the creaking basement stairs.

When they had the light, Hank directed the beam into the opening. Jack had gotten it open just wide enough for the spreader.

"Alright, stand back," Hank said. "We don't know what we're dealing with. For all we know, the thing could be booby-trapped or something."

Jack and Freddie backed up as Hank used the spreader. The metal groaned and squealed as the spreader put pressure on it.

"It's opening, but slowly," Hank said. "We may need those-" His sentence was stopped as, with a deafening *pop*, the plate flew open, sending the spreader down into the hole and Hank on his ass in the basement dirt.

He got up, dusted himself off.

"Fuck, I hope I didn't break that thing," he said.

"That sounded deep," Jack said.

"Ten feet," Freddie said. Jack looked over at him. "Give or take, judging by the length of time it was in free-fall, factor in the-" He paused. "Yeah, about ten feet."

"Hank, you brought your Maglite?"

Hank nodded, handed it to Jack. He made sure it was screwed on tight before dropping it down the hole.

"You trying to break *all* my shit!?"

"I'm not going down there without light," Jack said. "C'mon, it's a Maglite ..."

They all looked down the hole. They couldn't see much, as the Maglite had landed facing in their direction, but they did see an iron ladder bolted into the side of the tunnel.

The ground looked sludgy, and the smell was horrible; moldy, mildew, musty; Jack couldn't smell death in that mix. He didn't smell sewage, or garbage, either. He expected to smell them, but he didn't.

"I'm going down," he said. "When I say it's safe, we'll get you two down there." He grabbed a Mini Maglite out of his shirt pocket.

"Freddie; forget the forensic light source for now. That thing could get destroyed down there, and Harken will be on both of our asses. Just grab two more flashlights from my car; it's unlocked." He pulled out his service weapon. "Bring your camera, too."

Jack gripped the Mini Maglite with his teeth and descended the iron ladder, aiming his gun where he aimed his light.

As soon as his head cleared the tunnel, he scanned three-sixty. He focused on movement, human-sized shapes, quieted his mind for sounds, but other than the occasional squeak of a rat, nothing. No shapes, no sounds. His feet hit the floor with a sucking sound.

Once he felt no immediate threat, he traded the Mini Maglite for the big one, and got a better look. The walls were stained with various levels of rust. There were fissures, nothing major, but he did need to get Hank down there.

The ends of the tunnel in both directions were beyond the beam of light, but the tunnel seemed to run straight, parallel to Fourth Street. There were crumbling rails, broken in places that ran down the tunnel.

Jack heard Freddie's voice, and a beam of light shone down from the opening.

"Alright, Hank, Freddie … come on down," he called up.

When Hank and Freddie were down, Freddie immediately started taking pictures, being careful not to blind anyone with the flash. He took pictures of the plate mechanism that led to the house, and the ladder they'd come down.

"Will this hold up?" Jack asked Hank, shining light on the cracks.

"It's been here this long," Hank said. "The overall tunnel doesn't show any real warping. As much weight as the bedrock puts on it, it kind of keeps it in place."

"Guys," Freddie said waving his flashlight around. "Got something!"

Jack and Hank walked over to him. He had his flashlight pointed in the muck.

"Footprints," he said, "both ways. Recent."

Son of a bitch, Jack thought.

"The Ramos crime scene was further that way," Jack pointed his light south. "Let's go. Freddie, keep taking pics."

They went south quietly. Freddie snapped pictures when he saw a footprint or something odd, Jack kept scanning back and forth, gun in hand.

He tried to radio for back-up, but he couldn't get anything. Harken *would* have his ass for it, just on principle. But so far they'd found a tunnel; nothing more.

After ten minutes of walking, Freddie found something more.

All three of them stared down at it.

"What the hell is it?" Hank asked. Jack thought he knew, and a knot tightened in his stomach.

Freddie pulled a plastic bag out of his pocket, having donned his gloves before they got there.

"That … is …" Freddie looked at it closely before finishing the sentence. "Skin. And fat."

"Fuck," Jack said. "I can't radio in from here!"

"You want to go back?" Hank asked.

"No," Jack said. "I want to secure the crime scene.

Jack took his sidearm from his ankle holster, and gave that and his radio to Hank; "you okay to go back and call this in?"

"Shouldn't we all go back?" Freddie asked.

"We should," Jack said, "but if he knows we're down here, we'll just be giving him, or them, time to clean up."

Freddie laughed. "Clean up?" He said. "I don't know how he didn't track this scum along the carpet!"

"Good point, but later. Freddie, go with Hank."

"I'm not leaving you alone down here." Freddie said.

"Suit yourself," Jack said.

The original plan was to sit tight and wait for back up. That was the plan. It changed just a bit as Freddie glimpsed another fleshy lump in the distance. They placed Jack's Mini Maglite where they were to preserve their spot, and proceeded down the tunnel.

The lump turned out to be more skin and fat.

And it wasn't just there; there was a trail of skin-crumbs, and as they followed it, Jack's pulse quickened, his breathing coming in short, quick bursts. Freddie would've noticed if he wasn't going through the same thing.

Then there it was; where their marker light was a pin-prick - a heap of rotting flesh. The stench was overpowering, so much so that Freddie almost didn't take a full inventory of the scene. Almost.

"Umm, Jack?" Freddie asked with incredulity as Jack was stifling a good puke. "Does this, umm ... mean anything to you?"

Jack looked over to see what Freddie was talking about. Freddie's light was on the wall of the tunnel; words painted in what Jack didn't have to guess to be blood, its outline embellished in silver sprinkles. Just one sentence in two lines:

"Welcome Back, Jack!"

CHAPTER THREE

Jack's knuckles bulged white against his skin as he dug his fingers into the wooden chair outside of Harken's new office. They were in the North substation now. It was a sterile place, night-and-day from the main station. They closed the North Sub' because of budget cuts, but no one objected.

He felt like a perp' waiting for an interrogation. Harken called him back to the task force once back-up arrived. They let Freddie stay, why not him?

But he knew why. He shouldn't have gone down the tunnel. He should've called for back-up immediately. He knew damn well that cases swung on whether a cop followed procedure. He didn't know what had come over him.

Then again, maybe the words on the wall were why the brass was in Harken's office, and he was out there. *Welcome Back, Jack!* Jack wanted to think it was a coincidence, the chorus line from some long lost Louis Jordan song from the forties. And maybe it was a coincidence, and maybe the calls to 9-1-1 saying

Hello, Amy, or *Hello, Bill* were a coincidence too. Gamble, Malloy ... almost every detective *but* him was at the scene that day. He felt a tap on the shoulder ... Gamble.

Jack sat up straight. "Eddie, what happened down there?" he said.

"I can't tell you everything," Gamble said, claiming a seat next to Jack. He rubbed his face with his hands.

"I don't know *everything*; I think that's what they're going over in there." He aimed his thumb at Harken's closed door.

"The tunnel went south from where you entered it down to the cross section of Rose Street, where it was filled in – probably went all the way down to the port at some point."

"How far north?"

"Washington Street," Gamble said, "Walter was right. It splits in a 'T' shape, down to First and up the hill under Saint Mike's." He scratched his chin. "It had a cave-in, but there was a hatch that went up into the old crematorium."

"They find anything in there?"

"Don't know yet," Gamble said. "Jack, those doors, entrances, whatever ... they were all over that tunnel. The killer or killers would've had their choice of victims if you hadn't found it. No matter what Harken says or does, know that."

"Why don't I find that comforting?"

"That's the best I got," Gamble said, "it's been a long day, and all I can smell is that tunnel."

"Smells terrible down there, doesn't it?"

"Yeah," Gamble said as the door to Harken's office opened.

"Gotta go," he said, patting Jack on the shoulder, "good luck, man."

A line of brass and suits with grim faces and sunken eyes filed out of Harken's office. Not one looked at Jack, not even the Chief. Once the office was cleared, Jack swallowed back a gulp and slid over to the doorway, leaning in.

WELCOME BACK, JACK **61**

Harken looked like shit. He was shuffling papers about list-lessly. He had been in the tunnels too that day, long after he re-called Jack to the task force. He looked up, wiped his forehead.

"C'mon in, Jack," he said, "Cop a squat."

Jack grabbed a wooden folding chair that had a stack of pa-pers on it. The office wasn't fully set up yet, and his walls were decorated in briefings thumb-tacked to the sheet-rock. There was a window in the back, old wood, cracked open and held in place with a binder. The fluorescent light overhead dangled from the ceiling on cob-webbed chains.

"Captain, about today," Jack said, "I know I put Freddie at risk. I broke procedure; I needed to call it in as soon as I found something, I-"

"Fuck it," replied Harken. "Yes, all of that. But if that was it, I'd just bench you for a day or two."

"I don't get it," Jack said.

"Jack, I have to ask for your gun."

"My gun!?" Jack cried. "Do you want my badge too!?"

"Just your gun, Jack." Harken was calm. Too calm. Eerie-calm.

"Cap', I don't understand ..."

Harken rubbed his temple, his elbows digging into the desk.

"I'm in a spot here, bud," He said, "I honestly don't want to do, but I have to put you on a desk right now."

"Can you tell me why?"

Harken paused, motioned Jack to shut and lock the door.

"We found something at the crematorium, where one end of the tunnel ... terminates, I guess you'd call it," he said. "Bear in mind, Jack; we're still pulling evidence out of there."

"But what we found ..." He took a deep breath. "It's gonna be hard for you, or any one of us to make sense of. Jack, I honestly don't know how to tell you."

"Captain, just say it. Don't dance around it … won't make it any easier, and I want to know."

Harken was sweating. Whatever it was, Jack's previous fears were replaced by fear of the unknown.

"We found two drivers licenses placed on a slab in the crematorium." Harken said.

"Whose were they?"

Harken cleared his throat. "Jonathan and Louise Myers," He said.

Jack heard the words, felt them bounce around in his mind's echo chamber, but he couldn't process them. He had to close the floodgate of questions to a trickle, lest he drown.

"That's not possible!" Jack cried. "Coleman fried for that!"

"I know, Jack. I don't understand it. No one on the task force does."

"So the room full of brass earlier?"

"Yeah, they were here about your ability to work the case."

"They tell you to take my gun?"

"They told me to take you off the case completely. I convinced them to let you sit-in, but *only* to look at angles, sort through the forensic analysis as it comes in.

"You are *not* to do any field work on this case unless the task force requests it, and don't get your hopes up on that happening."

Jack got up, slipped his arm out of the right sleeve of his jacket and gently placed the shoulder-holster on Harken's desk. He stretched, his hands on his hips.

"So what am I going to do now?" Jack asked, of himself as much as Harken.

"We don't want the media in on any possible connection between Clyde Coleman and our killer or killers. But we need to look at it. Can you work it as a cold case?"

"Yeah."

"If you don't feel comfortable-"

"Captain, I'll do it," Jack said.

They were quiet for a while before Jack got up to leave. His shift was over, and he had the dull thud of his pulse shooting out the opening salvo of a migraine.

"Jack," Harken said as he was heading out. Jack turned his head.

Harken put his hand on Jack's gun. "Take this back," he said.

"I thought they said-"

"Yeah, they did, and I said I'd ask for it. And I did. You gave it to me; and now I'm giving it back.

"I gotta' consider that you and your family are in danger. And I'll be damned if I send you out of here with just that peashooter you carry on your ankle."

Walt just finished polishing the brass rail along the bar when Jack stumbled in.

The floor looked like it had been buffed. Jack slid his shoe across it. *Yup.*

The place was dead. Jack knew it would be. He'd been in a daze since he heard about the licenses. There was a dam his six-year-old mind placed on that night and, despite leaks here and there, it had held. But the day's revelation pushed the whole reservoir against it, and he needed to talk to Walt. Eddie was too close; so was Mary.

Still, he had to be careful; as much as he trusted Walt with regard to everything in his life, this was evidence that wasn't to be released to anyone. He'd have to keep it off the table.

Walter nodded as he started for a scotch glass.

"Seltzer, Walt," Jack said. "I don't want to drink alone."

"Eddie's not coming here tonight?"

"We don't have plans until tomorrow," Jack said.

"One seltzer, then." Walter grabbed a beer glass. "Anything on your mind, kid?"

"Yeah, lots." Jack sat down at the bar, eyes avoiding the mirror behind it. He didn't want to know what would stare back at him.

"What's on your mind?"

Jack shrugged. "I'm off the case."

"What did you do?"

"Nothing. They just think this is getting to me ... personally, ya know?"

"Is it?" Walt asked.

"Maybe it is," Jack said, "I don't know anymore."

Walter walked to the other end of the bar, where the papers were. He had them all: New Rhodes Sentinel, Capital Land, New York Post and the New York Times; and he rifled through them. It looked like he'd earmarked the pages that talked about the case.

"There's no mention of you in any of 'em," Walt said. "Not even a shot of you standing around one of the scenes. Have you been reading these?"

"Nah. And the Chief's been all over the media-handling," Jack said. "I'm good at dodging cameras."

"So they just took you off it?" Walt asked. "Did you blow up on somebody or something?"

Jack wanted to tell Walt what he knew. He didn't like keeping a tight lip around a friend and former cop. Plus, Walt had given him the first lead about the tunnels, and that naturally gave him something else to talk about.

"So I talked to your friend in the Historical Society; Mansfield?"

"Oh, yeah?" Walt said. "Did he help in any way?"

"Maybe," Jack said. "He said he didn't know where any tunnels were specifically, but he said they might be here. Where did you hear about that Boone Park tunnel? From him?"

"Yeah. He told me all about it one night when we were in here just before close. He was pretty drunk, but he sounded like he knew about it."

"Yeah, that's weird. You'd think he would've been more specific with me."

"He was trashed when he told me." Walt glanced at a couple coming in the door. "Probably doesn't remember it."

"Yeah, maybe not,"

"Did you guys actually find a tunnel?"

"Well," Jack hesitated, "No, I was just curious, that's all."

"You call yourself a detective," Walt said with a smirk. "You suck at lying."

"What do you-?"

"The chief was my partner for eight years. I heard about the tunnel."

Jack didn't know how to react. "What did you hear?"

"Enough to know why you're having the problem you're having right now."

"You're not going to talk to Ed Mansfield about it, are you?"

"I should snap you with my towel!" Walt said. "And I wouldn't go to him again about anything pertaining to this case."

"But you sent me to him in the first place!" Jack said.

"On a wild theory that I thought he could help with," Walt said. "Did you get any real help from him?"

"Not really."

"Then from here on in, treat him like you would any civilian."

"I want to give him a closer look, actually, but I'm benched."

"You won't be hurtin' my feelings." Walt said.

"But he's a friend of yours, right?"

Walt slung his towel over his shoulder. "I work in a bar. For all I know, I could be making Vodka Martinis for the killer himself every weekend."

Jack and Walt talked about his parents, Walt's wife, Joanie, Jack's standing dinner invite, and he felt a bit better; enough to make it home.

Jack drove up to the cul-de-sac where his house sat and noticed the war-beaten unmarked Chevy Caprice. Nothing flashing, and no ambulances told Jack it was a protective detail, official or not-so. He pulled in two cars behind and quietly got out. When he made his way to the unmarked, he pulled his jacket so that his badge was in view and tapped on the glass. Mary's brother Tony was in the driver's seat, with Gamble riding shotgun.

"What the fuck are you two doing out here?"

"Protective detail," Tony said.

"Yeah, I guessed that," Jack glanced up at the house. "I mean, what the fuck are you doing *out here*? Mary's home. C'mon in."

"We really should stay on the street, watch for anything suspicious ..."

"This guy's not an amateur. He's not gonna lurk out here. I'm sure Mary knows this car and is wondering why you're here. Let's go."

Tony and Gamble got out of the car and followed Jack to the house. They walked in to the smell of pumpkin pie, fresh-baked. Paul was reading a book on chess that Papa Taggart sent him. Paul was playing correspondence chess with the old man, who taught him the rules one Thanksgiving weekend.

"Hey, Uncle Tony, hey, Eddie," he said. Jack was ever thankful his boy had inherited Mary's kind eyes.

"Hey, Paulie," Tony said, ruffling his hair.

"Paul," Gamble nodded. Paul nodded back.

"Hey, Paul," Jack said, "Can you do me a favor? Can you go up in your room and read that?"

"Are you guys gonna talk about cop stuff?" Paul asked.

"Yeah, bud," Jack answered.

"How come Mom doesn't have to *go upstairs*; she's not a cop!"

"I heard you, son of mine," Mary said. "And I'm *auxiliary*."

"Fine ..." Jack could hear the dull thuds of Paul's footsteps on the carpeted stairs.

Mary came out of the kitchen wearing sweats and a pale blue tank-top.

"Why were you guys watching the house?"

"Told ya she'd know."

"Still haven't answered my question." Mary folded her arms.

"Protective detail, sis," Tony said, "just a precaution; they gave me second shift for the next week."

"They give you second shift too, Eddie?" Jack asked.

"Nah, I just tagged along," He replied. "I was waiting for you to get home."

"Okay, why do we need a protective detail?"

Jack gulped, tried to hide it, but Mary was a better detective.

"Spill, Jack …"

"Somehow, the killer, killers, whatever, left evidence that ties them to my parents."

"Your parents live in Buffalo, Jack."

"No; my *biological* parents." Jack said. "We recovered the licenses of Jonathan and Louise Myers at a new crime scene,"

"Wait; there was another murder?" Mary looked confused.

Jack and Gamble told Mary about finding the tunnels, the greeting painted on the wall, and then the licenses. Mary wasn't easily shocked, but Jack could see her scratching at the enamel of her coffee mug.

"Paul and I can stay with my Dad for a week or so, until this blows over. Should we do that?"

Jack thought about it, but only for a second. It was a good move, until he had a handle on things.

"Yeah, Mary, let's do that. He, or they, either want me in the game, or out of it." He said. "I have a gut feeling I'll get drawn back into this. I don't want it to be at the expense of you or Paul."

"I can take you guys tonight, Mar," Tony said.

Mary agreed without saying a word. In over ten years of marriage, Jack had never seen his wife blindly follow anyone's direction without putting a word in edgewise, but she looked dazed. Tony got her upstairs, Jack and Gamble sat in the kitchen as they heard the sounds of drawers opening.

"So you're benched?"

"Under house-arrest, more like," Jack replied. "I can't actively work the case. So Harken's got me reviewing my parents' closed case, looking for anything that might have been missed."

"Oh, I got one thing for you to help me with, though, if you can …"

"Anything," Gamble said.

"Edward Mansfield," Jack said. "He works at the New Rhodes Historical Society."

"You want me to check him out?"

"Yeah, but be careful," Jack said. "Online only, and below radar."

"You think he's in on it?" Gamble asked.

"I think he knows something," Jack said, "Not sure if he's in on it or not. Just see what comes up."

Tony came downstairs, followed by Mary and Paul, each gripping a bag. Tony was going to drive them over to Riverville that night to Jack's father-in-law's house. Jack kissed them both, hugged them tightly.

"Tell Dan I'll be over to check on you guys tomorrow," He said. "Also, tell him I'll need him to crack out the old bourbon I got him for Christmas."

"Why would you ask him to do that?" Mary asked. "He hates bourbon."

"He'll know ..."

He watched from the bay window as Tony drove them out of the cul-de-sac. Gamble patted him on the shoulder. Jack wanted to cry, or scream. But all that came out was a cough.

The news hit Jack like brass-knuckles as he woke from a two hour power-nap in the headquarters. He'd pulled twelve hours, coming into the HQ after Mary and Paul left. He just couldn't sit around their empty house.

"At around 6:30 this morning, a man walking his dog on Pine Street between First and Second lost control of the leash," Harken said to the quickly silent main room. "The dog led him to two naked bodies in a pile of trash. Two females, mutilated and wrapped in clear plastic.

"We have the State Police assisting with evidence collection, but this is something new.

"If he's out of his comfort zone, he may have left evidence, or been seen. We need to identify the victims and really push the canvass.

"As you all know, the media's outside, and we'll be issuing updates through Lou Jeffries, our Public Information Officer. If you're going out, coming back, all information goes through him.

"People, this is our case. After the man found the bodies, a second 9-1-1 call came in, identifying the dispatcher. This is not a copy-cat."

Jack wanted a cigarette, but the media trucks were camped out like tailgaters at a football game. He went out and snuck a couple of drags near the back entrance.

The main floor of the task force was a mosh pit of office work. Harken assigned him a desk, but not much else, so he made himself useful to anyone who needed a hand. He knew if he wanted to stay in the loop, he'd have to spend some time as a thread in that loop.

A lawyer, Papa Taggart told him that as much as the lawyers knew about a case, you could learn more from the people who worked for them; the paralegals. So Jack became the "paralegal" of the task force for the morning, and he kept his eyes and ears open.

He got chores from Harken, Sheriff Melfly, and Commander Teague. The Feds were playing close to the vest, but Jack didn't know any of them personally. He still made a run to the store for them.

Harken's assumption about everybody wanting to take the lead was wrong. Melfly and Teague were comfortable with joint-command, in case the killers left the city, or county. With so much media attention and so few answers, it sounded like taking the lead was a "no-win" situation.

The evidence from Leiah Marcusen's murder was back from processing, but even with the FBI's help, the backlog would be days, if not a week, for processing the mounting body count. They decided to use the State Police Forensics Lab to process evidence.

Jack skimmed the report on Marcusen. She had a blood alcohol level at time-of-death of 0.10; she had been legally drunk.

Also, the M.E. determined that the knife that had slashed her carotid artery was most likely a buck-knife, but without anything to compare it to, they couldn't determine a specific brand and model. They took a photo of the cleaned-up wound for future matching.

There were no signs of forced entry. One thing of note was the fact that the rose petals were dyed red; originally white. Maybe it meant something.

Jack realized that everyone was chasing down their own leads, like he had with the tunnel. Jack also figured out, in a roundabout way, that he was seen by some as the prime lead.

... Or suspect. It pissed him off, but he'd have done the same thing if it was someone else with a blood-painted target on his back.

It was really the Feds, because everyone who knew him knew he wouldn't do it, and the estimated TOD on the first two cases put him in a three-day conference in Tampa (Marcusen) and instructing at the New Rhodes Police Academy (the Ramos murders).

But the Feds were looking at a two-killer solution, like everyone else, so alibis didn't mean much to them. They, he found out, were the ones who wanted him completely off the case.

It gnawed at him as he sat at his desk, trying to make sense of probably the only combined collection of clues and leads in the whole place. He turned over to glance at the FBI's area, and caught Special Agent Haskell looking over. *Enough is enough ...*

Jack got up slowly, and with measured pace, walked over to the FBI desk. Haskell hadn't taken his eyes off him until they were looking each other face to face. Then Haskell glanced down at some papers.

"Special Agent Haskell," Jack said. Haskell looked up. "Can I talk with you for a sec'?"

"Not a problem, Detective. You want to meet here, or ...?"

"If you can meet me at my desk, that'd be great," Jack said.

"Can you just give me a minute?"

"Yeah, that's fine."

Jack walked back to his desk. He shuffled his papers, trying to leave a clean area.

He wasn't going to blow up on Haskell; not his style. But the air needed to be cleared.

A few minutes went by, and Haskell was at his desk.

"Grab a seat, Special Agent." Jack said.

"You can call me J.R.," Haskell said. "Informally, of course."

"Yeah, I hear you. And call me Jack; everyone else does."

Haskell took a seat, angled slightly away from Jack.

"J.R.," Jack said, "I know two things: one I know for certain, one I suspect." Jack leaned forward.

"I'm the biggest lead we have right now; this I know." Haskell nodded. "And, I know at least among your guys, I look good for this. How do I clear the second one off the table, so we can stick with the first?"

Haskell looked, for a moment, like the cat that swallowed the canary. But then he regained composure.

"Jack, you do look good for it," he said, "*on paper*. And my partners have asked me to observe you. But mainly because we feel this is too ... *personal*?"

"Look, I'm not involved,"

"But you are 'involved,' you see that, right?"

"You know what I mean," Jack said. "I want to be on this case. Is it personal? It was when we saw the writing on the tunnel wall … but not before then."

"The main concern is that you won't be able to be objective," Haskell said.

"I'll do anything you need to show you that I'm objective," Jack said. "It's tough to work a case when you have one of your joint-partners skeptical of you. Do you have any suggestions?"

"Do you have time to talk with me for a few minutes?" Haskell said. "Privately, without all of this," he motioned about the room, "flying about?"

"Did you score an office here?"

"I'm a psychologist," Haskell said. "One of the perks." He smiled.

"Let me just organize what I have on the desk here, and I'll meet up with you in your office."

"How do you know which room it is?" asked Haskell.

"I used to work out of this sub," Jack said. "There's only one room they'd give you here; north hallway, three doors on the right."

Haskell raised his brows. "Pretty good!" he said. "See you soon."

Jack sat in a beige overstuffed chair in the office, Haskell behind the old North Captain's desk. The room used to be his office, and was one of the only rooms that had decoration, aside from pure function. Haskell told him this would be informal, but Jack didn't feel so confident about that.

They had already interviewed everyone in a position to know dispatchers' names. Jack and Gamble were eliminated by IAB. Jack knew he didn't need to clear his name with the FBI, but he also knew that if he wasn't in good standing with them, he'd be contributing to any future breakdowns in the task force.

"Where do you want to start?" Jack asked.

Haskell folded his arms neatly on the desk. "Let's start with why you feel the need to clear yourself to me," He said. "You've been eliminated by your own Internal Affairs, so why do you care what we think?"

Jack slumped in his seat. "I don't know," he said, "I don't want the secrets, the whispers; I've spent all night catching them here, there ... not from the people on the force, but ..." Jack rubbed the back of his head. "We need to be on the same page."

"I was on a narcotics task force in 2003, multi-county, multi-agency – bigger than this," he said.

"The traffickers we were investigating seemed to be one step ahead of us at every turn ... turns out they had a mole in the task force; dirty cop, not one of ours.

"It took two years to get a break, mostly because information didn't get shared across agencies. It was mistrust, pure and simple.

"I don't want this asshole to keep killing because people think they can't open up in here."

"I don't think you're the reason things aren't open in here," Haskell said. "Look at us; do you really think your local guys want us here? We're running into that same wall.

"I've been monitoring you, yes, even profiling you, to see if you can handle being on such a personal case without damaging the integrity of the task force," he continued as he picked up a file folder and started flipping through pages. "You're a very smart man, Jack." Haskell adjusted his glasses. "Top percentile of all of your scholastic tests, aced your SAT, a few points from a perfect score on your LSAT ... but you chose to be a cop. Can I ask why?"

"I don't know ..." Jack said. "My dad and I were having problems; I took the LSATs to make him happy, but I never intended to go to college."

"You would have gotten a full ride ... anywhere," Haskell said.

"What can I say? Hindsight is twenty-twenty ..."

"But you had to have a reason to be a cop, right?"

"I know what you're getting at," Jack said, "You think I got into police work to avenge my parents' murder. Look, maybe, somewhere deep down ... but I was raised around the law. My adoptive dad, George has friends in the NRPD; I had my own friends because of the murders ... I was kind of a part of the force my whole life; hell, my wife is the daughter of the detective assigned to their case."

"What made you pick her for your wife, if you don't mind my asking?"

"We were high school sweethearts," Jack said. "I knew her growing up; she looked hot in tight jeans ... I mean, why does any guy marry any woman?"

"Alright, Jack. We could be here all day talking about your past. Let's talk about the present," Haskell said. "You found the tunnel. I don't remember seeing the lead-work at the central processing desk until after you found it. How did you even come up with the idea, if you didn't already know about them?"

Jack didn't want to bring Walt into it. But he didn't want to lie either.

"Walter Brinbey," Jack said, "He's a retired detective. He owns Emerald's, a bar in the South End."

"He told you the tunnels were there?"

"No, he told me that there were rumors about the tunnels. He heard it from a patron, Edward Mansfield, works at the Historical Society."

"And he helped you locate them?"

"Well, not really ... He explained why there were tunnels in New Rhodes, but didn't give specifics.

"Ultimately, it was just investigative work that led me there, Special-, sorry, J.R., You read my report on that, right?"

"Yes, I did," Haskell said. "Let me ask you, not to be off-topic, but ... if you had my job, profiling, this task force, not the suspect, what would you say?"

Jack gathered his thoughts. He had only begun to see the case itself, the big picture, that day; other days, he'd been as far away from the task force as he could be.

"There's a few things I would say about the cases," Jack said. "There are a lot of leads and actions that need to be filed."

"Things that are filed are sitting in our database; no one's cross-referencing anything. *I* don't even know everything in the database. It seems like, for each lead, I can see six or seven necessary follow-ups, but we don't have enough manpower to follow things up.

"There's only ten people from New Rhodes Police, six deputies from the Sheriff's Department, and three from the State Police. You're the only one from the FBI that's truly active on this case;

"Special Agent Decker is more focused on this spreading to other counties and states. So that's a grand total of, at best, twenty-one people involved, and ..." Jack paused.

"And what?" Haskell asked.

"... even if he wasn't involved in my parents' murders," Jack replied, "this guy, I think ... fuck, I know he's killed before. Probably here in New Rhodes, years ago."

"I've thought of that, too."

"He's playing with us, like you said in the beginning." Jack said. "I wouldn't be surprised if the 9-1-1 calls are just a red herring. He's escalating because he's bored, older; he probably wants to get caught, but he wants to end it with a show."

"That's it, Jack," Haskell said. He reclined in his seat, folded his arms neatly across his midsection. "I'm satisfied that you're good for the case, dare I say critical. And I'll stop us from giving you the cold shoulder; I'll reassure Decker."

"That's it, really?"

"Yes," Haskell said. "Your mind's on the game, you're just enough involved to be effective, yet detached enough to be objective. And I agree with a lot of what you've said. Just one more thing ..."

"What's that?" Jack asked.

"If we don't catch him, do you think he'll continue to escalate?" Haskell asked.

"My opinion, but the closer we get to him, the more drastic he'll become."

Jack let out a breath. "We gotta' catch him before he paints the town red."

CHAPTER FOUR

Jack sat at his desk, going over the files of his parents' murders. He looked at the evidence, the crime scene photos, and it didn't affect him as much as it had when he first saw them. He was looking at a closed case; two victims that he barely knew; it didn't feel like the most formative event in his life.

He couldn't see it that way. His parents or no, it was a double-homicide, one of three cases in the file for Clyde Coleman. Jack also had the case-files for the two other linked cases; Sarah Wexler, and Jeanine Burton.

His father aside, Coleman targeted women, nowadays, he would've been classified as an *anger-retaliatory* killer; when women in his life pissed him off, he took it out on other women – "substitute" victims.

Everything from the victim type, body placement, injury patterns, to the fact that items were stolen to simulate a robbery, were consistent. But in his parents' case, which had caused him so much turmoil when he first saw it, had some key differences.

Coleman knocked Jack's father unconscious with a lamp, and tied him to a chair in the bedroom while he raped Jack's mother. That's what they surmised, based on the crime scene. They didn't do a rape kit back then, but Louise Myers had bruising on her inner thighs. Jack shuddered at the thought that his dad may have had to watch it.

But in the end, his mother and father were stabbed over twenty times each. Wexler and Burton were stabbed eight and ten times respectively. All three houses had blood sprayed along the walls, but in the case of Jack's parents – it seemed excessive, even though there were two of them.

Coleman maintained his innocence until the day he took the big jolt. He was caught in a stolen car with Georgia plates. He was still wearing his bloody clothes, and the blood types matched Jack's parents. Coleman claimed that he tied up Jack's father, but didn't kill them.

But he couldn't give them a name for his mystery accomplice, and the description he gave was general.

The detectives on the case, his father-in-law being one of them, saw it as a last-ditch ploy. He claimed to have alibis for the other two murders, but his alibi references were cokeheads and drunks. And they couldn't remember the nights in question, much less alibi Coleman.

They tried him in a federal court. It wasn't clear what the reason was, but it was clear that people wanted him dead. That was five years after the moratorium on the death penalty was lifted, but New York still abolished it. It took the jury more time to eat lunch during that trial than it took them to return a guilty verdict. The sentencing went about as quick. Jack was thirteen when Coleman's appeals process petered out and he was executed.

Jack turned photos around like chess pieces. Like so many times when he played himself out of boredom, he played Coleman. His alibi witnesses were druggies and drunks; totally unreliable at confirming his alibis. But did that mean that Coleman was lying?

He didn't know his accomplice's name; he said the man offered him five-hundred bucks to help him with a B and E, but might that have been the truth?

After the Wexler and Burton murders, Coleman got away silently, but after the murder of Jack's parents, he jumped into a stolen car and drove erratically, wearing bloody clothes? Something didn't add up.

It was a big deal back then; the public, the media, screaming for the cops to catch the killer. Jack knew that pressure; they were facing it now. Did they miss the real killer back then?

Jack knocked on Harken's door.

"Come on in, Jack," he said through the door.

"How did you know it was me?"

"Repetition. What's up?"

"Captain, I think Coleman may have been telling the truth back then about not committing the murders," Jack said. "My father-in-law was one of the detectives that had Coleman in the box. I need to interview him."

"You won't be the one doing it."

"Why not!?" Jack said. "Who better than me!?"

"Who *worse* than you?" Harken said.

"I don't follow ..."

Harken stood up from his chair, stretched.

"You want to ask your father-in-law if he fucked up the case of the man who may or may not have killed your parents," he said. "Tell me one way that doesn't turn into a pile of shit."

Jack thought about it, and thought about a counter-argument that wouldn't likewise turn into a pile of shit. He had nothing; Harken was right.

"He needs to be interviewed," Jack said after a long pause.

"Have you even looked at the case management database?"

"Well, a little bit …"

"Interviewing him is one of the actions pending," Harken said, "because – another thing in that database you may not have seen – your parents' licenses had old blood stains on them, probably theirs."

"Dan would have had to be interviewed because it was his case." Harken said. "You sure your head's in the game? Dan's not just your buddy, ya know. I imagine you'll catch some grief from him if he thinks he missed something."

"Oh, I know." Jack said. "No matter who does it, I'm the one that has to face him later. Just thought it'd be softer coming from me."

"Like I said, *pile of shit*… either way." Harken scratched his stubble.

"Point made. Now, what about the blood stains?"

"Yes. At some point, we'll need to get a DNA sample from you to compare it to."

"Here, or at the lab?"

The lab, dumbass," Harken said. "Go tomorrow morning, and talk with the techs if you get an opportunity. They're swamped, but this is a high priority case, so maybe they can tell you something."

"Alright, boss."

"And by the way," Harken said, "look at the damn database for forensics that have come in *before* you talk to them."

A smoke never tasted as good as it did when Jack threw his black '70 Chevelle SS into *drive* and turned out on Sixth Avenue, headed for Riverville. Riverville was a quiet city, if you could call it that, just over the bridge from New Rhodes It had an Army base cutting the city in two. Dan lived on the south end, which, unlike the South End of New Rhodes, was a white picket-fence slice of American pie smothered in high school football spirit.

He didn't know what kind of shit he was getting into. Gamble and Malloy had been to interview him and they had just walked in the door before he left. Gamble gave him that look that said *guard your nuts before you go to wifey.*

Jack stayed a bit longer, and Eddie told him that Dan insisted Coleman was the killer. Jack figured he'd shut down no matter who questioned him. But he still had his old notes on the case, and he gave them over.

Jack stopped at the nearest Morgan's for a pack of cigs. He stood in line behind an old man spending a hundred dollars trying to win a little bit more than that. Gamble was a lotto nut; scratch-offs and the Powerball were his poisons. Jack busted his stones, saying he was cursed by his last name.

He felt a tap on his shoulder. The tapper was a scrawny guy in a black sweater with his dress shirt collar sticking out, horn-rimmed glasses, and tweed pants; couldn't have been more than twenty-one.

"Excuse me, you're Detective Taggart, right?"

"Who are you?"

"I'm Simon Smith, from the Sentinel," he said. "I'm working on a story about the South End Killer. You were the detective that found the tunnel under Fourth Street, right?"

"Who told you that?"

"I have a source ..."

"Look," Jack said, "all of our information goes through the Public Information Office." Jack got to the counter, and asked for his brand. Then he lowered his voice, tucked down to be at ear level with the reporter and said, "Do you have a card or something?"

The kid eagerly produced one as Jack paid for his smokes.

"I'll pass this to the Public Information Officer."

The kid was ecstatic. "That's great, Detective! Thank you!"

Jack tucked the card in his inside jacket pocket as he walked out the door.

Jack had a magic pocket. It was the inside pocket of his coat; he never kept anything in there, never reached in to look for anything – it was lined with a small plastic evidence bag. Took him forever to find good bags in a size that would fit, but he'd found them.

He was careful to only touch the edges of Simon Smith's business card before slipping it in there.

As he drove the Riverside Bridge, he pulled out the bag and opened the glove compartment. As soon as he got to Dan's house, he'd document it, and mark down the time he met Smith at Morgan's.

The tunnel's existence had leaked to the media; it was bound to. But Jack's finding it was not. Either the task force had a leak, which was possible, but unlikely – they all knew the killer watched the news and read the papers – or Simon Smith had come about direct knowledge some other way. In any case, it was a fresh lead.

Jack had to rule out two obvious sources – Walt, and Edward Mansfield. Walt, he knew, hated reporters, especially after a reviewer for the Sentinel gave Emerald's a bad review. Mansfield had to be considered. But it was just a start. A tantalizing bit to add to the matrix.

Jack hesitated before knocking on the door of 314 Sage Street, a split level ranch on a quarter acre of freshly mowed grass. Tony's car was there; probably getting ready for his shift. By the time he got used to the split shift, he'd be back on graveyard. Mary answered Jack's knock and hugged him tight.

"I was worried about you," she said. "Haven't heard from you. Are you okay?"

Jack saw Tony putting on his Sam Browne belt and waved. "Yeah, just pulled a ... triple? I've been working since you guys left yesterday."

"Jeez, you must be tired."

"Too tired to sleep, actually," Jack said. "Dan around?"

"He's out back on the deck, smoking his pipe," Mary replied.

"Oh, shit..."

"Just go talk to him, will ya?" She asked. "He's been in a funk ever since Eddie and Chris came over to talk to him."

"I'll go hang out with him, Mar'..." Jack said.

He went through the dining room to the kitchen. He could see the furrow in Dan's bushy blonde brow from the window.

He tapped on the sliding glass door. Dan looked back, nodded. Jack slid the door open and sat next to him, pulling a cigarette out of his new pack. Dan had the bourbon bottle and a glass of ice by his side.

"Ya know they had to, right?" Jack said.

"Yeah," Dan grumbled, "... could've been you."

"I wanted to be the one, but Harken wouldn't let me."

"They think I fucked up and an innocent man got executed. How do I live with that?"

"Dan," Jack said, "if Coleman was telling the truth ... *if* ... then he was an accomplice. He could have walked away as soon as he knew the killer's intentions. But he didn't. He tied up my dad and stayed long enough to get covered in blood. And for that much blood to be on him, he had to participate. *Even if* he was telling the truth, he was lawfully, and truthfully, charged with capital murder."

"And the real killer walked," Dan said.

"It stopped him for a good long while," Jack said. "No more killings like that until now. It may not be the same killer, and hell, Coleman may have been lying. Point is, the licenses were never recovered and they show up now. We have to pursue every angle to explain it. And that's just ... it."

"I couldn't give a damn about what the department thinks," he said. "But you ... you ..."

"I worked five years in narcotics," Jack said. "Every time we thought he had the top guy, it wasn't the top guy."

"More people got killed while I was working narco than this guy has killed now.

"Maybe we could've prevented some of those deaths if we'd believed everything a perp' said, but maybe we'd have chased our tails and not caught *anybody*. It comes with the job, Dan. I don't blame you for shit."

"That's good to hear. I needed to hear that from ya, Jack."

"It's the truth," Jack took a drag. "So, Eddie said you gave those guys your personal notes?"

"Yeah, I don't know if they'll help, though ..."

"They'll help, Pop,"

Dan laughed. "Haven't heard you call me that in a while."

"Sleep deprivation," Jack said. "Anyways, is there anything at all that wasn't in your notes? Any wild theory you had, a weird observation, anything?"

Dan puffed on his pipe; the smell of cheap cherries filled the air around them.

"One thing," Dan said. "Well, two things."

"Okay, shoot."

"When you go back, look at the crime scene photos. From all three cases," he said. "The first two cases, the stab wounds were ... I don't know ... it looked like there were a few hesitation marks around the actual stab wounds, but they were tiny; like the killer was lining up the stab. Best way I can describe it. But with your parents – no hesitation, and twice as many stab wounds."

"Do you think the first two were ... practice?"

"No clue," Dan said, "just thought it was odd, that's all."

Jack rolled it through his head for a minute. If it was true, then his parents might have been the *real* targets.

"What was the other thing?"

"Oh yeah," Dan said. "Your dad got a lot of hate mail for his design of the Agora, and we recovered that, but one letter stood out. Do you have those?"

"Yeah, they're in the case file," Jack said.

"Most of them were directed at your father. Some were general threats against your family, but not specific. We never followed up on the hate mail because we caught Coleman. We only collected them to see if he had written any of them, but one caught my eye." He went on,

"It seemed like it was about the Agora, but I had this weird feeling about it. It mentioned your mom, almost in a familiar sort of way, like the writer knew her.

"Also, it was hand-delivered; no postmark. We couldn't match it to Coleman, and the media was then, as it is now, anxious to see a killer behind bars, and we had one ..."

"Thought we did ..." he added.

"I'll check it out tomorrow when I get in," Jack said. "Thanks, Dan."

"Go get something to eat," Dan replied. "Mary cooked you dinner, and you look like a hungry piece of shit. Get stuffed, and get some rest tonight."

Jack laughed. "Sounds good," he said. He went in and ate meat loaf and mashed potatoes and fell asleep in Mary's arms watching old episodes of *Dragnet* on DVD.

Jack picked up Freddie before he went to the State Police Forensic Investigation Center in Albany to give his DNA sample.

Harken wanted him to try to chat up the techs, and Freddie was both chatty, and a tech, and, as usual, tired. But he agreed to go.

"What do you expect me to get out of them?"

"Rapport; pure and simple," Jack said. "You know their language, and I don't. Harken knows we probably won't get much, as swamped as they are, but if they give us anything, you'll understand the shit, know the follow-up questions."

"But, I mean ... alright, look," Freddie said. "The person we need to talk to, her name is Amy Barenski. She's the best, and she's coordinating the forensics on our cases. But, in the past, I've had to talk to her, and ..."

"And what?"

"It's like she barely notices me."

"You like her, don't you?" Jack smiled.

"I don't know ... maybe."

"She single?"

"Haven't gotten that far," Freddie said. "Look, she handles major cases for the state all day, every day. What would she see in a guy like me?"

WELCOME BACK, JACK **89**

"Yeah, you're right," Jack said. "You're just a lowly tech. Not like you've ever put yourself in danger to collect evidence, or would chase bits of human flesh down a murder tunnel and *choose to stay there* to help secure the crime scene. *That* kind of guy might impress her ... but I see your point."

"So I'm supposed to brag about that?"

"Nope," Jack replied. "If she's as good as you say she is, she already knows."

"Just keep it professional. If she asks about it, down-play it. Trust me on this."

"You a ladies man, Jack?"

"I'm a married man," Jack said, "but I'm good with people ... kinda my job."

Freddie laughed. "Okay, so play it cool,"

"Close to the vest, Freddie."

With a sample of his DNA on a cotton swab, Jack and Freddie went up to see Amy Barenski. Her office reminded Jack of his own desk, but he'd guess she knew where every paper and every file was in the mess. *Disorganized-organized*, as Mama Taggart called it.

She had her hair up, very organized in her appearance, a spotless white lab coat with the State Police symbol on it. She was attractive, in her mid- to late twenties, tall with long brown hair, pinned up in the back. She was very direct, with piercing brown eyes. Freddie had his hands full.

"Dr. Barenski," Freddie said, "this is Detective Taggart, from the NRPD."

"Pleased to meet you, Detective," Amy said, then turned to Freddie. "I've never heard you call me 'Dr. Barenski' before ..." She cracked a slight smile. "Are you becoming formal since you've hit the big-time?"

"Big-time?" Freddie asked. "No, no ... I just realized that I should've always called you 'Doctor' – you have a PhD."

"I have two," Amy said, "but thank you, Freddie. So what can I help you guys with?"

"We don't want to waste your time," Jack said, "but I always value what people think, even if it's something they can't put into the reports.

"I'm asking, has there been anything striking like that? Is there anything you guys maybe don't have an explanation for?"

"Off the record?" she asked.

"I won't put it into our database unless I can independently verify it. Your name won't come up ... unless it breaks a case wide open. Then I'll give you credit, of course." He smiled. Amy's eye darted up in her head, like she was searching her mind with her eyes.

"There was something," she said, "came in with the Fourth Street murders."

Amy led them to the lab. Jack was afraid to even breathe around the multi-million dollar equipment. There was a long white table in the center of the room covered with pictures, evidence bags and plaster molds.

Amy held up one of the evidence bags. "This is from the vacuuming for trace evidence." She said. "We found the usual carpet fibers, dead skin cells... the normal stuff you see in trace evidence with a carpet."

She walked over to a microscope. "But there's a minute trace, and I mean truly minute, trace of something I can't explain."

"May I look?" Freddie asked.

"By all means."

Freddie peered into the microscope. He grunted, said a few things under his breath.

"Do you have the bag this came in?"

"Yeah, it's right here." Amy slid the bag over, and Freddie put on a pair of gloves. He opened up the bag and held it under his nose. His eyes went up in his head like he was tasting the stuff.

"Does he normally do this?" She asked Jack.

"Not this in particular, but… he gets into his work."

"There's not enough of this." Freddie said.

Amy looked puzzled. "Umm… there are other bags…?"

"No; not that." Freddie said. "It's the sludge in the tunnel, Jack."

"Where?" Jack said. "In the bag?"

"Yes, in the bag, on the slide…" Freddie said. Now he looked puzzled. "But not enough."

"How much should there be, Freddie?" Amy asked.

"In the tunnel, the sludge was about an inch deep." Freddie said. "If the bodies were brought in through the tunnels, there should be more of that sludge embedded in the carpet, no matter whether or not the scene was cleaned up by the killer afterward."

"This is just a trace of what's in the tunnel." Freddie said. "The barest trace at that."

"So could it be some other kind of transfer?" Amy asked.

"Yeah… but what would leave so fine a trace?"

Freddie and Amy stood face to face, arms folded, thinking deeply. Jack had to break the silence.

"You guys go into a crime scene with those booties, right? For your feet?"

"Yeah." Freddie said.

"Do they keep *everything* clean, even if your shoes were filthy with crap?"

"No, in that case, you'd probably have a trace of leak-through." Amy said.

Freddie looked at her. "Would you say that's about what we're seeing in the microscope?"

Amy paused. "Not tentatively..." She said. "But I wouldn't rule it out. I'd need a sample of the muck in the tunnel." She smiled at Freddie. "Plan on going down there again?"

Freddie laughed nervously. "Sadly, no." He said. "But I imagine they'll be getting some to you soon."

They all discussed the evidence (and lack thereof) for a few minutes, but Amy did have to get back to work. And so did Jack.

"What do you think?" Freddie asked as they drove the arterial to New Rhodes.

"I think she's warmed up to you," Jack said.

"That's good, but I was asking about the theory?"

"I think it's as good as the tunnel theory," Jack said. "But remember, it was only a theory until we could prove it, and I hate to say it, but it's gonna get tossed in the pile of evidence and leads we already have."

"So no go?"

No;" Jack said, "go. Just, you know ... on your own time."

The Hudson River lapped over its banks, releasing waves of putrescence; dead fish with a hint of rotten eggs and dirty diaper. Jack was used to it; hell, everybody was. But some days it was more potent than others.

They flew over the Route 460 Bridge into the South End. Jack treated Freddie to lunch at Ginny's.

"She called you 'big-time,' Freddie," Jack said as they ate. "Looks like she notices you now. And calling her 'Doctor' was a nice touch."

"I might ask her out," Freddie said.

"Slow it down, bud," Jack said, "we have a killer to catch first."

Jack took the evidence bag, indexed, with Simon Smith's business card to Harken and informed him of the contact made. Harken was only mildly intrigued.

"You told him you'd give it to the PIO, right!?"

"I needed to get his info and a business card," Jack replied. "I had to say *something*."

Harken put his hands to his temples. "Let's hope he doesn't consider that as an admission that you found the tunnels, throw you in the spotlight. The killer's got a boner for you as it is. What's gonna happen if he sees you in the paper? On the news?"

"I'm sorry, Captain," Jack said. "I was tired, he ambushed me, and I figured either he had a source in the task force, which would have been bad, or he had a source close to the killer, which would have been a workable lead."

"Jack, you're cowboying this, working it like a regular case, but it's not," Harken said. "It's not just you; everybody's doing it. We got all our agencies, all our detectives and staff chasing down leads one by one when we have probably a thousand leads in the database. We're all grabbing pieces of hay hoping for a needle."

Jack was quiet.

"We need to get our ducks in a row here," Harken said.

"Everyone has to have a role, and stick to it, including you. We're going to have a meeting this afternoon to reorganize the task force. I want you to be there."

"Cap', I'm sorry. I know you're at the end of your rope."

"Tomorrow, the mayor's breaking ground on the new Arts Center," he said. "The Chief's gonna be there. He wants me to be there, and ... I want you to be there with me."

"Why me?" Jack asked.

"To keep me from using the Mayor's shovel to dig my own grave," he replied.

There were six people in the conference room as Harken discussed reorganizing the task force.

"Everybody," he said, "I know it seems like we've gotten off to a rocky start, but I want to begin by saying that we've been proactive with this, and even though some of us might be discouraged, we were quick to recognize that we had a serial murderer; we were conferencing after the first murder.

"We haven't been communicating at well as we could, which plagues many multi-agency task forces, and even though not much has panned out, each lead we bring in is getting us closer to the identity of the killer. But we face challenges.

"The media has the pressure on us, and that's not going to get better, especially if he kills again, which he probably will. But we need to clear every bit of information through our Public Information Officer. No more talking about the case in any public places, among friends, and, while I know this is tough, family members."

Harken looked down at a piece of paper. "At the same time, we don't want to interrupt the flow of ideas between people in the task force.

"The local VFW just got a new building, with a bar and pool table, nice place. But the old property's owners are allowing us to use that building for R&R and conversation. Only people on the task force will be allowed in. There will be a map posted for those of you who don't know where it is."

Harken cleared his throat. "With that out of the way, let's discuss how we should shift our personnel to be more effective. Before I turn the floor over, I just want to say that I know we don't have enough people. But let's try." He nodded to the man next to him. "Commander Teague?"

Teague straightened out his shirt as he prepared his words.

"I've been in contact with Superintendent Miles, and today he authorized ten additional troopers to work the task force. Since we have the crime lab and the day-to-day forensic resources, we'll be covering the crime scene analysis on any future cases."

He cleared his throat. "

We also have a forensic accountant, George Millibank. He's never worked homicide, but he's got expertise with IT. We would like to have him coordinate with New Rhodes PD on the case management database."

"Okay, all agreed?" Harken asked. Everyone nodded. "Okay, then. Sheriff Melfly, what do you have for the sheriff's department?"

Sheriff Melfly propped his elbows on the table. "We can keep a total of ten deputies, no new adds there, but we can bring in five clerical folk," he said.

"They're good, vetted and can free us all up some. We will be focusing our efforts on following up on leads. We have a good relationship with the courts, and as long as we got probable cause, we can get search warrants quicker than anyone else."

"Okay, thanks, Clem," Harken said. "Special Agent Decker, what will be happening on your end?"

"We won't be adding anybody to the direct task force," Decker said, "but we have agents on reserve if anything in the case overwhelms us.

"Adding personnel isn't a problem for us, but the Field Office wants the Bureau to play an assistive role.

He stood up, walked over to a computer and rested his hand on it.

"We will be working on a more developed profile, case linking support with VICAP and watching other jurisdictions around the country for similar cases.

"We'll assist the State Police with any evidence that we would be uniquely qualified to examine, as well as assisting with their workload, when needed."

"Thank you, Special Agent Decker," Harken said.

"The New Rhodes PD will be concentrating on interviews; witnesses, suspects; also we'll be coordinating any covert surveillance operations in the city limits should any come up.

"Does anyone have anything else to add?"

"I do, just one quick thing," Haskell said. "So far, we've all been operating under the premise of there being two killers, and that may very well be true.

"But it's hard enough to find one killer, much less two at the same time. I think we need to stay aware of the possibility of a team-up, but we should consider them, just for the sake of simplicity, one killer.

"Find the one, and let him lead us to the other."

Leaves flew up from the cold, muddy ground as a brisk wind flapped the jackets and dresses of the handful of men and women at the groundbreaking ceremony.

Three local news outlets and a couple of cameramen were on scene, as were the Mayor and, quietly in the background, Chief Detmer. He was in full dress; *better you than me,* Jack thought.

It was a silly sight, to be sure. The land was at the edge of the East Hill, just before it got steeper. It only recently became accessible because of the Canal Street Connection they finished last year. Canal Street was one of the two main roads that went east from the city, up the hill, eventually turning into Route 26 to Vermont.

But Canal Street used to have a hook that merged with Union Street, side-skirting the old Roy Jackson Tower and the scrub lands on the edge of Independence Park, a large hill-top recreation area with tennis courts, a swimming pool and more than one scenic vista of the valley. Its entrance was on the continuation of Canal Street.

Last year, they built a road through the rubble of Jackson Tower, making Canal Street continuous from the river to Route 26, opening up the whole east-slope barrens for development. Before the project, the barrens was a hideout for degenerates, a party spot, with beer cans, cigarette butts and the occasional baggie.

The Rhodes County Sheriff's department sent a work crew from the jail to clean all that out. The Mayor had a gold-painted shovel and in the background was a backhoe, fully painted in psychedelic patterns and designs.

The guy running it was a blue collar type with a skull tattoo on his arm. Jack tried not a laugh at that.

"So basically, the Mayor is going to say some stuff, and shovel a bit of dirt, and then the backhoe will take out one scoop for the photo-op."

"That's it?"

"Yeah, Jack," Harken said. "I think they just want something good in the news for a change."

"I think we all do, Cap."

"New Rhodes has come a long way since the times when it was a small trading post on the Hudson River," Mayor Erickson said.

"We were one of the first cities to industrialize, one of the first to have electricity and we have been a pinnacle of success in architecture and character.

"But we have seen our rough spots too. Urban decline, loss of jobs; we are a reflection of the history of America. And I know, recently, we have had tragedies to endure."

The Mayor raised his shovel. "But we will get through it. We will survive, and we will revive. And this land, once a symbol of urban decay, will become the New Rhodes Collaborative Arts Center, a state-of-the-art facility for the promotion of the creativity that will, one day, renew our city.

"To my left is Susan Williams, the director of the New Rhodes Cultural Arts Council. Her hard work and passionate dedication has turned this dream into a reality." He looked over. "Susan, would you like to say a few words?"

"Thank you, Mayor Erickson," Susan said. "I would just like to thank all of the volunteers, who have been the true driving force behind the revival we have seen in New Rhodes.

"Thank you all for inspiring this collaboration between the city government and our Council to create a place that will breathe new life into the arts community of New Rhodes. Thank you all so much!"

With that, the Mayor took a couple of heaps of dirt from the ground, to the flash of cameras. Then Susan Williams, who would presumably become the director of the Arts Center, dug a couple of shovels full.

Then everybody backed away, and the cameramen repositioned their equipment to catch the backhoe as it prepared to take its turn. Jack and Harken walked over to the Chief.

"You doin' alright, Chief?" asked Harken.

Detmer sighed. "This is the only peace I've had in the past week. How are you boys?"

"We're holdin' up," Harken said.

"Jack, how about you?" the Chief asked. Jack could hear the backhoe bearing down.

"Yeah, I'm just happy to be out in the open air for a-"

He was interrupted by shouting and a woman screaming.

All three of them ran over to the backhoe. The crowd of media staff and the attendees were gathered tightly, obscuring the view, but the Chief cleared them away to see what caused the commotion.

Inside the bucket of the backhoe, sticking up at obscene angles, were bones. Other bones were poking through the gouge in the ground. Dangling from one of the bucket's teeth was a jawbone, larger than life against its neon butterfly backdrop. Its teeth were cracked and stained from age and dirt.

The Arts Center site was now a crime scene. What was worse, what raised the bumps in Jack's flesh, was that they had just publically broken ground on a body dump.

CHAPTER FIVE

"Authorities are still uncovering the remains of what may have been previous victims of the South End Killer," the anchor woman said, in voice-over to a live feed of the groundbreaking site. The New Rhodes PD, the State Police and the FBI were pointing, directing and darting in every direction as crime scene units from all across the state were digging up what the Sentinel had quickly dubbed *The Killing Ground*.

"Police have confirmed that at least twelve different sets of remains have been found," she continued, "This morning, New Rhodes Police Chief Michael Detmer made a statement. We'll go to that now."

Mary wrapped her arms around Jack as the Chief spoke into the crowded sprig of microphones.

"At this time, we can confirm that there are bones from twelve separate victims, but that number could, and probably will change. This was only discovered yesterday, so we still have a lot of ground to cover."

Or 'uncover'. Detmer looked like he felt. Harken wouldn't let Jack out of his grip yesterday, and Detmer wouldn't let Harken out of *his.* Jack got home at midnight. He drank Dan's bourbon bottle down to the label and passed out.

"Do you think this is the work of the South End Killer?" asked one of the reporters.

"We're not ruling it out," the Chief said, "although it's too soon to say anything definite at this point.

"The key thing right now is catching the South End Killer based on recent murders; if these offer insight into that, we'll use the information. But we have to consider the possibility that these murders may have been committed by one or more individuals.

"This area, in the past, was a high-crime area." He coughed into his hand. "We're not ruling anything out, but we can't afford to get side-tracked."

"Right now, with the help of the State Police, the Rhodes County Sheriff's Department and the FBI, we will be working around the clock to identify the victims and make notifications."

Jack tapped the power button on the remote with his toe, and slurped down the slurry of cereal from his bowl.

"Fucking nightmare," he said.

"You think it's him?" asked Mary.

"I have no idea ... really."

"If he's connected to your parents, I mean, that would be consistent, right?"

"Nah, Mary; not necessarily," Dan said as he came down the stairs. "That spot was inaccessible before the Canal Street Connection. It was just a big brushy field that every decent person avoided, in a gang neighborhood.

"Coulda' been druggies, dealers, lowlifes, snitches ... anybody," he added.

"Yeah, work is gonna be fun today," Jack said.

"Just keep your chin up, honey." Mary said as she lifted his chin with her finger, wiping off a dribble of milk out of habit.

"... and don't follow the crowd," Dan said, "the pressure's gonna make everybody jump on any little thing. Whatever you were working on before, just try to keep at it."

"I had a lead I thought was good," Jack said, "that letter you mentioned. Maybe I can find someone who was a friend of my mother. Any prospects?"

Dan rubbed his balding head. "Look in my notes when you get into the office. I wrote a list of Louise's high school friends."

"Her best friend's name was up top. I think she was the only one who still lived in New Rhodes when I was doing interviews. She might still be living here. You should look her up."

"Thanks," Jack got off the couch and stretched. "I best get dressed. Harken told me to come in whenever I wanted, but there's no point loafing."

"Eager to get to work?" Mary said. "You, of all people?"

Jack laughed. "I just want to see what kind of rubber they're padding the walls with today."

Harken was unshaven, his sideburns were starting to creep down the sides of his face. Jack could smell the dark-roasted mud coming from the Styrofoam cup on his desk. He looked like shit. He wasn't leading the task force that day; the Assistant Chief was. It wasn't permanent, just a temporary refresh for the command. Teague and Melfly had taken the day off to get their affairs in order for an extended job. Plus, reinforcements had come in because of the body dump, so they knew they had at least a day to catch their breaths.

Detmer told Harken to take a day, but Jack knew he wouldn't take it. His wife died last year of breast cancer; his kids were off to college, he'd just sit home and watch old westerns on a nineteen inch tube set or tool away in his basement, making furniture, or fixing the dirt bike he never rode.

"A fuckin' mess, Jack… A fuckin' mess."

"I've been here an hour," Jack said, "I don't even know what they want me to do today."

"Do whatever you want," Harken said. "I'll back ya."

Jack tossed a letter in a clear plastic bag on Harken's desk.

"This was a piece of hate mail sent to my father," he said. "No postmark, so it was hand-delivered. Dan turned me on to it."

"Got any leads off it?"

"It's not like the others," Jack said. "Most were pissed about the Agora, but this one's personal. And Dan gave me a list of my mother's high school friends."

"Go for it, but out on the floor, keep it impersonal. Call them Jonathan and Louise Myers, not your mother and father. Here, I know you.

"Out there, already there are twenty new people we don't know … so just keep it impersonal, okay?"

Jack nodded. "Got it."

"Oh, Jack," Harken said, "we got something for you at the station, postmarked Buffalo. Must be from your dad." Harken searched his desk for a letter, found it and passed it to him.

Jack opened it, wondering why George would send it to the station. The letter inside was a photocopy of an image; a chessboard in play. Jack laid it out on Harken's desk.

"That didn't come from George," Jack said. "Those are plastic pieces. George only uses jade, marble or wood. Never plastic."

"Maybe he was on the road?"

"Nah; he sets up correspondence chess problems in notation, not a picture."

Harken grabbed a glove and picked up the corner, inspected the picture. Can you make sense of it?"

"The board's pretty static, but the black knight's got white in a fork," Jack said.

"A fork?"

"The knight has the king in check, see?" He pointed at the knight. "Since you can't block it with another piece, and nothing on this board can take it, the king has to move. But the queen's also able to be taken by the knight." He traced out the path to the queen with his finger.

"So you move the queen?" Harken asked. "I barely know chess ..."

"No, you have to spend that turn moving your king, and the knight then takes the queen."

"What takes the knight? Anything?"

"The rook on this board, but a knight's easy to sacrifice for a queen."

Harken shook his head. "When are these surprises gonna end?"

"Captain, if he's in Buffalo ..."

"I'll call the Buffalo PD," Harken said. "I don't want you out there."

"But he's my dad!"

"... and Mary is your wife, and Paul's your son. I don't know shit about chess, but it sounds like he's trying to put you in that, what was it?"

"Fork."

"Yeah, fork," Harken said.

"But Captain, Mary and Paul have Dan and Tony-"

"He's trying to spread you thin, and take you out of this investigation. You go to Buffalo, he succeeds. Let us deal with it. I'll have Decker call the Field Office in Buffalo. Your parents will be safe, Jack.

"Besides, George has a .357."

"What!?" Jack said. "You're kidding me!"

"Nah. Dan and I gave him a reference."

"When?"

"When they moved to Buffalo," Harken said.

"Why didn't he ask me?"

"Because he thought you'd try to talk him out of it."

"Why the hell does Dad need a gun?"

"He's more afraid of Buffalo than he was of New Rhodes, I guess..."

Jack laughed. "Go figure."

Parkwood was in the northeastern corner of New Rhodes. It was the upper echelon neighborhood, landscaped yards, parks with crystal pure, running marble fountains and posh houses. Jana Mayes lived in a mansion, by any standard Jack knew.

A circular driveway wrapped around a fountain, lion statues perched in front of the two pillars that formed the entrance. Jack grabbed his "Parkwood clothes" before he left the station; custom tailored Navy cotton blazer, matching slacks, silk tie and patent leather shoes with a mirror polish. Parkwood was a tough sell for anyone dressed in "off-the-rack."

Jana Mayes had been Louise's close friend all the way up to the time she was murdered. Her picture looked only vaguely familiar to Jack when he ran her name through DMV.

Jana greeted him at the door wearing a flowing floral dress, her grey hair done up in a bun.

"My, Jack, I have not seen you in ages!" she said after she let him in. "What a handsome man you have become! You have your mother's eyes, you know. I bet you drive the ladies crazy."

Jack felt like an embarrassed kid. "Thank you, Mrs. Mayes, but just one lady." He showed her his wedding band.

"She must be very lucky," she said. "And call me Jana, please, darling. Come, have a seat. Would you like some coffee?"

Jack had been drinking coffee for a week, so he asked for tea, despite his distaste for it. She called out to her maid in the kitchen.

"I wish you had come around some when you were younger, Jack," Jana said. "I was empty for a long time after your mom, and of course I worried about you...." She paused, wiped the side of her nose.

"It's okay, Jana. I've long ago come to terms with it. That's actually what I'm here about today."

Jana patted Jack's arm. "Well, I will help you any way I can, dear."

Jana's maid brought in two cups, and poured them some tea, returning momentarily to lay out lemon, cream and sugar. Jack took his straight. Jana waved her hand over the tea, bringing the vapors up to her nose.

Jana's living room was luxurious; all Parkwood homes were like that. Parkwood was where the owners of the mills lived, and their mansions were extravagant for the time. In the late 1800's, Jana's house would've been considered a palace. Now it was simply an elegant, spacious mansion with Waterford crystal chandeliers, pink satin drapes, antique, early-nineteenth century furniture remarkably restored, in rooms with ceilings that had intricately carved wood in crown moldings, and trim made of mahogany-and-ivory interlaced. The moldings and trim alone was worth Jack's house.

Jack briefed himself on Jana before he arrived. She came from the Rose family, a prominent family in the history of New Rhodes. Steam pipes, or something; a business that New Rhodes was famous for. Of course, she married a successful venture capitalist after college, and he died a few years back. She was worth quite a bit. Jack didn't look much further than that.

"Jana, I know this is going to be difficult," he said, "but I need to know about my mother."

"I'm surprised it took you this long," She said as Jack pulled out his notepad and pen. "You're taking notes?"

"I have to, Jana … it's regarding a current case."

"You don't mean …" She hushed her voice so that her maid wouldn't hear. "… *the South End Killer?*"

"Yeah," Jack said, "there may or may not be a tie-in; I just want to get it out of the way."

"I'm not sure how much I can help about the … *murders,*" Jana said, "it was thirty years ago."

"We'll take it slowly, and if you don't remember, we'll leave it at that," Jack said. "Now, I saw that the detectives interviewed you back then. What kinds of questions did they ask?"

"Oh," Jana said, "they showed me a picture of … *him …*"

"Coleman?"

"Yes," she replied, "Coleman. They asked me if I'd ever seen him before, or ran into him, but I didn't recognize him."

"And what else?" Jack asked.

"That was pretty much it," Jana said. "They asked me if Louise had talked about someone following her, but there wasn't anybody."

"Okay," Jack said. "Now, I'd like to try to have you remember what was going on in Mom and Dad's life at the time; you know … the kitchen-table talk.

"I know you two were best friends in high school and room-mates in college, and whatever it might be, you won't be hurting my feelings. And please take your time. I'm here as long as you'll have me." He smiled.

Jana stirred sugar into her tea, breathed it in again to test its aroma before she took a sip, like the smell of the tea would take her back through the decades.

"Louise was having problems with Jonathan around the time they were," she hesitated, "you know,"

"What kind of problems?"

"You have to understand the situation, Jack, dear," Jana said as she sipped her tea. "Jonathan was not having a good time living in New Rhodes.

"His Agora Complex was completed a year after you were born, and it replaced four whole blocks of a historical district." Jana looked down at the coffee table as she spoke.

"It was very modern for its time, but it replaced some of the city's most familiar landmarks. It had attracted attention, both positive and negative, but the positive reviews were coming more from New York. Jonathan had gotten an offer to work for a New York firm. But Louise ..."

"She didn't want to go?"

"Not really," Jana said. "She would have, of course, but she wanted to keep you in the Mellville Academy and, to be honest, this is all she knew, this area."

"So how tense were they?"

"It wasn't so much that they were tense, except that Louise ran into an old acquaintance from high school in an ... *odd* sort of way, and Jonathan suspected that she was having an affair."

"Who did she run into?" asked Jack. "And what did you mean, an '*odd* sort of way'?"

Jana held her teacup in her hand, traced the rim with her finger.

"One day in the market, she was, well, *confronted*, if you will, by a man we went to high school with."

"Do you remember his name?"

"How could I forget?" Jana said. "Jeffrey Bowman. He dated Louise briefly in high school, freshman year."

"So how was he memorable?" asked Jack.

"Well; he wasn't *then*;" she said, "I mean, it was complicated ..."

"Take your time, Jana."

"Jeffrey carried a torch for Louise long after she broke up with him," Jana said. "She paid it no mind, and, by the time she was a junior, she was dating Jonathan, but in secret."

"Why in secret?"

"Jonathan came from the Myers' fortune, as I'm sure you're aware." Jack was well aware. He had his *de facto* inheritance piling up in an investment portfolio.

"And Louise; she was ..."

"I know; it's okay. She grew up poor," Jack said, not wanting Jana to feel uncomfortable. He needed the information.

"So, they kept it a secret until the prom, when Jonathan and Louise went together."

"So how does ... Jeffrey ... fit into the picture?" asked Jack.

"He went as Louise's date," Jana said, "uninvited, naturally; he must have thought nobody had asked her. And he and Jonathan had it out in the parking lot. Since they were both drunk, they spent the night in the drunk-tank."

"Okay, so where does this lead to the confrontation they had before my parents were murdered?"

"Well, she wouldn't go into detail about it, but she was scared. And Jonathan's friend saw it happen, so Jonathan confronted her about it. Louise was under a lot of pressure."

"And you're sure she didn't tell you what was said between her and this ... Jeffrey Bowman?"

"No, nothing I remember," Jana said. "But she was scared. I thought then it was because of Jonathan and divorce and whatnot, but now ..."

"Jana, I just have to ask you one thing," Jack said. "Do you know what Jeffrey Bowman is doing now?"

"I remember he was at our twentieth high school reunion," she said. "He told me he was a doctor in New York City. Don't know if it was true, but ..."

"Okay. Thanks, Jana," Jack said. He reached for his wallet and gave her his card. "If you can think of anything else, don't hesitate to call me, okay?"

"I won't, Jack," she said. "But do stay in touch. I *did* watch you grow up, after all ..." She smirked. "Even babysat you once or twice."

Jack chuckled. "I'll keep in touch," he said on the way out.

Jack spent the rest of the afternoon checking records for Jeffrey Bowman. He wasn't in the system, but he had been in the military, having served in Vietnam from the time he graduated high school in 1970 until 1973.

He did indeed move down to New York, but he was never a doctor. He was an M. E.'s assistant in Brooklyn, where he regularly received his VA benefits. He retired from the city's employ in 2009; no work complaints.

Jack knew it would be an impossible sell to get the time to go to Brooklyn and interview him. He knew he'd be walking a fine line with any person of interest in his parents' murders, no less a man living in Brooklyn with no obvious red flags.

He wrote up the report, logged it into the case management database and filed it with his parents' case file. If it was Bowman, his name would be bound to pop up again.

Or so Jack hoped.

On a positive note, Harken told him that the State Police had tried to track the letter they'd got, but the postmark was a fake.

Harken was right; it was a ploy to get Jack rattled. But he still couldn't get the chess move out of his head. One of the things he'd noticed was that the knight in the fork was black.

At the time, he'd thought the sender was using black for effect, but the game was well played up to that point in the picture. The sender knew chess. So they knew that white always made the first move. And in this whole case, the killer had been making the first moves. What was the sender, or the killer, really saying with the picture?

Jack went to the old VFW Post on Mott Street in the Marnesburgh section of the city, north of the task force by about a quarter mile. It was a small square brick building with steel trim on the outside, with a drive that dipped down into a large gravel parking lot with a grassy area that held two old picnic tables and a horseshoe pit.

Jack had been there before with Walt and Eddie, the latter of whom he was going to see. The top floor only held two or three bare offices, a bathroom and the staircase down to the much larger bar in the basement level.

Jack saw two Sheriff's deputies smoking cigarettes outside. He waved, and they waved back, uneasy. They were new; they didn't know him very well.

The bar hadn't lost its smell of stale sweat, mildew and cigarette smoke. Jack noticed the 'No Smoking' sign on the front door; that was new. The actual bar was small, but central. Surrounding it were shiny black barstools and red naugahyde-padded booths.

He saw the flags on the pole in the corner: Old Glory, POW-MIA and New York State flags. For a moment he flashed to Willard's living room. There were stained glass over the lights above the booths and a fluorescent light over the bar. The place was dim and awash with the buzz of its patrons.

Dick Moran was by the door, presumably to check badges. There wasn't a cover.

Jack shot the shit with him for a second, and then saw Eddie sitting in one of the booths. He walked over.

"What're ya drinkin', Eddie?"

"A Mojito," Eddie said. Jack laughed.

"What in the God-awful hell inspired that one?" he asked.

"I don't know," Eddie said. "They say ya gotta count your blessings ... never said ya can't order one of 'em."

"Hear ya..." Jack went to the bar and ordered a highball.

"How's things? Sarah and lil' Eddie?"

"Junior's doing alright," Eddie said. "He's sleeping better, at least."

"And Sarah, dare I ask?"

"No, don't dare. I want to enjoy the Mojito." Eddie had the look.

"Got it," he said. "So what have they got ya doing?"

"So just like that? Right into the case, huh?" Eddie said.

"Hey, you wanted to meet here," Jack said. "We could've gone to Emerald's."

"I'm just fuckin' around ... hoping you had something; I've been turning over stones for snakes and comin' up with earthworms. How about you?"

"Kinda the same," Jack said. "I got a lead today, or so I thought, a guy that had an unhealthy thing for my mother back then ... a 'Jeff Bowman.' Turns out he shipped out to Nam and relocated to New York City. Still lives there, according to records."

"Did you call him? Make sure?"

"And say what?" Eddie asked. "Hey there, you stalked my mom. Just want to make sure you ain't killin' folk up here."

Eddie laughed.

"He would've been half-good for it too. M.E.'s lab assistant; some skill with a scalpel. And there was another thing. This guy came up to me the other day, Simon Smith, works for the Sentinel. He knew I discovered the tunnels, so he got that somewhere."

"The task force leaks. Shit, he could've just overheard it."

"Yeah, that's what I'm thinking ..." Jack said.

"Oh, and we got a letter." Jack described the letter, the picture, the fake postmark and the chess move.

"You know more about chess than me," Eddie said. He sipped his Mojito and quickly put it down, wiping his mouth with a napkin. "Wait! It was a fake postmark, you said?"

"Yeah."

"Where was it delivered?"

"The main station."

"That's a good fuckin' lead right there!"

"I don't follow ... I mean, it's easy to fake a postmark ..."

"Only if you hand-deliver it!"

"Shit, I didn't even think of that!" Jack said.

Joe swirled his cup around on the table. "I helped Bennie Moretti install a security system to watch the garage across the street from the station." He said. "It catches our outside drop in the background. Bennie'd be happy to make us a copy of the video ... We won't even need a warrant."

"Think about it, Jack ... either we got him on camera, or he works for the local post office ... Only two ways to get that letter to the station.

"We gotta get back working together,"

"No kidding," Jack said. "Who ya got with ya now?"

"They got me with Pembroke."

"Oh, man ... really? Pembroke?"

"Yeah ... I'll give it; he's good at records searching, ya know, paper searching. But man, he's a human *off-switch* to every interview. He needs to be behind a desk."

"You miss having Magic Man, eh?"

"Only *you* call yourself that, Jack," Eddie laughed, "... but yeah. Really."

"I'll talk to Harken," Jack said. "I know he doesn't really want me digging into my parents' murders ... fine line as it is ..."

"He put you on it in the first place, though, didn't he?"

"Yeah," Jack said, "but I think it was to soften the blow of getting desk duty. But since I had a successful interview, he might be more open to putting me back in. He knows we're a good team."

"Just one thing," Eddie said, "you know how you asked me to look up Edward Mansfield?"

"Yeah," Jack said. "What'd you get?"

"Well, one thing; he was one of the loudest voices against the urban renewal project."

"I have all of the hate mail they all sent to my father." Jack said.

"Nah; I mean, he was on public record about it. Doubt he'd resort to hate mail. But I found something else out. It might be relevant. There was a company, really old, called 'Webb & Mansfield.' We're talking 1820s. Records of it ended in 1890. They were a mining company."

"There were mines in New Rhodes back then?"

"Nope." Eddie said. "No mention of that ... anywhere."

"We gotta talk to Mansfield," Jack said.

"Think he'll give anything up?"

"Not a damn thing. He's a sly one; I could tell when I first talked to him. We're gonna need an 'in' to get his guard down. He isn't the type to just go down to the station."

"You think he's good for this?" Eddie asked. "Guy's seventy-two."

"I don't know if he's good for it, but he's strong for his age. Probably works out. But I don't think that he's good for it as much as I think he knows the person who *is*."

"So, kid gloves," Eddie said.

Jack swirled the melting cubes in the bottom of his glass.

"For now ..." he said.

Jack and Gamble went into Harken's office together to talk about the letter. Harken had the red-eye express going, but he agreed to have Gamble go over to Bennie's and get a copy of the tape from the time between the last picked-up delivery to the day they got the letter.

Jack stayed behind to talk about being reassigned.

"About fucking time ..." Harken said.

"You're not gonna give me shit about it?"

"I couldn't afford to have both you and Gamble on a desk, but I would rather have done that than split ya up," he said. "But you're out, ya did an interview, so there's no reason not to put the two of you together.

"I want you two to go talk to Walt," Harken said. "He said something about someone lurking around the bar last night. Probably nothing, but a lot of cops hang out there, and I just want to get his statement.

"I also want you to re-canvass the block that Leiah Marcusen lived on. I've been looking over reports, and I'm not really convinced we got everything there was to get."

"Sure thing, Captain."

"And I should take both of yer golds. The pair of ya' walked right by me in the Post last night. Didn't even notice me. Detectives ..."

"No way!"

"Yeah ... you had a highball and Gamble had two Mojitos."

Jack laughed. "John could've told you that ... he was running the bar last night."

"He wouldn't remember a highball ... maybe a Mojito; what the hell is up with that, anyway?"

"I don't know... I asked, he gave me some 'blessings' crap. But they didn't have his beer either."

"Yeah, he drinks that weird Irish shit, doesn't he?"

"Yeah, 'Pride of Eire'," Jack said.

Harken nodded. "I'll have them order it from the beverage mart."

"I'm only telling you so that you know who schools you, right?" He smiled and pointed, shaking his head.

"Ya got us, Cap'," Jack said. "Enjoy it while it lasts."

"I plan on it," Harken said. "Now go drag your ass, find Gamble and get that tape. Then off with ya both."

Jack found Gamble over at Bennie's, two blank CD-Rs in his hand. Probably weren't blank by then.

"Hey, Bennie. Thanks for helping out," Jack said. Bennie smiled. "Harken's got a yoke on us today," he said to Gamble. "We'll probably be pulling double-shift."

"He put us back together?"

"Yeah, and did you know he was in the bar last night?"

"No way!"

"Yes, way, he knew what we ordered," Jack said.

"He could've-"

"No, he didn't," Jack said. "The man's a fuckin' mountain lion in wait. He wouldn't brag about schoolin' us if he didn't."

"Oh, *schoolin'* us, eh?"

"Yup."

Eddie chuckled. "But anyways…"

"We caught a real big break with this," He said. "Let me bring it in, and I'll meet you in the car. I'll tell you all about it when I get back."

"Okay," Jack said. He walked over to the side of the main building, where he'd parked. He switched cars, having driven down in his own car.

As he slid his hand over the gleaming chrome trim, he wished they could use his car to ride around in. At least his heat worked.

Gamble got back and hopped in the passenger seat.

"Knew that wouldn't last," he said.

"What?"

"Being the driver. Pembroke hated driving."

"You wanna drive?"

"Not right now," Gamble said. "I burned us a copy of the surveillance tapes. Two clips, anyway."

He pulled his laptop out of the back.

"What's the big break?" Jack asked.

"Okay," Gamble said, his hand up, fingers shaking. The last time Jack saw him like that, he'd found out how to hack into the hospital's records to find out he was having a baby boy. Sarah didn't want to tell him. So this must've been big.

"Bennie's camera, the one on the police station, at 3:37 a.m. shows a man, slight build, wiry-looking, judging by the height of the mailbox, maybe five-eight, five-nine, I'm guessing a hundred forty pounds. He's wearing ..." Gamble loaded up the video clips.

Jack saw the man he was talking about. He was wearing a half-sleeve black hooded sweatshirt with a white full length shirt underneath, and jeans. He had on black sneakers. He was also wearing sunglasses, and Jack's mind had to run the lyric of the Corey Heart song; *I wear my sunglasses at night...* Hard to see any facial features from the angle of the camera and the hood.

Something about him looked familiar.

"But that's not it," Gamble said. "I installed a hidden pinhole camera, high quality, in the back parking lot of the garage. Bennie wanted to be able to read the license plates of any car parked there.

"Well, this guy was stupid enough to park there." Gamble clicked on the second clip. Jack's jaw dropped as the delivery boy drew down his hood and took off the glasses as he fiddled for the keys to a black Mercury Sable.

It was the reporter, Simon Smith.

CHAPTER SIX

"I know that guy!" Jack said. "He's that reporter for the Sentinel!" Jack remembered the card. "We have his prints on the business card he gave me!"

"The car belongs to Edward Mansfield," Gamble said. "I just punched it up when I was in Harken's office.

"Did Mansfield report it stolen?"

"Not reported stolen," Gamble said. "Think we should go check in on Mr. Mansfield."

"Wait a minute," Jack said. "Smith doesn't know we're on to him. We don't want to tip our hand until we're ready to move on him. We should take this to the whole task force first."

"We can get him on mail fraud right now," Gamble said.

"True, but that's federal," Jack said. "So let's talk to Decker and Haskell at the HQ."

"Deal," Gamble said.

"And we learn everything we can on Simon Smith,"

"This is Simon Smith, thirty-seven years old; a freelance re-porter for the Sentinel," Harken said of the image captured from Bennie's parking lot camera. "We have him on tape slipping mail into the box at the main station at 3:37 a.m.

"The letter in question had a false Buffalo postmark," he continued. "A few days ago, Detective Taggart was approached by Smith, who indicated that he knew Taggart was the one who found the tunnel; that information was not released."

"Jack got a business card from him, and the prints on the gloss laminate matched the prints on the letter.

"Detective Gamble ran the plates on the car. Owner was Edward Mansfield. He's also been on our radar."

"We should go pick Smith up," Decker said. "We can charge him with mail fraud until we can figure out his role here."

"I think we need to do some research on him and Mansfield before we make a move," Harken said. "Hit them both at once."

"Wait," Jack said. "What if they're not the only ones involved?"

"So you say we just sit on our hands?" Decker said. "Let them drop other bodies?"

"No. But we should tail them, set up surveillance," Jack replied. "They've been playing us this whole time; we finally have something on them they don't know about. The moment we start dragging them into the box, we lose that advantage."

"We need to put the heat on them," Melfly said. "Jack, I understand what you're saying, but we have the public and the media breathing down our necks. If he, or they, kill again, even if your way pans out in the long run, there'll be hell to pay … for all of us."

"OK, let's everybody calm down. This is the first solid lead we've had on suspects," Harken said.

"Jack, I want you and Gamble to go out and do what you were assigned today. Teague, Melfly, Decker … let's meet in my office and figure out what we're going to do."

A re-canvass of Leiah Marcusen's neighborhood brought one new lead in: a list of license plate numbers of people stopping in the house at all hours. The woman who wrote down the plates had just gotten back from vacation when they first canvassed; they missed her.

She suspected drug dealing by Leiah's boyfriend. Only one name was marginally interesting; Jason Smith. Jack flagged that plate for follow-up; could've been a relative of Simon Smith, but then again, the name *Smith* was common.

They went to Emerald's, and Walt was mopping the floor. He waved them in, directing them to the bar area where he hadn't mopped. Walt stopped, and hopped behind the bar to pour two cups of coffee.

"Glad you guys stopped by," Walt said. "I called Harken. Had a weird incident last night."

"Well, we're all ears …" Jack said.

"Okay, so I get done with the bar, Ralphie went home and I lock up. I turn the corner to go to my car and there's this guy fidgeting around …"

"Get a good look at him?"

"Nah, the light's shitty in the alley, so not really. He's wearing a hooded sweatshirt and an army jacket, one of the ones we used to have, before they changed them up."

"You were in the Army?"

"Yeah, I was drafted in seventy-two," Walt said. "I was only there for a year."

"So what did he say?"

"He said that I should've kept quiet about the tunnels," Walt said. "He thought I was a friend, and how could I betray him, and just some other jumbled rants. Then he walked to his car, got in and drove down the alley."

"And you really didn't see his face?"

"He had a beard, like mountain-man stuff." Walt said. "Other than that, no."

"The car?"

"Mid-eighties sedan, dark color, brown or black?"

"Didn't get the plate?" Gamble asked.

"Nah, it was too dark, and the plate lights were out."

Jack wrote down everything, and Eddie went outside to look around the alleyway.

"How did he know you talked about the tunnels?"

"I have no idea," Walt replied. "You two are the only ones I mentioned that to."

"From what you're saying, it's like he knew you; like you were friends."

"My friends all talk to me to my face," Walt said. "And I didn't recognize his voice.

"Look, I was a cop, I know I should've ran in the bar, grabbed my gun, chased him, anything but just sit there slack-jawed, but that's just what I did. I was caught off-guard."

"Walt, why did you wait until today to report it?" Jack asked.

"Same reasons, I guess … it wasn't until this morning that I put it together that he might have been the South End Killer. I thought maybe it had something to do with Mansfield.

"I'm sorry, Jack,"

"It's alright," Jack replied, "but you have to call us immediately if this guy shows up again."

"I will," Walt said. "After this, I think I might just keep my gun on me."

"Let me ask you something," Jack said, "does the name 'Jeff Bowman' mean anything to you?"

"Never heard it before. Do you think that was his name? Who is he?"

"Just a name at this point. And just keep that between you, me and Eddie, okay?"

Walt nodded.

Gamble came in with something in his hand.

"This is the only odd thing I found in the alleyway," he said. He placed it on the bar.

"It's an Army patch," Jack said. Walt's eyes dropped and he shook his head.

"It *my* old Army patch," Walt said. "My old unit, I mean – Eighteenth MP Brigade. But how!?"

"Are you *sure* you don't remember him from the war?"

"All I remember about the war was the heat, humidity, bugs and drunken derelicts I had to watch in the brig. So many people passing through; I only remember my sergeant, and that wasn't him."

Jack turned the patch around in his hand.

"We gotta' bring this in." Jack said. "Are you sure it's not yours?"

"The only ones I have are sewn into my old uniform." Walt said.

"Okay." Jack and Gamble got up to go.

"We'll get back here to catch up, Walt... under better circumstances, hopefully. If you remember anything..."

"I know the drill." Walt finished the thought. "I'll call ya back."

They stopped at the Java King for coffee. Mindful of Harken's words about talking outside the taskforce or the Post, they drank it in the car in the parking lot. Gamble tapped away on his laptop as they spoke, as was usually the case.

"So where are we, Eddie?"

"I'm assuming you mean the case ..."

"Yeah, Eddie, the case," Jack said. "Simon Smith, Edward Mansfield, Jeff Bowman ... Walt ... assuming they're all involved; how are they related?"

"They're related," Gamble said.

"I'm sure they are ..."

"No, I mean, they're *related*," Gamble said. "Well, not Bowman and Walt, but Smith and Mansfield."

"How?"

"Okay," Gamble moved the laptop so the screen was in Jack's view. "Edward Mansfield had a sister, Joanna. She was killed in a fire in 1962. She had a son, Jason, who was adopted by Mansfield. And he has a son named Simon."

"So Smith was her married name?"

"Yes. Smith."

"So where does Jason Smith play into this?"

"Doesn't seem to," Gamble said. "No record; no priors, damn-near squeaky clean. Works in the County Clerk's office."

"So, Mansfield was a city planner, Jason Smith works in the County Clerk's office, and Simon Smith works freelance for the Sentinel. That all equates to knowledge, information; the locations of tunnels, the calls to 9-1-1 dispatch ... but it doesn't equate to what we saw when we walked into those crime scenes.

"There was a confidence, an *ease with the acts*. That's easy for office guys to fantasize about, but not easy to do."

"Besides, they needed medical training, forensic training, some military training, maybe ... Bowman has those in spades, but he's living downstate, and Walt ..."

"And then there's Walt ..." Gamble said, nodding.

"I know he looks good for this, but ... you know..."

"We can't exclude him, Jack."

Jack set his coffee on the dashboard. "He just looks *too* good for this."

"What do you mean?"

"I mean, twice, he's implicated himself in this investigation," Jack said. "He has the forensic training, the military training, apparently."

"I remember him when he was a cop. He was good; I don't mean decent, I mean *good* at being a cop.

"Why would he go to such lengths to make himself a suspect?"

"I don't think he's a suspect," Gamble said. "He's like you, though; *involved*. The Killer is trying to make him look like the prime suspect.

"Now, what about this Bowman guy. You talked to him?"

"No, not yet," Jack said. "And I checked with the VA. He's getting his checks sent to Brooklyn still."

"Let's say I have a summer home in Lake George." Gamble said. "Sometimes I get to go there for a summer, and my checks come here. So hypothetically, in the summer, where am I living?"

"So what are you saying?" Jack said. "He's a commuter?"

"I'm just saying we can't rule the guy out."

"Okay, so how does he fit into this picture?"

"Bowman has motive, and skills," Gamble said, "but the Smiths and Mansfield provide some degree of means and opportunity."

"But what's *their* motive?" Jack asked. "They wouldn't do this for nothing."

"No idea." Gamble tapped on the laptop. "I can only get so much from here."

Jack burned his mouth on the coffee, but was careful not to spill any on himself. Outside of their office, the sidewalks were lined with kids with back-packs and cellphones, sharing their nasty homework assignments or test jitters with the world in one-hundred and forty characters or less.

"We're missing something." Jack said. "Something big."

They arrived in the task force to see Harken with a sullen look on his face. He motioned for them to go into his office.

"They arrested Simon Smith for mail fraud," Harken said. "They tried to sweat him in the box, but he lawyered up."

"Son of a bitch!" Jack shouted, loud enough for the sound to escape the office. "He's related to Edward Mansfield!"

Harken let out a sigh. "Fuck," he said. "The D.A. told me he'd be out by tomorrow on bail, and he ain't talking."

"How did you-?"

"Listen, Jack!" Frustration and anger seethed in Harken's voice. "I went to bat for you! Don't treat me like I didn't back your play!"

"Sorry, Cap," Jack said calmly. He knew Harken was being honest. "So what actually went down in the meeting?"

"The Feds have been waiting to take jurisdiction on this, ever since we found the body dump. They say that they're just here to assist, but I know better.

"They're waiting for anything federal to take over the task force. It was a power-play, Jack."

"Take Smith in or lose the task force," Jack said.

"But Melfly was the one who brought this up in the first place. What's his angle?"

"He's up against a tough opponent next year for the Sheriff's race," Harken said, "He's our only elected official, and he wants to show the media, and through them, the public, that we're actually getting something done.

"Plus, the Party Chairman is putting pressure on him to make his own power-play," Harken said. "I'm just about ready to let them take it."

"Sorry I yelled, Cap," Jack said. "So what now?"

Harken leaned back in his chair.

"We play it your way," he said.

"Decker told me they only asked questions about the mail fraud before he lawyered up. No questions on the murders. He'll be out by tomorrow afternoon. Teague's got his hand in the power-play too, but he wants to keep it local, like us. So he managed to get a search warrant for Smith's place and Mansfield's car.

"Surveillance and reporting only; do not approach Smith *or* Mansfield about the murders. We'll set you up with anything you need … *within reason.*"

"Captain, Smith and Mansfield will make me," Jack said.

"That's why I'm putting you in charge of the operation," Harken said. "I got everyone to give up a couple of under-covers, even the FBI's giving up an agent from Albany to assist …

"I think they agreed just to save face, though. You and Eddie run it, they work it. They report to you, you report to me, and I report to the senior command.

"No, and I repeat, *no*, sidetracks," he added. "Bring any leads to the task force, and let 'em go.

"You got until the eight o'clock brief to come up with a basic plan, both of you," Harken continued. "You'll meet us in the conference room, and go over your plan. No one's gonna be happy that you're running it, so make it *that good*."

Jack and Gamble went over a plan that they hoped would stand up to the senior command. They decided that Jack would need to keep up the appearance of doing interviews if they didn't want to tip Smith off.

He would interview Mansfield about his car, directing it as if they were focused on Smith. Jack wouldn't mention the fact that they knew the two were related.

Gamble would be in charge of running tactical computer support for the members in the field. He would be paired with a support person from either the FBI or the State Police.

They would adopt a strategy utilized by many military campaigns of the past; their operation would *live off the land*, basing their strategies as new information came in, while keeping standard reporting to Harken.

It was critical that every member of the team relay what they get to Gamble for processing and cross-linking as soon as they got it. Gamble would run the intel up the chain, and he and Jack would plot next moves. They would make the fixed points simple to relocate and the undercovers would make it highly mobile.

They'd need wiretaps on Smith's phone and to bug his residence. They knew they could get that for Smith, but they'd have a harder time getting one for Mansfield.

Their key to their success, or failure, would be how few people knew what they were doing.

They decided that operations involving wiretaps and bugs should be handled by the FBI or the State Police, as the Smiths and Mansfield seemed to have connections in Rhodes County.

But the information stream couldn't go dead in Rhodes County, so Sheriff Melfly would have to work with the operation to coordinate internal misinformation as it involved anything going outside of the task force.

Jack and Gamble knew with all of the power-playing going on, they needed a plan that brought all agencies in, and gave the senior command at least the appearance of control, while allowing them to adapt.

They bought it at the eight o'clock. They dicked with it, tweaking this and that, but Jack knew they would. He was flexible, and since they included everyone, nobody wanted to tie up the operation's hands.

They decided to use the third floor of a vacant property across from Triumph Park, facing the window of Mansfield's office in the Historical Society, for the main base.

They also set up a more visible dummy surveillance post outside of Smith's house, and a smaller post in an apartment across the street from Mansfield's home.

They were hoping to use the three posts to not only get audio and video evidence, but also force Smith and Mansfield to interact.

In addition, they had three undercover teams to track movements.

The FBI worked that night with the State Police to set up the three bases, two of them little more than two chairs, a table and some surveillance equipment. The apartment across from Mansfield's office had everything they could get into the place. Jack went to his house that night and slept alone, called Mary to let her know he was okay.

He woke up early, ate two cups of yogurt as he got dressed. He and Gamble decided that he should interview Mansfield before Smith made bail. He needed to throw some chum in the water.

He mulled over his approach as he drove down Route 6 toward downtown. He couldn't go in directly accusing Mansfield of being involved with the killings; He'd shut right down.

It would be the easiest way to see if he was involved or not, but he needed something incriminating to get probable cause. However, He would suspect something if Jack tried to feign complete ignorance. He needed to build rapport with Mansfield, then give enough out to make him nervous. Make him think it.

Jack arrived at the Historical Society at eight-thirty. Mansfield was the only person there.

"Hello, Detective," Mansfield said. He looked a little rattled. "How can I help you today?"

"I have a couple of questions. I was wondering if you could help me out."

"Sure thing," he said. "Come on in."

They walked into his office. Mansfield offered him tea, which he accepted.

Mansfield went out into the kitchen to brew a pot, and Jack jumped up really quickly to scan the room.

He noticed a thick, box-like frame on one of the pictures along the back wall that Mansfield wouldn't notice. He reached in his pocket and turned on an untraceable bug he'd brought in, something he had from his days in narco, just in case a warrant came through later. He placed it on the frame, within earshot and out of sight.

Mansfield got back to the office with two cups of tea. His hands were shaking, but barely. Could have been his age.

"Ed, I remember asking you about the tunnels early on in the investigation. Do you remember that?" Mansfield smiled. "Yes. It looks like they were there. How on earth did you find the one you were looking for?"

"Well, Walter told me where it was, and you confirmed that they existed. It was an easy matter of looking up archives of the mills on the East Hill.

"We found one that had hired a mining company. It was called Webb and Mansfield. Coincidence, right?"

Jack saw it; the twitch in his left eye.

"Yeah," He said, "must be."

"How long has your family been in the area?" Jack asked.

"Oh, I don't know ... That company name is new to me. I'd be surprised if I was related to them."

"But it is possible, right?"

"Well, I guess anything's *possible* ..."

"Is it possible that maybe you saw maps or something? You know, as a kid, of course ..."

"Yeah, that would be possible, but I hardly remember back so far." He laughed hesitantly. "I'm an old man now. May I ask where you're heading with this?"

"Well, Walter said that you told him exactly where the tunnel was that we found. Pretty much right as we found it." Jack leaned close.

He saw the faintest sheen of sweat on Mansfield's brow. "Between you and me, I don't think either of you are involved in this, but I have to know exactly where that information came from."

"I don't remember ever saying anything to Walt," Mansfield said as he crossed his arms. He swiped his hand over his head in a poor attempt to get rid of the sweat. His forehead had acquired new creases, as if the skin was shriveling under the heat of the truth.

"And you're sure of that? Not even if you guys were drinking late one night?"

"Oh, no, it's only tea for me." He smirked.

"Don't drink?" Jack had his notebook open by then, and wrote that down.

"Nope," Mansfield said.

"Ever drink?"

"Not with Walt," he said. "I'd always drink seltzer when I visited him. Long drive home."

"Where do you live, if you don't mind my asking?"

Mansfield hesitated slightly. Jack was getting too close.

"Outside of the city?" he prompted.

"No, in the city, just across town."

"Oh, okay," Jack said. "Sorry if I sound like I'm grilling ya here. Just haven't gotten a lot of sleep lately. You'll have to forgive me."

"It's no problem, Detective. You boys are pretty busy, I imagine ..."

"You have no idea," Jack said. "You heard about the bones they found, right?"

"Yeah, I saw it on the news. Are they linked to the South End Killer?"

"Too soon to say," Jack said. "We've got a lot of identifications to make."

"I don't imagine it's easy. They say the count's up to twenty bodies now?"

"Close to that,"

"Jesus ..." Mansfield said. He sounded sincere; a little *too* sincere.

"I just have one thing to ask you about," Jack said. "Kind of the reason why I came here ..."

"Okay, go ahead," Mansfield said. Jack pulled out the mugshot of Simon Smith.

"Do you know this man?"

"Yes, actually," Mansfield said. "That's Simon Smith. He's a reporter for the Sentinel. He also helps me around here sometimes."

Jack took out a still from the camera behind Bennie's, showing Simon and Mansfield's car.

"At three in the morning, a couple of nights ago, he parked this car at a garage next door to the police station." Jack said. "We caught him on the camera in front placing a letter in the police station's mail box, possibly implicating himself in the killings. Do you recognize the car?"

"Well, yes, that's my car," Mansfield replied. "Simon has a copy of the keys. He runs errands for me sometimes."

"Did he have you're permission to use your car that night?"

"No, he didn't."

"Would you like to press charges on auto-theft, then?"

Mansfield stopped and rubbed the side of his face. This was the moment Jack had prepped for. *What would he do?*

"I'll talk to Simon," Mansfield said. "Today."

"So you're declining to press charges?"

"He may have thought he had my permission; either way, I want to get to the bottom of this."

"I would urge you to let us do that," Jack said.

"Do I have a choice?"

"Of course; it's your car, after all."

"Then I'll talk to him," Mansfield said.

"Okay," Jack said, "just be careful, Ed. If he is implicated, he's likely to try and drag anyone down with him. I don't want to see it happen to you. You've been pretty helpful in this case."

Mansfield took a sip of his tea, keeping his eyes on Jack. "I'll be careful, Detective."

Jack thanked him and got up. He gave the man his card.

"If you change your mind, or have any questions, don't hesitate to call."

"I won't," Mansfield said.

"And we'll let you know if we have more questions. Is that okay?"

"No problem." Mansfield nodded nervously.

Jack left with the bait on the hook.

Jack, Gamble and their contact, Agent Walson, ate bagels and drank coffee when Simon Smith was released. They had a team in place following him.

He took a cab to a house on Fifth Street, stayed there for an hour. The team relayed the address to Gamble, who already knew it.

It was Jason Smith's house. They didn't have any audio set up in there, and Jack only wished he could've been a fly on the wall. Simon left and walked to his own house, seven blocks away. Dressed in street clothes, the team had to follow on foot, careful not to be noticed. Simon got to his house around noon, where the team set up across the street had a rifle mic.

When Simon was arrested, they had cloned his phone, and they had a tap on his land line. He used his cell to make a call.

"Historical Society," Jack heard. Gamble pressed *record*.

"It's me," Simon said.

"Now is not a good time," Mansfield said. "But we need to talk."

"When and where?" Simon asked.

"Meet me here at the office tomorrow at six," Mansfield said. There was some interference.

"Six in the morning?"

"Yes. Six in the morning," Mansfield said. "Be here at six sharp."

"Yes, sir," Simon said, then hung up.

The rest of the day was largely unproductive. They watched the Historical Society. Simon stayed in his house, leaving only to get lunch and dinner. He didn't go to the Sentinel. Not that that was expected, seeing as the only story he could give them would violate his Fifth Amendment rights.

Jack, Gamble and Walson spent most of the time shooting the shit.

"So why does the FBI want to take jurisdiction on this?" Jack asked.

Walson laughed. "Who said we wanted to?"

"C'mon ... I hear the office gossip,"

"The Bureau comes in to assist," Walson said.

"If you're gonna hang out with us for the next week or so, you're gonna have to do better than that," Gamble said.

"Alright, look," Walson said, "we come in to assist. But once our name is attached to any case ..." He paused.

"It's like people have impossibly high expectations of our ability to solve crimes. So when the case, especially a case like this, doesn't seem to be going anywhere, the pressure on us from the top is to try to wrestle jurisdiction.

"Even when we get it," he added, "we're usually not happy about having it."

"Nobody wants their name on a turd," Gamble said.

"Exactly."

Jack went to bed on one of the cots at five. It was God-awful early to go to bed, but Gamble and Walson could back each other up. Jack had to make his own arrangements.

He woke up at one in the morning, surprised he had gotten a full eight. Gamble was at the post; said Walson would relieve him at five.

They sat there in the stillness of the night, watching a gentle breeze blow the flag around in the park below, a small space with a towering obelisk surrounded by a bit of grass that separated three streets.

"When's Mary and Paul coming back?"

"They're thinking this weekend." Jack said.

"How are you on that?"

Jack shrugged. "I won't have to drive to Riverville every night." Jack said. "But still, I don't know..."

"Do you think they'd go after your family?" Gamble said. "I mean, you gotta' admit, we're close..."

"But are we?" Jack said. "Say these guys are our killers. They slip up on wiretap, we catch 'em, case closed. But the case was closed before..."

"Coleman."

"Yeah, Coleman." Jack said. "I just kind of feel like we're chasing pawns here... Simon? Too bold to be physically involved. Mansfield? Not good under pressure; I saw that when I interviewed him this morning, and Jason Smith; we don't know enough about him, or if he's involved at all."

"So you think we're chasing a dead end?"

Jack yawned. "No, not that... they're *involved*, I'm sure of that, it's just, I don't know... I'm just afraid of Mary and Paul coming home, and all we manage to do here is stir up a hornet's nest."

"They made it personal for ya." Gamble said. "But even I'm nervous about Sarah and Junior. And Sarah does *not* want me on this case."

"What have you been telling her?"

"I told her I've been on a desk the whole time."

Jack laughed. "I *wish* I could tell Mary stuff like that."

"What do you tell Paul?"

"About as much as you tell Sarah."

Gamble let out a sigh. He scanned the streets with binoculars.

"Let's hope that this time next week, we'll be working good old homicides again." He said.

"So I take it you and Sarah are a little better off?"

Eddie shrugged.

"Doc says she's got 'post-partum depression'... He gave her pills. She's been calmer, but she's gained a couple pounds. So now she's complaining about her clothes not fitting."

"I just don't want her to go off the pills, ya' know?" He continued. "I'd much prefer 'chubby Sarah' to 'bowl-throwing-at-my-head' Sarah."

"Wow... Got that bad, huh?"

"It's not her fault, Jack."

"I'll just consider myself lucky that we didn't have to go through that." Jack said.

"For a while, I was just locking myself in my study and writing apps for my phone."

"Anything good?"

"Mostly music players and search tools... Some good shit, I guess. But one draws devil horns on any person's image through facial recognition."

Jack laughed. "Really?"

"Guess who inspired *that* one..."

Around four, Jack noticed something. A man, camouflage jacket and jeans, walking between the Historical Society and the adjoining Hudson River Museum. He had an olive drab backpack. He kept watching.

"You think that's the guy Walt saw?"

"Maybe," Gamble said. "Or he might be homeless. Hudson Park's back there; a lot of them sleep there."

"Did you see where he came from?"

"Nah, didn't catch it."

They kept their eyes fixed on the building. About a half-hour later, the man came out to stand between the two buildings.

He eyed the street, right to left, ducking his head out to do it. Then he tucked his hand in his side pocket and started walking South on River Street. No backpack.

"Wake up Walson," Jack said as he reached for his jacket. "We gotta go after him."

Gamble was only too happy to oblige, having sat on his ass for the better part of sixteen hours.

Walson was half-awake when they told him to man the window. He nodded and rubbed his eyes.

Jack and Gamble thundered down the stairs and out the front door of the apartment. They spotted the guy heading around the curve in River Street, going toward the riverfront.

"Let's go!" Jack reached for his Glock 17 as he started running, Eddie close on his heels. They rounded the corner where they saw the guy disappear. They could see him about a half a block away, walking quickly.

Jack put his finger to his lips, and he and Gamble took a quick, quiet walking pace, using the dumpsters' shadows to cover themselves. The shuffling of the man's feet got louder. They were almost on him. Jack could see his outline casting its own shadows. The man got to an old sedan and unlocked the door.

"Stop! Police!" Jack screamed. "Right where you are! Hands up!"

The man turned around briefly, opened the door and, crouching behind it, put a gun through the window and opened fire.

Jack returned fire, but the man got into the car and turned the ignition. He yelled at Eddie to go after him, but he realized he was wasn't yelling too loudly from the ground.

He was hit; hot blood soaking his shirt, followed by sharp, searing pain. He heard Gamble shout into his radio. His head hit the pavement, his gaze fixed at a brick wall as the dark shadows grew even darker, until all that was left was black …

"10-13, officer down! Corner of River and Union Street!

CHAPTER SEVEN

Jack drifted in and out of consciousness. Flashes of antiseptic fluorescent light and the glint of steel railings of the gurney, the faces over him as he felt the movement toward the OR... not that he knew a thing about where he was. Just flashes. Then, lights out.

He opened his lids to a fluorescent light above and one behind him, guarded by a semi-opaque beige plate. He felt the IV in his arm just before the pain. It was dull; they must've loaded him up with morphine. He turned his head to see Paul sleeping in the other bed. Mary was curled up in one of the padded chairs. Gamble was in the other chair, reading a paper. He could tell it was Gamble by the way he hooked the sides with his thumb and forefinger.

"Eddie," he whispered, not wanting to wake up the others.

Gamble looked up and sprang to his feet. Mary and Paul stirred. Mary opened an eye and then she got up.

"How long have I been out?"

"About twelve hours." Gamble said.

"Honey, how do you feel?" Mary ran her hand across Jack's head.

"I feel high ... and like I got run over," Jack tried to laugh, but that was a *no-go*.

"Yeah, don't laugh," Gamble said. "And try not to cough. You were lucky, man; don't push it."

"So what's the damages?"

"Well, one bullet, they had to sew up your guts a little, and they were able to pull out the slug." Gamble said.

"No through-and-through?"

"If it had been through-and-through, you wouldn't be lucky. They spent six hours on ya; Doc said one more inch deeper and it would've severed your spine."

"Damn ..."

"You're right, *damn!*" Mary said. "What were you thinking!? *Both* of you!?"

"No fair, Mary ... I'm on morphine ..."

Mary crossed her arms, sulked. "Well, at least it'll be good to have you back home for a while now that you're off the case."

"What do you mean, *off the case*?"

"We're both suspended with pay until they investigate the shooting," Gamble said.

"Oh, yeah ... the shooting." Jack rubbed his eyes. "They're going to have a field day with that."

"I don't think so. A witness that came forward about it."

"Did they see the guy?"

"No, but he saw what went down. Just so happens, he's a member of the civilian review board."

"You're shittin' me," Jack said.

"He didn't get a good look at the guy, though, and I couldn't see him so well from where I was standing. Did you get a good look at him?"

"It's fuzzy, Eddie. Last thing I remember clearly was us chasing him."

"I memorized the plate on the car," Gamble said. "It was stolen; they just found it an hour ago abandoned at an old factory on First Street. State Police and the Feds are processing it."

"I wish I could remember his face."

"It was dark," Gamble said, "I wouldn't sweat it."

"Maybe if I see his face again, it'll trigger it."

"Maybe ... Just give it time. You need to rest."

"What about the surveillance footage?"

"Nothing really useful," Gamble said. "The guy didn't look up."

Gamble took off after that, and Mary sat by the bed, stroking Jack's arm until he fell back to sleep.

He awoke the next morning to Captain Harken.

"Mary and Paul are downstairs getting breakfast," he said.

"So I'm off the case, I heard," Jack said. "Me and Eddie both."

"Yeah, but Eddie will be back on once IAB clears him."

"Why not me, then?"

"Jack," Harken said, "I admire your enthusiasm, but no. You're injured, ya almost got killed. I'm not putting you back into this."

"I'll be fine ... Just need to heal up. I could still work a desk..."

"Have you even talked to the doctor yet?"

"I'll see him today at some point ..."

"So how do you know you'll be fine?"

"I'll heal…" Jack said.

"And just what in Baby Jesus's name was that stunt the two of you pulled?" Harken said. "No body armor, chasin' a guy in a dark alley… Are you both in somebody's death pool?"

"Cap', it was a clean shoot. And we had to take action. It was exigent circumstances."

"I know," Harken said. "I read the incident report. You guys did what you had to do; I'm not faulting you for that."

"Then what are you faulting me for?"

Harken sat down in the chair, scratched at his moustache. "Stupidity," he said. "You had no idea who you were chasing, what he was capable of. You wanna' know why I'm here this morning, and not stuck at the task force cleaning up your messes?"

"I'm getting a medal?" Jack tried to make it sound like a joke, but without being able to laugh, it sounded sarcastic.

"I'm no longer leading the task force." Harken said. "Smartass…"

"Why? Because of us?" Jack felt the pain slithering in his gut.

"Not you guys," Harken said. "Because of *him*, I imagine."

"I don't follow," Jack said.

"Yesterday morning, a bomb went off in the Historical Society building. It killed eight people. Six were living above it, and two were found in the Historical Society itself. They've yet to be confirmed, but based off of your operation, we think it was-"

"… Smith and Mansfield," Jack said.

"Yeah. So the ATF is co-leading with the FBI now," Harken said. "And Homeland Security is knocking. All we'll have left are the first four murders. Anything thereafter, they're gonna' claim it.

"Look, you'll go through the same stuff as Gamble, plus a psych eval, so go through it, and then, once you're cleared by us, you have to be cleared by your doctor. Then, by all means, you're welcome back."

"To the case?"

"To Homicide," Harken said. Jack slumped back and sighed.

"You can still come to the Post," Harken said. "The Feds haven't made any use out of it, so I guess it'll just be for us expatriates." He grinned.

Jack got cleared by IAB in a closed session in Room 608A of the hospital. Totally cursory; they might as well have given him a survey. He'd gotten grilled more on the policy break, but there really wasn't much of one.

Turned out the civilian review board, long known for harassing cops for everything from excessive force to illegal parking, went out of their way to push IAB to clear cops they actually saw doing their jobs.

The psych evaluation was another story. He had to spend a week in the hospital before he was able to get out. He wasn't totally healed; the doctors said he shouldn't do anything involving bending for at least three weeks. They normally did the evals at the shrink's office, but they agreed to meet him at Dan's.

Haskell asked to perform his own psych eval as well. Jack could've declined it, but he figured it would keep him closer to the case. Since the Feds were in the lead, wouldn't hurt to cooperate with one.

In the meantime, he got visitors, and lots of them. Even Teague and Melfly stopped over to ask how he was doing. Melfly joked with him that when they caught the killer, after the trial, they'd make a pendant out of the bullet they pulled out of him. Jack respectfully declined.

Teague was quiet. Jack didn't know him starting out, but he was a warm man; a family man, bunch of kids and churchgoing, the whole family was. But he was cold, barely said a word, looking around like he was lost. Maybe the case was starting to wear on him.

When he was discharged, Dr. LaPlace met him at the house. They picked Dan's study, a tastefully decorated little room with a leather recliner and a bookcase built into the side-wall.

The bookcase made him envious, filled with books on every subject, an encyclopedia set, and law books. Dan told him once that if it wasn't in there, he didn't need to know it. He also had a small wet bar in there.

Jack sipped on some of Dan's Scotch as they talked about the shooting. Jack thought it was going to be like pulling teeth, but not so. Dr. LaPlace was a warm woman, older than him, and he felt comfortable opening up to her.

He had been rattled by the shooting. He thought about Mary and Paul, and what would've happened to them if he hadn't made it. As far as discharging his weapon, he still didn't remember it. LaPlace told him that the memory might never form.

She couldn't tell him if he'd passed his evaluation, but she told him not to worry about anything. Coming from her, it felt comforting.

Haskell came over, dressed in blue jeans and a white button-down shirt. His hair was ruffled, and he looked like he had more on his mind than Jack had on *his*.

"Jack," Haskell said as he sat in the side chair, "you know that anything said in here is confidential, right?"

"Yeah, I know."

"Good." Haskell took a sip of the tea Dan poured them. "The Bureau's holding off on interviewing you," he said.

"They know you don't remember the shooter's face, and for everything else, they're just using the video that Agent Walson shot when the bomber left the Historical Society."

"Heard they won't get much off of that," Jack said. "But why are you referring to the Bureau as *they*?"

Haskell laughed, rubbed his head. "Slip of the tongue," he said, "Freudian slip, if I must say ..."

"They giving ya grief?"

"No, it's not that," Haskell said. "Just, since the bombing, ATF has come in, they and the Bureau are running over this case like a tank, and I'm just ..."

"Getting rolled over, eh?"

"They took over my office, if that tells you anything."

"Well, they took me off the case, if that means anything."

"Yeah," Haskell said, "I heard that. That was a decision made by your Police Chief."

"Detmer took me off of this?"

"You gotta understand, at the time he did it you were still in surgery. He was worried about you."

"Worried that what, I'm letting this get too personal?"

"No; I'm thinking more that this guy's gonna succeed next time in killing you." Haskell said. "He's made it personal, and he's been making it personal."

"If they take me out, then he wins," Jack said.

"Your chief isn't going to put you back on this case. He couldn't right now if he wanted to. You have a bit of healing up to do."

Jack sat back, lit up a cigarette.

"Spare one?" Haskell asked. Jack was surprised, but handed over the pack. Haskell lit up.

"There are some people on the task force who don't think you should be entirely off the case," Haskell said.

"Go on," Jack said.

"He's made it personal to you. And there's at least a tie-in to your parents' murders."

"Isn't that why they're keeping me off?"

"They don't want to bury you, Jack," Haskell said. "And they don't want to see you lose family members. And you don't want either of those things."

"So, how do I stay involved?"

"Work with me," Haskell said. "Work with your partner. Go to that VFW Post and keep your ears open. Stay in this, Jack, but lay low."

"Why do you care, Haskell?"

Haskell set his cigarette in the ashtray. "You need a break from this, a rest." He stopped for a second. The lines on his face softened suddenly.

"There was this case," he said, "child-killer near Philly. Fifteen abducted women, ten found buried in shallow graves." He took a shallow, ragged breath. "One of them was my girlfriend at the time.

"I wasn't a profiler then, just a field agent assigned to the task force. At the time, Jersey had three murders, same M.O."

"They took you off the case?"

"Yeah," Haskell said. "And I hated them for it."

"So what happened?"

"Well, they killed the prime suspect in a shoot-out, the abductions stopped, and I left the field to study at Quantico.

"That made me become a profiler," he said. "I know what you're going through, Jack. I know what it's like when it's personal. My only wish back then was that I'd fought harder against being reassigned. But ... different times."

They talked for a while longer. Haskell talked about his girlfriend, their life before and the dark road that he staggered down after they dug her out of a ditch. Jack talked about his parents and about Mary, and how he wouldn't know what he'd do if he had to face what Haskell had faced.

After the session ended, he invited Haskell to the back porch for a Scotch.

"I'll help you out," Jack said as they drank. "God knows I don't want to be benched. But I don't want to lose my job either. Can you do anything for me there?"

"I'll be able to hire you as a consultant," Haskell replied. "I'll be utilizing your skills and experience in enhancing a profile of the killers."

"I'm pretty sure I know who it is," Jack said.

Haskell cleared his throat. "I saw your notes about Bowman," Haskell said. "But I think Simon Smith's father is also involved; Jason Smith."

"So why do we need a profile?"

"Smith didn't show up for work today, and he hasn't been located. Based on your work, I did some digging. Jeffrey Bowman's address was searched in Brooklyn. Dead end. He doesn't live there. Used to, but we're looking for someone who picks up his mail. That's all we have on his location; squat.

"And Walter Brinbey was in Vietnam at the same time as Bowman, but there's no evidence they crossed paths. We can't rule him out completely, but he's not really a suspect.

"We need a profile based on everything we can find out about both Bowman and Smith." Haskell continued; "I'm trained in crime scene analysis and serial killer behavior, but that's not enough. I need someone who can help me, help us all figure out their next moves."

"And you think I'm the one for that?" Jack said.

"Let me ask you something," Haskell said, "you went to London with your father and entered a chess competition. When I looked you up, it said you came in second against one of the top grandmasters back then. I was able to look at the game. You made one move that cost you the game. A move you didn't make with any of the other players. A bone-head move. Now, I know you're good under pressure. So, why did you lose?"

"I'm assuming you know the answer ..."

"You took a dive," Haskell said.

"So what?"

"You were good enough to wipe the floor with grandmasters, yet you took a dive. Why?"

"It was Dad's thing, chess ..."

"Well, dive or no, do you still wonder why I think you're the one to figure out their next moves?"

Jack raised his glass. "Point to you," he said. "Alright, so how do we work this?"

"We'll have to do it somewhat discreetly," Haskell said. "Low profile; you won't be interviewing or doing field work, but if we get anyone in interrogation, you'll be behind the glass, and whoever's inside will have an ear-piece.

"And I cleared it with your chief," He added.

"He agreed to that?"

"You won't be his problem now, and he doesn't want to bench you either; just circumstances ..."

"So when do I start?"

"Not right now," Haskell said. "Get on your feet, Jack. Then we'll talk."

Jack took in the bitter smell of the desiccated Historical Society. He told Mary he was going to Beacon Park for a walk. He hated lying to her. He also hated being on this side of the tape; a crime scene ghoul. Feds in suits stood outside, huddled together making plans he wasn't privy to. Men in dark blue jump-suits came in and out of the area they'd cleared.

The building was caved in from the left side; Mansfield's office. Jack had to wonder if the bombs were only meant to flatten that room. A piece of charred paper wafted through the air like an errant spark from a campfire. Jack saw it, made up his mind that the bomber didn't care.

There were others standing around; on-lookers. Jack didn't understand why death filled so many with awe, why the traffic slowed on the highway during an accident because everybody gawked, but there he was. At least his fellow on-lookers wouldn't face hell over being here.

One of the agents looked over. Jack didn't get a good look at him at first, his back turned and all. But it was Decker.

Decker spotted him and motioned for him to come over with his index finger.

'Aw, shit... here we go'... Jack walked over to the tape-line. Decker walked over and put his hand on it, like he was going to raise it, but he didn't.

"What's your business here, Detective?" He asked.

"None." Jack said. "I'm off the case."

"So I heard..." Decker said. "How are you feeling?"

"Still hurts a bit, but they're lowering the dose on my pain-killers."

"You almost didn't make it."

"I was lucky, I guess. It was dark; he couldn't see me too well."

Decker pointed to a street lamp on the corner where they chased him.

"Does that work?" He asked, "Did it work that night?"

Jack played back the tape in his head.

"Yeah, it worked." Jack said.

"Then it was *you* who couldn't see *him*; he could see you just fine.

"You think he wasn't trying to kill me?"

"I'm not sure what to think when it comes to you and this case."

"You're glad I'm off the case, huh…"

"Nothing personal, but I would've taken you off the case permanently when we found your parents' licenses in the crematorium."

"Guess that would've made sense…"

Decker turned his head to look at the crumpled building

"For what it's worth," he said, "if I was in your shoes, I'd have fought tooth and nail to stay on too."

"You gonna' tell Harken I was here?"

"No." Decker replied. "Wouldn't want to spoil his vacation."

"Oh shit, that's right…" Jack said, "He invited me up to the lake this week."

Decker checked his watch. "I'd suggest you get up there." He said. "Get a little R and R yourself."

Jack sped down the gravel road doing thirty. He'd been there enough, and fifty was top speed before a spin-off would send you into a ditch. But Paul went with him. Mary was worried that they hadn't spent enough time together lately, which was true. Plus, Paul wasn't showing it, but the shooting had rattled him. So they drove to Harken's cottage in Port Henry, on the coast of Lake Champlain in the Adirondacks.

They emptied out on to the main road that led into town. Jack rolled down the window to catch the smell of cow shit and country air.

"Ray's not really my uncle, you know..."

"Yeah, Paul... I know that. Why?"

"Do you think it'd hurt his feelings if I didn't call him 'Uncle Ray'?"

"I don't think so. Why don't you want to call him Uncle Ray?"

"Because he's not really my uncle, and I'm getting older now."

"But you called him your uncle last summer!"

"Which means I'm six months older."

Jack looked over at him. "What's this really about, kiddo?"

"That too..." Paul said. "Kiddo. I don't like being called that."

"I'll stop. I'll just call you short stack." Jack grinned.

"C'mon! I'm serious!"

"Paul, you're growing up... Just faster than we are, that's all."

"We all grow up at the same rate, Dad."

"At least you're not calling me Jack now..."

Paul folded his arms, closed his posture.

"I mean this, kid-... 'Paul'... You're fourteen. I'm thirty seven, and Ray is too old for me to tell you." Jack said as they neared the village center.

"In four years, your voice will get lower, you'll start having to shave... probably hook up with a girl or two... You'll change a lot in four years. But me, Ray? We'll just be four years older. That's what I'm getting at."

"You lost me." Paul said.

"We want to see you as a kid forever," Jack said. "Because seeing you become a man makes us realize how old we are."

"But I *am* a man. I have to be. What would've happened if..." He didn't finish his thought as it bounced in his head.

"Oh, I get it." Jack said. "Look, Paul. My job... carries risks. Some I have to take; others..." Now Jack couldn't finish the thought.

"Anyways," He said. "You will be a man. And if anything happens to me, I know in my heart you'll step up and *be* a man if you have to. But for now, you can still be a kid. Don't give up being young out of fear. Any one of us can die by accident. It's no way to live your life. You hear what I'm saying?"

"Yeah, dad..." Paul said. "...I like calling him 'Uncle Ray' anyways..."

They stopped for a bite at the deli on East Main Street. Port Henry had the charm of a small town on a big lake. There were no fast-food chains, or big box stores, but some of the creature comforts of New Rhodes were there. They had a Morgan's, after all.

They got to Ray's around two-thirty. He had a rustic, two-story house, stained pine siding, black window trim and a screened in front porch. Ray was out back. Jack saw the smoke from the driveway.

Ray came up there to hunt in the winter, had a snow-blower to clear the two- to three-foot drifts in front of his driveway. But the season was light on snow. Warm too; Jack was wearing his NRPD hoodie, which was little help against a normal winter.

Ray looked up as they rounded the house. He was burning garbage, not legal, but he did it anyway. He had a beer in his hand, tipped it up and motioned them to the plastic lawn chairs by the fire pit.

"Glad to see you boys!" He said.

"Hi, Uncle Ray."

"Paul…"

"Hey, Ray…"

"How ya been shittin'?"

"How have I what???"

"Shittin," Ray repeated. "How ya' been shittin' since the surgery?"

Jack laughed. "C'mon, Cap'… Not in front of Paul…"

"He's a man, now, Jack… He can hear it."

"Fine, I guess." Jack said.

"Good to hear."

"What's got into you?"

Ray leaned back in his chair. "I don't know… I got to thinkin'… I know your gut hurts, but the real test is how ya' shit, isn't it?"

"You're drunk."

Ray burped. "Yup."

Jack and Paul had a seat by the fire. Ray started putting real wood on it, and the smell improved. It was alluring.

"So Paul," Ray said, "How's school been?"

"Alright, I guess…"

"You getting' any girls yet?"

"Ray, he's-,"

"I'm going out with a girl from my science class."

Jack looked at him, eyebrow raised. "You plan on telling your mother and I about this?"

"Not if I don't want to freak her out."

"Are we that weird?" Jack felt a little hurt.

"No… you'll just…" Paul hesitated. "*Look into her.*"

"She's your age," Jack said, "What are we supposed to find?"

"I don't know…"

"C'mon, Jack. Like you never did anything behind George and Emma's back when you were their age."

"I didn't say I'd look!" Jack said. "If I did, you'd be my daughter, not my son."

"What's that supposed to mean?"

"Grown up stuff." Ray told him. "Good for you, havin' a girl. What's her name?"

Paul looked to Jack, who shrugged, his palms out.

"Amelia."

"I like that name." Ray said.

"You don't have to hide stuff from me," Jack said. "I won't look into someone unless you want me to. You're mature; I trust you."

"Hey Paul," Ray said, "You wanna' go play with Alpo?"

Alpo was Ray's German shepherd. He was on in years, but he loved Paul, and Paul darted off into the house to play. Ray also had cable in there, so Paul had other reasons for parting company.

They sat around the fire as the dark mass of wood was invaded from beneath by the flames of the embers.

"Thanks for inviting us out, Ray." He said.

"I'm glad to see ya'…" Ray stared into the flames.

"You know, Angela and I would just sit here for hours every weekend in the summer." He said. "Even if we never made it to the door of the house. When she got sick…

"It was quick, you know. Three months from diagnosis to death, but time doesn't mean much when you're in it, watching the love of your life get weaker and weaker, knowing there's nothing you can do… not even to make her comfortable."

"I'm sorry, Ray." Jack said. "I loved Angela too."

"I know." Ray stared blankly at the fire, his beer reaching his lips without guidance. Jack knew he had to get Ray off this topic; he'd been punishing himself for two years. But Ray beat him to it.

"You know how much shit I got into for putting you on this case?"

"I can imagine…"

"The Chief wanted to relieve me of command *before* you got shot."

"I'm sorry, Ray… I didn't know…"

"I'm sittin' in the waiting room while they're working on you, not knowing whether you'd live, die or be a vegetable. All I could think was that I'd done it. I put you in; *I* put you there."

"Ray, you don't have to-,"

"I want you to listen." He said. "You watch your back out there. You may be off the case, but he's gunnin' for you.

"Watch yourself." He said.

They headed back later that night, Port Henry awash with home strung Christmas lights. Jack pointed out a house in full display to Paul, until he realized that Paul was asleep in his seat.

Jack spent Christmas with the whole family. He felt a little useless as they had gotten a really late start on putting up the tree.

Dan and Tony pulled it out of their cluttered basement, entertaining Jack as he sat on the couch watching them bicker over what pole went with what other one. They used to get trees fresh from a stand in Clerving, a small village north of Riverville, but the stand went belly up during the recession. Jack nearly wept at the sight of the plastic tree the first time they put it up.

Jack did help decorate, to the best he could. Paul would give him decorations to hang on the high parts of the tree. He still wasn't supposed to bend over.

He had to admit, when the tree was done, and the Christmas music played on the radio, the real pine garland with mini pine cones that Mary strung along the banister, he felt festive, as if for that one moment, the weight of the world had climbed off his shoulders.

Tony and Dan cooked Christmas Dinner, which in the Taggart family, happened Christmas Eve.

Jack learned long ago that Paul got too wound up on Christmas Day playing with his toys to enjoy the dinner.

Not that it was still the case; Paul was older, so he knew most of the stuff he was getting. But Christmas Day had become a visiting day for family and friends.

Jack's parents were driving in the next day from Buffalo. He told them not to, for their own safety, but George wouldn't hear it. Despite his concern, Jack would be happy to see them. So would Paul, Mary and everyone else. On top of that, the house would be filled with cops.

Christmas dinner was incredible. Jack gave many compliments to Dan and Tony for the spiral ham, mashed potatoes and gravy, and assorted vegetables and, for dessert, New York-style cheesecake.

Mary did the dishes, as per their agreement. At eleven-thirty, with eggnog (spiked, in some cases) in everyone's glasses, and Bing Crosby on the radio, the ripping of wrapping paper began in earnest.

Paul got loaded up with video games, no surprise to anyone. Jack got Dan what he got him every Christmas; a can of Old Spice shaving cream, a pack of razors and a bottle of Bourbon. It was a running joke, as Jack got a flannel shirt and a box of god-awful cigars.

Every year; it had been a tradition that went back to the first Christmas they spent as a family.

Jack got Mary a massage chair, something she had her eye on, but didn't want to spend the money. Mary got Jack a silver pocket-watch. Jack loved pocket-watches.

The one she got was emblazoned with the NRPD seal – she had to have special ordered it. They weren't sold anywhere.

"Open it." She said.

Jack opened it. The inside face was an emblazoned portrait of Jack and Mary, taken the day they were married. Jack reached up and gave her a kiss.

"I love you, babe." He said. "It's perfect."

On Christmas Day, everyone showed up. Jack's parents arrived at noon. Harken came over at around two and stayed till well into the night. Eddie and Sarah came over briefly, but Eddie Junior was putting up a fuss. It was warm, busy and hectic, but in the afternoon, George and Jack found themselves in the study sharing a cup of coffee.

"Did you pack heat this trip?" Jack asked.

George laughed. "So Ray told you, huh?"

"Yeah." Jack said. "You know, you could have told me. I might not have written up a reference, but I wouldn't have stopped you."

"Easy to say now," George leaned back in his seat. "So, do you normally go out without bullet-proof vests on?"

"Oh Dad, I've gotten bitched at thirty times over about that. Can we just say 'lesson learned'?"

"Sure, kiddo… Just happy you're still alive." George said. "So, what's your game plan now?"

"I don't know. I'm off the case, but I have a chance to do some consulting work with the Feds."

"When?"

"A couple of weeks, I guess?"

George set his coffee down. "Jack, based on what the doctors said, you could get six months off, flat, with pay. Why aren't you taking it?"

"I want to nail this guy to the wall! He's dangerous! And he's made it personal!"

"Jack, I taught you well about taking things personal. If you're gonna' get back into this, you have to be objective. And if he's making it personal, you've got to be even more objective."

"You're trying to catch a serial killer that may have a long history with you. I couldn't be more proud of you as a detective, Jack, but… you are just one man. And you have people who depend on you."

"I know, Dad, I know…"

They drank their coffee in the din of the merriment outside of the study.

"You may see this as redeeming your past," George said, "but don't let it be at the expense of your present… or your future."

Jack spent the next two weeks avoiding the task force. He couldn't drink yet, so New Years was a quiet night at home. He spent his mornings getting coffee at Beans, Inc., a trendy little café across the street from the Agora.

He wasn't much for the ambience, the smell of patchouli and jasmine that filled the shop, opting instead to sit out on the bench, across the street from the Agora.

There was plastic covering most of it. A developer was renovating it to make it a mall again. Graham Developers, some outfit out of New York; some faceless entity making an investment in Jonathan Myer's memorial in glass, steel and concrete.

Jack spent most of his days with Mary and Paul, dreading the day he'd have to tell her he was getting involved with the case again. He went to the Post to hang out with Gamble on occasion, keeping up to date on recent developments.

The task force hadn't, in fact, been taken over by the Feds, It was still a joint command, but each agency was compartmentalizing information. The case management database had gone all to shit, and everyone was going out, chasing leads on their own. Jack only wished he could judge that, but he and Gamble had done it too.

Gamble did tell him that the explosive used at the Historical Society was RDX, which wasn't easy to come by. The ATF was tracking it, but if they'd found it, they weren't sharing. Jason Smith was still nowhere to be found. That left Bowman, who himself was nowhere to be found.

Gamble had been chasing down leads from the murders they had, but now he was getting results, all tying, in some way, to the Smiths or Mansfield.

The license plate list he had received from the canvass of Leiah Marcusen's house did indeed have Jason Smith's car on it. Smith had left his car, and they found traces of blood in it. The DNA matched Marcusen.

They got a search warrant for his house, and they found the buck knife that killed her. Curiously, the also found a box of shoe covers. Jack told him about the trip he and Freddie took to the crime lab. That conclusively linked Jason Smith to all four murders.

A BOLO had been issued for Smith, giving his picture, height, weight, and some pictures rendered to show him with different hair colors and facial hair.

Gamble understood Jack's desire to work the case as Haskell's consultant, but he warned him that, with the way things were in the task force, it could be dicey with his fellow detectives.

"Expect some angry glares," he joked.

Jack was eating dinner with Mary, Paul and Dan at Dan's house when he let them know he was going to work the case again.

"Jack, are you serious!?" Mary said.

"I need to, Mary," he said.

"You know, I've been nothing but supportive with this," Mary said, "having to stay in Riverville, no offense, Dad, pulling Paul out of his school, sitting there every day wondering if you were going to come back alive, and you barely escape death in the middle of the night?

"I can't take this, Jack," she said. "You have to make a choice; I've grown up around cops, and I've also grown up around divorces and widows and dysfunctional families because you all get *married to the job*."

"Should I just give up every time it's tough?" Jack said.

"He's targeting you!" Mary said. "Don't you get that?"

"I can take care of myself, Mary …"

"Like you did in that alley the other night?" she shouted. "It's not just *you*, Jack. *You*'re not just *'you.'* You're *me*, and *Paul*."

"Mary, I'm doing this to protect you both! Do you think he's going to stop just because I'm off the case?"

"It doesn't matter, Jack! You're *obsessed* with this case! Let me ask you; when was the last time you had a bad dream? Or a migraine?"

"Not in a while …"

"Exactly what happens when you're obsessed with something!"

"Mary, I'm not going to be out in the field. I'm just going to be in an office, consulting."

"That's what you said when you found that message in the tunnel. You'd just be in the office doing desk work."

"What do you want me to do, Mary?"

"Stop. Wipe your hands of this case. Let the task force worry about it, and go back to working regular cases."

"And if one of them turns out to be our guy? Should I just walk away then?"

"Jack, now you're just being an asshole."

"If they'd caught him back then, we wouldn't have to-" Jack caught himself a bit too late. He looked over to Dan.

"Dan, I'm-"

"Jack, you'd best go back to your house tonight. Mary and Paul will be safe here," he said. Jack could feel the chill.

Jack walked out the door with a tear running down his cheek.

He sat in the dark in his empty house with a cigarette in one hand and a bottle of Jack Daniel's in the other. The place was trashed; mostly his shit. If any of Mary's or Paul's stuff had been broken, it was accidental. His gut was sore. His head hurt. He hoped it was a migraine. He hoped Mary wasn't right.

What the hell was happening to him? Two months ago, he shelved three cold cases without a thought. The leads dried up, he had new cases to investigate, and into the basement they went.

He *was* obsessed. He could try to justify it any way he liked, but he knew he wouldn't rest until they caught the sons of bitches … even if they never did.

He looked at an angel figurine lying on the floor. He got up and picked it up. The wing was broken. He had given it to Mary after she gave birth to Paul. Mary was brought up in a Catholic household, and the Taggarts were lapsed Methodists. But the angel was the only religious thing the hospital had in its gift shop. *The angel will protect you*, he'd said to his glowing wife. The angel with the broken wing.

Jack took the figurine, and the bottle, down to the basement where he kept his work-bench. He glued the wing together as his eyes welled up. He wanted to give up the fight. He wanted to be sleeping in Mary's arms that night, drinking Irish coffee with Dan in the morning. But he knew it was fantasy.

They were in danger. And as long as Smith and Bowman were off the grid, they wouldn't be safe. They'd been one step ahead of the investigation the whole time, one step ahead … until they were identified.

Well, Smith was positively identified; Bowman was assumed, but they really didn't have proof it was him, did they? Eddie told him that Walson's pictures didn't show his face clearly, so how could they even prove their hunch?

Mary didn't understand. He *needed* to be on this case. Haskell could help him get access to what the FBI knew, build the profile, and once and for all, confirm it actually *had* been Bowman who shot him.

Haskell asked Jack to meet him at a conference room at New Rhodes Tech Park on Route 4 in South Creek, a rural town to the south of New Rhodes. It was a small office space, big enough for two people and, Jack hoped, mountains of leads.

As he arrived he saw a small box of files, and Haskell marking up a whiteboard.

"Glad to see you, Jack. You look tired. You okay?"

"Yeah, just ... problems at home."

"Your family doesn't want you back on the case, I take it?"

Jack nodded, yawning.

"Well, we'll keep it light. We don't have to spend much time each day."

"Doesn't matter," Jack said. "She's staying at my father-in-law's."

"Oh ... are you sure you still want to do this?"

"Yeah," Jack replied. "I want to find this guy."

"Okay," Haskell said. "Let's start off with recent developments. I've been gathering leads and organizing them in your absence. We have three main things."

Haskell pointed to the board. "One, the remains at the Canal Street Connection. We've been able to identify ten of the victims through dental records. We focused on any possible connection they had to Jason Smith or Jeffrey Bowman, and we found something."

"Good news?"

"Definitely," he said. "They all had business with either Code Enforcement or the County Clerk's office."

"In either case, the ones with Code Enforcement occurred when Jason Smith worked in Code Enforcement, and the same for the County Clerk's Office."

"Also, we found his car, and we found blood. It was matched to Leiah Marcusen."

Jack wanted to say he knew that, but he figured he'd leave Gamble out of it.

"So, we got Smith for all four murders," Jack said. "Same signature."

"Yes," Haskell said, "and now we have to find him. But first, this." He pulled an old yearbook out from the box. New Rhodes High, Class of 1969.

"That's my parents' yearbook."

"Not specifically, but yes," Haskell said. "Flip to the pages I marked."

Jack flipped to three separate pages. The first one had Jason Smith's junior picture. The second marked page had Bowman's picture. Jack studied his face, trying to trigger his memory. Nothing.

The third page had a picture of Bowman and Smith, hanging out on the bleachers, too close to each other to be coincidental.

Jack studied the picture. "It's not proof, but it's not coincidence either."

"My point," Haskell said. "I got Bowman's military records unsealed."

"He was a *tunnel rat*. They worked in the tunnels that the Viet Cong built. A year into his deployment, his unit was killed in North Vietnam when they were on a secret mission, and he had been declared KIA. He resurfaced in the demilitarized zone a year after the declaration, which was then amended. He stayed for one more year before he completed his tour."

"Nobody else survived from his unit?"

"No," Haskell said. "Oh, and the third thing: the ATF determined the type of explosive used in the bombing of the Historical Society. It was RDX wired to the support columns, set off by a timer.

"They'll be able to trace its source, but we don't know how much Bowman might have left, or where he's storing it."

"Which brings us to Smith." Haskell said. "Your thoughts?"

Jack was still staring at the year-book. He'd found a prom picture of his mother and father. Louise looked nervous; Jonathan, top of the world.

"Smith is on the move, but I don't think he's going far," Jack said. "He seems too much like a 'comfort zone' guy.

"If anything, he'll have thought of an abandoned place to hide out in. But by now, he's probably making short runs to stores outside of New Rhodes for groceries, shit like that."

"So, what would you recommend?"

"I'd suggest having Melfly keep the other counties in the loop about Smith. He'll go out at night, go to stores at off-hours, and drive with exceeding caution. Noticeable caution."

"Another option would be to release his picture to the media," Haskell said.

"If you do, do it carefully," Jack said. "Stress that his family members were victims of the bombings, and he's not a suspect. Maybe put him out as a missing person?"

"Yeah … I like where you're going," Haskell said.

"So, now for the profile," Jack said. "What's your take on Bowman?"

"A loner," Haskell said. "No friends, no relationships. He uses the torture, the murders, as a proxy for human contact."

"He needs to be in control. Anything that threatens that proxy or control makes him escalate, change tactics.

"I'd also say that he can influence others to do things they'd never ordinarily do, then lock them in to help him do what he does. He views loose ends as expendable."

"So, why do you think he's been targeting me?"

"Honestly?" Haskell said. "You're a loose end. And through you, he's able to reclaim his loss of control back in high school ... with your mother."

"No offense, but that doesn't make a lot of sense." Jack said. "It sounds good, but he's had years to take me out, years. Why, all of the sudden, would he go after me now? If what you're saying is true, what thing happened in his life that said to him, *Now is the right time to go after Jack!*"

Haskell smiled.

"Profiling's not an exact science." He said.

Jack spent the rest of the afternoon piecing together the murders, clues, and leads, and everything pointed to either Jason Smith or, presumably, Jeffrey Bowman. The only thing they couldn't pin down was the knowledge of the names of dispatchers.

They couldn't make heads or tails of that from the research, but Haskell decided that catching Smith would reveal more about it.

Jack hit the VFW Post that night, at Harken's invitation. The place was dead besides them, and Sheriff Melfly was tending the bar. The jukebox was playing country twang instead of the classic rock that had wafted through the place before.

There were a couple of Sheriff's deputies, and Commander Teague was sitting next to Harken. Jack almost felt like the place was dead *on purpose*, but that could've just been guilt.

"Hey, Captain... Sheriff, Commander ..."

Teague and Melfly nodded, deadpan.

"How's the gut, Jack?" Harken asked.

"Still hurts a little," Jack said. He turned to Teague and Melfly. "I imagine you all are pissed at me."

"You're fucking nuts to stay on this, Taggart," Melfly said. "Now, I can't say what I'd be doin' if I was in your patent leathers, but you had an 'out'; you shoulda' took it."

"You're too close to this, Jack," Teague said.

"Why in the *fuck* didn't you talk to me first!?" Harken asked. "Hell, I'd have found some way to keep you in the loop, but this? Working as a 'consultant' for the Feds with that snake oil peddler?"

"Captain-"

"It's Ray; I'm not your captain right now."

"Aw, Jesus, Ray! Is it gonna be like that?"

"You're making it like that," Harken said. "We're getting pushed out by the Feds, and you're joining them!"

"*Captain,*" Jack said, "You are still my captain. You will be my captain even if you fire my ass. I'm a *New Rhodes Police Detective.* And if you had *offered* to keep me in, I would've snapped on that. But Haskell came to my house, offered me the *in.*"

"But why didn't you at least *ask* me before you accepted?" Harken said.

"He told me it was already cleared through the Chief, so I assumed you knew. And I knew if you had a problem with it, I'd have heard by now."

"I spent two weeks doing squat, coming in *here* of all places, and nobody's said a fucking *thing* to me about this being a problem until now!"

Jack felt a sharp pain in his gut; he braced with his arm, grabbing the rail to steady him.

"Whoa, Jack," Harken said. "Slow down, everything's okay."

Jack regained his composure. "Look, if you guys want me to quit, I will. I'm not on *their* side; I just want to catch the sons of bitches. And Commander, I am too close, I know, but I just think if I fall back, he'll draw me in no matter what."

"Jack," Teague said, "first off, just call me Willie. Second, I think we're all feeling cast off since the Feds have moved in on the senior command. They've been keeping us in the dark for the most part."

"I can keep you in the loop as best I can," Jack said. "But here, between us. And Eddie, of course."

"We wanted Eddie to come here," Harken said, "but he's having some problems at home, I guess."

"Okay, Jack, we'll forgive you, but we still have to punish you for treason." Melfly slid a *Pride of Eire* across the bar.

"I hate this shit. It gives me a hangover."

Kind of the point!" Melfly said.

As they drank, the mood lightened up, but Teague was right. The FBI and ATF had been pushing the locals, even the State Police, out of the heart of the investigation. The case management database was now being coordinated by the FBI, and local law enforcement had been assigned to investigating the bodies found at the dump site and being visible to the public.

The NRPD Public Information Officer still ran point on the information going out. But the Feds were giving him crumbs, so the media outlets were conducting investigations of their own, and they were all playing catch-up, chasing so many red herrings, just to show the media they were following every lead.

Jack told them everything he and Haskell had talked about, including Haskell's decision to go public. Like Jack, the three of them had reservations about that.

Taking the assumption that Smith was hiding out nearby, they talked about every major and minor route out of the region.

New Rhodes and Albany were the intersection between two interstates, not to mention close to a dozen county routes and state highways. They identified fifteen likely routes, and Melfly and Teague plotted a blanket patrol along those roads.

They talked about the bombing of the Historical Society. They told him that a search of Smith's house had revealed a turn-of-the-century map of some tunnels in New Rhodes, probably not all of them. Teague gleaned that the bomb was made of RDX, which Jack knew, but that the remote detonation system was suspected, probably a cell phone trigger.

"Haskell told me it was a timer," he said. "The detonator was wired to a timer."

"I don't know why he said that," Teague said. "They found pieces of a cell phone with wires coming out of it; said it was so badly burnt up that it was most likely on the main bomb."

"They told you guys that?"

"No," Teague said. "They didn't tell us shit, but I overheard two of them talking when I was in the bathroom taking a two."

"Ya know, I don't trust that Haskell guy," Melfly said.

"He's alright," Jack said, "but not if he's gonna lie to me about inconsequential shit."

"Hey, keep that between us," Harken said. "There's enough gossip in the office as it is."

"I will. Don't get me wrong, I don't trust him over you guys; I just think he's harmless."

"He's just weird," Melfly said. "Always asking us how we felt while we're trying to do some work."

"He's a psychologist," Jack said.

"He's a profiler, as far as this case goes," Harken said. "And he should be profiling the killers, not us."

Jack took a big gulp of his beer. It was like a pill; best swallowed whole. 'Eddie actually liked this shit?'

"We have an office in the tech park now, so you guys won't be seeing much of him, I imagine," Jack said.

"No offense," Harken said, "but good riddance.

"So I don't imagine Mary is taking this well?"

"She's staying at her father's house. I'm not. Do the math..."

Harken buried his face in his hand.

"You're so smart, you're dumb, and I mean no disrespect, but I mean it."

"Look, it isn't making things easy for me, but what are my options?"

"Back off. Just... put the cards down and walk right back into the homicide division."

"He's gone through the effort to involve me like he did. Do you think he's gonna' care where I go, or if I pack up and ship out, even?"

"Ray, he's got a point," Melfly said. "This guy's got it out for him. Maybe being in that office out there is a good thing."

"We gotta' catch Smith, and have him give up Bowman." Jack said. "I'll be a part of this until there is no... *this.*"

They talked, Jack drank, but the mood was lighter. Harken went at length about a boat we was restoring from a husk, and Melfly was worried about his up-coming campaign.

Teague was still quiet, sipping his beer and peppering the conversation here and there, but he seemed out of place. Jack knew the feeling.

Harken agreed to give Jack a ride home.

They hazed him pretty good, and he'd need Eddie to give him a ride back to the Post for his car in the morning. The drive home was uneventful, stop lights peppered with Harken's observations.

He prided himself on noticing things that no one else saw. Not that Jack could see anything but triplicates.

"Be careful, Jack," Harken said as he let him out. "You can't let this eat ya up. Tell Mary I said hi, when you can."

"Mary's not too happy with me right now."

"I know," Harken said. "But she still loves you, though."

"Thanks, Captain."

Harken sighed. "Stop saying 'Captain,' Jesus … I'm off the clock."

"Sorry," Jack said. "Thanks, Ray."

Harken gave a salute and took off.

CHAPTER EIGHT

Jack woke up sprawled across his bed, soaked in sweat. Could've been a nightmare, or a hangover; he couldn't tell which. After a puke, he brushed his teeth and washed his mouth out with Listerine. He took care of the "S"s sluggishly, each one, and got dressed. He chased dry waffles with a lukewarm cup of Alka-Seltzer.

He called Mary, but Dan answered. He said they were out at the market. Dan didn't chew him out, or even sound pissed, but he was quiet, choosing his words ... distant. Jack knew he'd hit a spinal nerve when he said what he did, but he couldn't think of what to say now. He needed to cool down, get a grip. In his heart, he knew he needed everything back to normal. Mary was right; he wasn't just *him*. And he was missing two parts of himself something fierce.

He turned on the local news. It was nine o'clock, and Smith's photo was the top story. The picture was replaced by their Public Information Officer, a live shot.

"We are looking for this man," he said, holding up the picture. "He has gone missing, and two of his family members were killed in the bombing of the Historical Society.

"We just want to talk to him. If you are him, or if any of you see him, please contact ..."

Jack shut it off. He knew the task force would be a madhouse, with everyone calling from the nosy neighbor with junk vision thinking they saw the guy twenty-five yards away, to self-styled psychics who would tell them they "feel he's near water ..." Pleas to the public brought out all types. About the only person guaranteed not to call was Smith himself.

Gamble picked him up around ten. He had extra rumples in his attire, and bags under his eyes.

"Wow, Eddie, I thought I'd be looking worse than you today ..."

"Funny," Gamble said. "You do look like shit though. Drink much last night?"

"How'd you tell?"

"You always wear that cologne when you're hung-over," Gamble said. "You told me once that it's the only one you got that doesn't make you puke."

"I forgot I told you that ..." Jack fished a pair of sunglasses out of his pocket and put them on.

"Damn, must've been a night!"

"Harken, Melfly and Teague punished me at the Post last night ... with beer. *Pride of Eire.*"

"Ah, that explains it," Gamble said. "You didn't kill my stash, did you?"

"Not even close. They ordered cases for you. I think they got a discount because it's piss. Don't worry ..."

As they neared the Post, Jack's cell went off. It was Haskell.

"They arrested Smith," he said before Jack could say hello. "Where are you?"

"I'm in the city, just getting to my car. Where'd they find him?"

"He tried to get on the Thruway," Haskell said. "The State Police sent his picture to the toll-booth collectors, and they had a car there waiting for him. He's in custody now."

"So where are they taking him?"

"State Police barracks, in Albany," Haskell said. "We get to observe the interrogation. How fast can you get there?"

"Twenty minutes," Jack said.

"Good," Haskell said. "I'll meet you there. We might just get a confession out of this!"

"We might get *Bowman* out of this."

Jack sped down the highway and hooked the interstate, arriving at the State Police barracks on Route 9. It was an old dormitory, a large, imposing building, grey stone with octagonal domed turrets capping the ends of two wings connected by the main building, also domed.

Jack pulled into the back parking lot, where he saw Haskell and Teague talking.

"Still waiting for him?" Jack asked when he walked over.

"No, he's here," Teague said. "He's sitting in the box; we're just waiting on you."

"Sorry," Jack said.

They reviewed the strategy as they walked down the hall.

"Teague and Decker will be conducting the interview, but they've agreed to wear earpieces," Haskell said. "To keep it simple, only I'll be telling them anything. But if you notice something, tell me, and I'll bring it up."

"Okay, sounds good," Jack said.

The *box* was a gray room, windowless, with a steel table jutting out from the side of the wall. In it sat Jason Smith. The room was designed to give everyone in the observation room a full view of a suspect's body language. Smith was wearing a stained sweatshirt and grimy jeans. His hair was combed, though – sort of offset the 'bum motif'. His leg was shaking. He was edgy, as could be expected. He kept scratching his head, scratching his nose and cheek. He knew what he was facing, but Jack had to wonder what he was more afraid of: them, or Bowman?

Teague was the first to walk into the room. He had a notebook and a file folder. He sat down, not looking at Smith, setting his folder and notebook up, clicking his pen over and over. It was rattling. Finally, Teague began.

"Hello, Jason. I'm Commander Teague with the State Police," he said. He then Mirandized him, and Smith signed the card.

The first question asked after Mirandizing someone was crucial; as Jack knew well. It could make or break an interrogation. Suspects could lawyer up real quick.

"Would you like something?" asked Teague. "A cup of coffee, soda, anything like that?"

"No thanks," Smith said.

"Now, I see they confiscated a pack of cigarettes when they took you in. Do you smoke?"

"Yeah," Smith said nervously.

"Do you want a cigarette?" Teague asked. "Sure looks like you could use one right now."

"You can smoke in here?" Smith asked.

"Well, no," Teague said, "but where you're going, you won't be smoking for a long time, so I don't mind bending the rules just this once."

"Where am I going?" Smith asked.

"Let me go get you that cigarette," Teague said. He got up and walked out, leaving his notebook and file folder.

"He left the folder in there," Haskell said. "Do you think Smith will open it?"

"Nope," Jack said. "He knows people are watching in here. But it's killing him that it's so close.

"I like Teague's style." He added.

Teague walked back in the room with a full pack of cigarettes, a lighter and a cup of water. He placed the cup of water on the table to be used as an ash-tray and then offered a cigarette to Smith and sparked the lighter. Smith eagerly took the smoke, and Teague put the flame to it.

"Why didn't he take in a plate?" Haskell asked. "The water will degrade the DNA."

"He doesn't need DNA," Jack said. "It's like the folder; the water's there, just sitting there, inducing Smith to get thirsty so he wants to ask for a drink."

"So, what did you mean, 'where I'm going'?" Smith asked. "Do you mean jail?"

"Well, let's take one thing at a time," Teague said. "I just have to ask you; why didn't you get rid of your car?"

"My car?"

"Yeah, your car. We tracked you as a possible suspect because your car was spotted multiple times at Leiah Marcusen's house. And when we tried to find you after the bombing, we found Leiah's blood in your car. All over it, actually … "

"Yeah, ya never really get all the blood out; it just streaks under the black-light when you spray Luminol."

"I don't know what you're talking about."

"We have enough physical evidence to convict you for Leiah Marcusen's murder," Teague said. "That's a slam dunk life sentence. No confession required. But that crime was linked to seven other murders. Someone called 9-1-1; knew the dispatchers by name each time, and reported the murders. Confessing to them. What was that all about?"

"That wasn't me, I swear!"

"Well then, who was it?"

Smith hesitated, scratched his elbow.

"I don't know ..."

"Sure you do," Teague said. "If we know who did, surely you do."

"Who did it, then?" Smith challenged him. Teague ignored the question.

"Then the bodies from the dump site, so far we've got ten of them whose only connection to each other is that they came across your path in Code Enforcement, and then in the County Clerk's office."

"I don't-"

"C'mon, Jason! Simon, your son, injected himself into the case, taunting us ... then he goes to your house, and the next day he's killed in an explosion that, by the way, also killed your uncle and six other people. You want to tell me you're innocent?

"Now, we're working with the FBI and the ATF, and they want to try you in Federal court. Now, New York no longer has the death penalty, the Feds do. And they'll aim to put a cocktail in your arm. Did you ever hear about lethal injection before?"

Simon's face crinkled. Teague had him scared almost to the piss point.

"They say it's humane, painless ... but I've been to executions by lethal injection."

"You see, a doctor takes an oath to *do no harm*, so they can't administer the lethal injection. Technicians have to do it, and I mean people that don't have the medical expertise of a doctor. And the machine, well, it's a machine, not an anesthesiologist. It just pumps the drugs; it doesn't gauge the effective dose. It's kind of *one size fits all.*

"It can take twenty minutes, sometimes more, for a man to die, and, since he's paralyzed, he can't scream ... just twitch, and jerk. It's sad. I actually feel sorry for those guys, no matter what they did."

"This is a mistake!" Smith said. "I didn't bomb the Historical Society!"

"Yeah, but according to you, you didn't do anything, and I know that's not true. I mean, maybe you did bomb the place, maybe you didn't. But we know about Leiah Marcusen, we have the physical proof of it, and you can't even admit to that, or the other South End Killings."

Smith bit his lip. His leg shook fiercely, eyes darting around the room.

"Alright," Smith said. "I killed Leiah Marcusen. But I didn't kill the other ones, and I sure as hell didn't bomb that building!"

"Okay, we're getting somewhere," Teague said. "We don't think you were acting alone in any of this, but it looks like you're gonna take the full blame, unless you can help us out."

"I can't," Smith said. "He's nuts; he'll kill me."

"We can put you somewhere he can never touch you. Jason, I promise you this. And we know who he is; we'll catch him anyway. But without your cooperation, we'll have no problem handing you both over to the Feds."

Smith scratched his face, his hand going straight up to rub his combed hair wayward.

"There are two other guys." He said. "One of them; the one who's been calling the shots - I knew from high school. His name is Jeff. Jeff Bowman."

"And the other guy?"

"I don't know who he is. I don't even know his name. Jeff said he was a war buddy."

"Can you describe him?"

"He's about your height, older ... He's in good shape, greyish hair ... I'd know him if I saw him."

"Can you tell me anything else about him?"

"Not really," Smith said. "He made the calls, though. Can I get another cigarette?"

Haskell spoke into Teague's earpiece. "Okay, have him write down his statement first. Make sure he admits to his and Bowman's part in every murder. Then come out and send Decker in."

"Teague's doing great," Jack said. "Why take him out?"

"I think he's getting too used to Teague," Haskell said. "This 'other guy'... Smith and Bowman have motive, means, and opportunity.

"I think he's trying to bring a third man in to mitigate his own involvement, to throw us off of Bowman. It's more probable that he made the calls."

Teague took his statement, and Smith admitted to being involved in the South End Killings and nothing else. Then Teague left, and Decker went in. Smith asked for a cigarette, and Decker said he couldn't give him one. And that's when Smith lawyered up.

Jack just shook his head.

"I'll talk to my contacts in the Marine Corps, find out if there's any truth to his claim that Bowman had a war buddy," Haskell said on the ride back to their office.

"It was a mistake to pull Teague," Jack said.

"I agree," Haskell said, "but it was my mistake. I'll have to deal with it."

"Has Decker ever run an interrogation before?"

"Yes. And he normally gets results," Haskell said. "He just let his frustrations get the better of him." Haskell paused. "We're going to have a second bite, don't worry."

"How do we get a second bite?"

"We know Smith doesn't want the needle," Haskell replied. "And we have enough evidence, including the confession, to give it to him. His lawyer will want to cut a deal."

"So we have a confirmation on Bowman, at least," Jack said.

"I'm going down to Brooklyn to dig up as much about Bowman as I can," Haskell said. "And I hate to say this; I mean I know you two are close ..."

"We have to look at Walt, I know," Jack said. "*War buddy...*"

"Once Smith is arraigned, we'll do a photo-array with Walt's picture in it. If he doesn't pick Walt out, we can eliminate him, at least."

Jack agreed to continue the conversation at their office. He drove fast, staring at nothing, drumming his fingers along the steering wheel.

No music; he just listened to the symphony of rants and doubts that rose and fall between red lights, stop signs and highway slowdowns. He made it to the office in a half hour, in no hurry.

"I know I should've left Teague in there, Jack, and I'm sorry," Haskell said as Jack got into the office. "I have to fix this."

"It happens, J.R.," Jack said. "I know you didn't do it on purpose."

"I should have listened to you. I thought he was trying to pass his part in the murders away to others. I thought Decker could find new avenues to help us track Bowman."

"We'll get him," Jack said. "Like you said, we'll have another bite, but don't release a picture this time, please?"

"Why not? We got Smith that way."

"Smith tried to leave," Jack said. "Bowman will go underground *literally*. You saw the maps of the tunnels. Bowman was a tunnel rat. I can only imagine that he's got a hideout in one of them."

Jack slugged down coffee as Haskell spent the afternoon on the phone. What kind of profiler was Haskell anyway? Couldn't he see that Teague's technique was working?

Jack shuddered to think of the hell he was going to get from Teague when they met up that night.

But Haskell was dogged in the office, talking away on his Bluetooth, his fingers flying lightning on the keys of his laptop.

Jack tried to look busy, going over Smith's file, but there was nothing in it that he hadn't already known when he went into the interview.

He had been looking at Smith's file for the past three days, even before he was caught, searching for angles to use to get him to give up Bowman.

But all hope wasn't lost. Smith knew more about Bowman's habits than Bowman would think he knew. Smith needed a chip in the poker game they'd be playing with his attorney after arraignment.

That wouldn't be until Monday, as it was Friday afternoon. He'd have a weekend to sit around and wait. Haskell was going to spend the weekend in New York chasing leads, and he wanted Jack to be on stand-by, in case they needed to follow-up.

He wasn't happy to spend that weekend in New Rhodes waiting for Haskell's calls. He wasn't enjoying being a *consultant*.

He wasn't happy watching a repeat of what must have been the interview of Clyde Coleman, either. He damn sure wasn't going to let Smith, and Bowman, for that matter, die alone and leave a killer behind.

Jack smoked a cigarette outside of the building, his hand trembling.

Jack caught a cab to the Post that night.

He still felt like shit from the night before, but he figured he'd just get coffee or sodas. The parking lot was packed; looked like the whole task force was there. Jack lit up and smoked outside the door. No doubt he'd be on the receiving end of the anger over the interrogation. He knew by now that, with few exceptions, everyone on the task force saw him as working for the Feds.

He walked through the narrow hallway into the dimly lit bar. He felt the dismissive glances burning into him, heard the murmurs and whispers.

He wished he could've been angry about it, but he didn't blame them. Eddie was the only one who nodded as he walked over.

He saw Teague, Melfly and Harken in the back at a booth. He patted Eddie on the shoulder and motioned him back toward the booth. They slid over to let him in, and Eddie grabbed a chair to cap the end.

"What the hell was that?" Teague asked.

"You had him; I know …" Jack said. "I don't know what the fuck Haskell was thinking …"

"Smith isn't gonna give up shit." Harken said, "He's got Jim Harrison for a lawyer."

"Jim Harrison? How'd he afford Jim Harrison!?"

"It's pro-bono … Harrison just wants face time."

"What kind of chips does Smith even have?" Eddie asked.

"Where he's tried," Jack said. "My guess, he doesn't want to get the needle. He knows he's not getting off, but if it's tried in State, he gets life; Federal, he gets death."

"He gave up Jeff Bowman," Teague said. "What else does he have?"

"I don't know," Jack said. "When you were in there, what was your read on his 'third guy' proposal?"

Teague sipped his vodka. "I think it means he either knows how to find Bowman, but is afraid to say, or he doesn't, and he needs a bargaining chip."

"Guess we'll know Monday," Jack said.

"So, you still like working for the Feds?" Melfly asked.

Jack shook his head. "Don't feel like I'm working for anybody," he said. "Haskell's holding me at arm's length."

"You're kidding," Harken said.

"Sarcasm deserved."

"Look, we appreciate the fact that you're trying to keep us in the loop, Jack," Teague said, "but at some point you're gonna have to step back from this deal you got going."

Jack took a deep breath. "I know," he said. "I just also know that if I walk on this, Chief will make sure I'm off the investigation for good."

"Not like you won't have a job," Harken said. "You'll still have regular old homicide."

"I'll know after Monday," Jack said. "Haskell's either gonna bring back real information, or he's not. If I don't have something usable, I'm back on homicide."

They drank, talking about the missing pieces of the investigation.

"Walt's figuring in on this as a possible," Jack said. "I don't want to believe it, but he seems to be popping up in the investigation. And if Smith's 'third man' is real, Walt did serve in Vietnam at the same time as Bowman."

"So did over a hundred thousand other people," Harken said.

"I know, but Bowman made contact with Walt."

"And Walt told you this!" Harken said. "If he was a perp, why would he tell us?"

"I don't know," Jack said. "He looks good *on paper*; that's all. I love the guy; *I* don't believe he knows anything about it. Haskell told me he's gonna put Walt's picture in a photo-array, see if Smith can identify him."

"Wait," Teague said. "If Bowman made contact with Walt, then for all we know, both of them know his face. He might just pick him out to throw us off."

"All I'm saying is that we have to consider Walt as 'involved' in this ... the same way you all consider me 'involved,'" Jack said.

"If Walt's not helping, he's a key somehow, like me. Now, we know why I'm a part of this. My parents and Bowman had a ... *history*."

Jack told them about Bowman and his mother, the prom, and the fact that his parents' murders were practiced on the first two "Slasher" victims.

"So where is Walt's, umm ... *history* here?"

Jack mulled it over, his Scotch glass in his hand.

"Vietnam," Jack said. "There's gotta be a connection there. Something that Walt doesn't remember; an interaction. I mean, it was a big war; something that may not have meant much to Walt may have meant everything to Bowman."

Teague set his drink down. "So how do you propose we find something like that out?"

"We can have Haskell unseal Walt's military service record, see if there are any intersections between his and Bowman's service."

"Or we can ask Walt ..."

"Not if he is a suspect," Jack said, "not until we've ruled him out, or he's our last resort for information."

"I don't like this, Jack ..." Harken said.

"I don't, either," Jack said, "but Walt's a lead. So please, no talking until we rule him out."

"So we trust Haskell," Teague said.

"Look, I know he fucked up that interrogation," Jack said, "but he made a bad call. Who here can say they never did that?"

"He'd probably let you go if he knew you were talking to us about your work."

"I think he's being left out now, too," Jack said. "And he told me to stay involved on the local action."

"Why, to spy for him?"

"Doubt it; he hasn't asked anything about you guys," Jack said.

"Yet." Harken said.

Jack went home that night and pondered many questions as he sat in front of his computer, playing chess in "expert" mode. When he didn't play by himself, he played against the machine. Sometimes he beat it; sometimes it beat him, but it was a great way to drift.

So they had three sets of killings: The "Slasher" killings that took his parents' lives, the "body-dump" killings, of which at least ten had a circumstantial connection to Jason Smith, and the South End Killings. Bowman could be linked to the first and the third, and motive was clear for Bowman in the first murders, but something didn't gel.

The first two victims had hesitation stab-wounds. Bowman was just back from Vietnam, and judging by his military history, it wasn't likely he'd be shy about killing.

If Bowman had killed the first two victims, there'd be no hesitation. So if Clyde Coleman wasn't his accomplice back then, had Smith carried out the first two murders?

As Jack made moves on the screen, he made up his mind to find someone to interview, even over the phone, if he had to, to find out what kind of relationship Bowman and Smith had in high school. He also needed to dig deeper; what about Smith's parents? Bowman's?

He'd need Gamble's help to do some digging ... maybe Haskell's. But his mind hit a brick wall. As a consultant, he couldn't act as a detective. He couldn't do interviews. Haskell had him painted in a box.

Smith himself held the key to many of the questions, but his lawyer wouldn't dare let him answer any that might implicate him in prior crimes. So aside from getting information on Bowman, or Walter, Smith's value would be limited. Smith's lawyer would file motions to keep it a state case, and might win that. Short of offering him twenty-five-to-life instead of life without parole, Smith wouldn't have much to gain from a plea bargain. He'd probably have more to fear from Bowman for talking.

Jack made the move that put the computer in checkmate, and shut down his laptop. Haskell was taking off the next day, so it followed that he had the day off, too. He decided right then that Monday would be his last day, regardless. He fell asleep in the study, an empty pack of cigarettes sitting by a full ashtray.

Jack sat in the Chevelle, the steam from his coffee and wisps of smoke from his cigarette dancing with each other as he stared at the house.

It was no stranger; he couldn't avoid driving by it when he was doing his job. When his parents owned it, that section of North Central was well-to-do; now it was a crime ridden shit-hole the city tried to keep under its rug. He had watched the house go from rented to for sale and back again. He could have bought it when it was for sale, had it torn down, but he didn't.

He could've easily bought it then, and, as the "For Sale" sign was back on the front lawn, he could have bought it that day, too. But he wouldn't. He knew he wouldn't.

He drove to Riverville around ten. He needed to talk to Mary and a phone call wasn't going to work. He missed her, Paul, even Dan.

He was tired. Of the investigation, of being "involved," of being at Haskell's beck and call, a hand-out job just to let him stay in a losing game. Catching Bowman wasn't his sole responsibility – he had done enough. And he knew what it could cost him; his gut reminded him every five minutes.

He pulled up to Dan's; Mary's car wasn't in the driveway. He thought of passing by, but he had apologies to make to Dan, too. Dan answered the door wearing a crimson bathrobe.

"They're not here," he said after inviting Jack in. "They're staying at Susan's house. She didn't tell you?"

"No," he replied. "I don't blame her, though. You still talkin' to Susan?"

"Yeah … not that her new husband likes it all that much," Dan said.

"Can you tell her that after Monday, I'm off the case?"

"You have Sue's number, Jack," Dan said, "maybe you should call her and tell her yourself … save me the headaches with Sue."

"Okay," Jack said. "Hey Dan, I came to apologize to you too. I didn't mean-"

"Don't," Dan said. "You had every right to say it. I know you didn't mean it to come out like that, but it was true. We should've pressed Coleman, and we didn't. Now that they got Smith, I know we fucked up.

He leaned back against the door.

"We all join the force to make a difference, ya know," He continued, "Protect our communities, put our lives on the line ... I can never count the number of lives I may have saved in my time on the force.

"But every day I read the paper on the job, I'd get an exact count of the ones I didn't save."

"Dan, I don't think you would've gotten Smith anyway." Jack took a breath. "Smith didn't murder my parents. I believe one of his school mates did it. And he's the one out there now."

"Who?"

"His name's Jeffrey Bowman. He was a friend of Smith's, and they work, well, *worked* together, but I think my parents were murdered by Bowman and Coleman."

"They need ya, Jack," Dan said. "Mary, and Paul ... they need you. They're worried."

"I know, Dan," Jack said. "I need them too."

Jack was heading to his mother-in-law's house when Harken called him.

"I got some bad news, Jack," Harken said. "About Smith."

"Oh, Jesus ..."

"He was killed in the jail a little while ago," Harken said. "Ya might want to come to the task force. Melfly's gonna brief in a half-hour."

Jack sighed. "Alright, I'll be there," he said. His tires squealed as he pulled a U-turn on Arcadia Street and floored it. He'd have to catch Mary and Paul around dinner time.

Sheriff Melfly stood up in the center of the main room. He had a booming voice, sure to reach every nook and cranny of the office.

"At approximately six o'clock, in the dining hall during break-fast, Jason Smith was stabbed to death by another inmate with a shank. And this one lands on us," he added.

"Why? What happened?" Harken asked.

"He was killed by Ethan Marshall, who was doing six months for assault. Marshall was Leiah Marcusen's boyfriend. He was immediately eliminated from the investigation early on, be-cause he had an obvious alibi," Melfly said. "We just never cross-linked him and Smith as enemies in jail. We should have."

"Fuck!" someone said. Jack couldn't tell who, but they were all thinking it. Chips or no chips, Jason was their last living link to Bowman, or whomever else was with Bowman.

Jack met Gamble in the back of the task force building. Gam-ble was smoking; rare.

"Well, there goes that," he said.

"I'm off of this, Eddie."

"Haskell get rid of you?"

"No," Jack replied. "I'm just … done. I'm tired of being a pawn in this, and Mary's damn close to drawing up divorce pa-pers. I gotta throw it in, go back to Homicide."

"I don't blame you," Gamble said. "I'll be joining you. I gotta' have time with Sarah."

"You know Bowman's still on the loose."

"If he hasn't skipped town by now," Gamble said. "I think we were lucky to get Smith."

"Yeah, point," Jack said. "Anyways, I gotta go talk to Mary, patch things up while I still can."

"Do that, Jack. You have a good woman there. Don't lose her."

Jack went to see Mary and Paul around dinnertime. Mary was happy to hear that he'd be off the case, but she asked him if it was official. He couldn't lie to her.

"When you tell Haskell that you're off the case, and you're working your regular job again, we'll come back … home. Not to Dad's house, but *our* home."

"I want to make sure you're safe, Mary … until we find him."

"What if you never do?" Mary asked. "What if it's years, or he moves to another state? I just want this to be over, Jack. I want us to live our lives again."

"Okay, okay," Jack said. "We'll do it your way."

"We miss you, Jack."

"I miss you guys, too."

"So you promise you're done with it?"

"Yes. Monday, I'll talk to Haskell, and have Harken reassign me."

Mary gripped Jack tight.

"It's gonna be okay, Jack," she said. "You've done your part. Just let this go."

Haskell took it as well as Jack expected when he told him that he needed off the case.

Jack kept his frustrations about Smith largely to himself, only mentioning that it was *just* a frustration, not the reason he was packing it up on the investigation. Smith really wasn't a reason, just an excuse he could hold onto, something he could live with in light of everything else.

He wanted Bowman in cuffs. He wanted this to end. But since the bombing of the Historical Society, there had been no new murders. Not since Smith had been brought in. And with Jeffrey Bowman just a name, Jack realized that he could easily have quit while the getting was good, spread his malignancy on some other city, or gone underground completely.

Jack could very well have lost his wife and son only to wrestle with shadows and whispers.

And he realized that this *was* personal. Everyone in the task force that thought he shouldn't have been on it was right after all. And the city wouldn't be absent of new, unrelated murders for long. The task force had exhausted the homicide division. They could use him as an anchor.

Harken said as much as they talked about it over the phone Sunday night.

"I'm glad to hear you say this, Jack," he said. "Eddie and I are going back to homicide, too. Chief's orders."

"So who's going to work the task force?"

"Lieutenant Billings," Harken said, "and Montclaire is replacing Eddie."

"So where are they at now?" Jack asked.

"They're concentrating on the bombing, trying to trace the RDX," Harken said. "They're still trying to identify remains at the body dump. But they're under the assumption that Bowman took off. The task force is shedding personnel."

"I hope they're right, Captain," Jack said.

"Me too. Still want to catch the bastard, though …"

"Ya know, Captain, I should've never been involved in this case once I found the tunnel."

"Oh, that's bullshit," Harken said. "We wouldn't have caught Smith without you; wouldn't have learned a thing about Bowman.

"I'm not just walking away, Jack," Harken said, "and I recommend you don't, either.

"This is our city. That asshole kills someone else, it's on *our* streets. You're coming back to Homicide; you'll need to stay abreast of the investigation – it comes out in the daily bulletins … You'll still need to read those, right?"

"Yeah; I guess you're right."

"If he's still out there, we'll get him, Jack," Harken said. "Don't you worry about that."

"I'll miss the coffee at the office …" Jack said.

"What's wrong with our coffee?"

"Nothing … it's just, ya know … *new coffee* …"

Harken laughed. "Then I'll steal some," he said.

"It'll be good to be home, Jack."

"Yeah." Jack thought of Mary and Paul, of great dinners, movie nights and homework help. "In more ways than one."

Harken tore his desk apart as he lifted his coffee, small slivers of particleboard jutting out from the bottom of his mug. Half of his coffee shot skyward. Jack laughed. Gamble shrugged.

"Damnit, Taggart!" Harken shouted.

"Super Glue?" Gamble said from his desk. "Really?"

"What kind of jerk would I be if I used Super Glue?" Jack said.

"Oh …"

"Epoxy," Jack said.

Gamble laughed. Harken grumbled, told Jack it was coming out of his pay. *Whatever.* It was good to be back to old tricks, pranking each other on a boring day.

They spent the morning doing follow-up calls on the Raymond Arrizo murder; a drug deal gone sour about a month before the South End Killer struck.

It was routine shit; Detective Hernandez was his old partner in Narcotics, and they'd been working the murder together. Hernandez went undercover, and Jack hadn't been around for new leads.

They had read the bulletin put out by the taskforce, but Jack felt useless on that front. Jack and Eddie were planning on stopping by the Post that night, see if they could catch a whisper or two.

Not that it would do them any good. They were off the rollercoaster, back on dope dealers with scores and batterers with cheating wives. *Motives*, something that had been absent as of late.

But he couldn't get case out of his brain. Because there *was* a motive … thirty years ago.

But for all that had happened in the past two months, where was the motive? How much of it died with the Smiths and Mansfield? And, most importantly, was Bowman gone, or just "dormant"?

"Umm … Jack?"

Harken walked into the squad room, a tissue in his hand grasping an envelope.

"This is addressed to you," he said. "Grab some gloves."

Jack found a box of gloves from the supply closet, and grabbed three pair, figuring Harken and Gamble would need some, too.

"The return address is 169 Turner Street," Harken said. "Familiar with it?"

"That's the house I grew up in … my parents' house," Jack said. "But that's impossible! No one lives there right now."

"Postmark is New Rhodes," Gamble said.

"Open it up," Harken said, "carefully …"

Jack opened the envelope, and was relieved that it only contained a letter. It was basic; copy paper, hand-written. He read it, mouthing the words under his breath.

Dear Jack,

So I hear that you're out of the game now. That just won't do. I have more fun with you on my tail. I have to say that tomorrow won't be as much fun without you. But I do have a surprise for your friends. Maybe you'll catch the first call. One can only hope.

My associate was unlucky. Not to mention a big mouth ... I was listening to the bug you planted.

The hangers-on almost gave me up. I didn't mean to cause the collateral damage, but the Historical Society ... Well, call that my own version of "urban renewal."

I do hope the ball-and-chain lets you play again. I'd love to see you around when I light up the night.

That's all for now.

South End's Favorite Son.

"Son of a bitch," Jack said.

"We have to get this to the task force," Harken said.

"He left clues," Jack said. "For starters, the return address. What if he was hiding out in there? We have to search it!"

"We have to let the task force do its job," Harken said. "For all we know, he did squat there, but he left, and wired the building to blow up."

"He's gonna kill someone," Gamble said. "He said we might *catch the call.*"

"If he does, he might change his M.O., make it look like a regular homicide," Jack said. "How will we know it's *him*?"

"Maybe that's the point," Harken said.

"And how did he know about the bug in the Historical Society?" Jack asked.

"Good question," Gamble said. "He could've tapped the transmission, but how did he know it was there in the first place?"

"Jason Smith could've had a source in the task force."

"Well, we better find that out pretty fucking quick," Harken said. "If there's a leak, it probably hasn't been plugged."

"I hope to God that the 'third guy' Smith claimed there was doesn't have eyes and ears on the task force," Jack said.

"Why would you think that?" Gamble asked.

Jack held the letter up to the light, hoping to find a smudge, stain, or anything to confirm that the *South End's Favorite Son* was, as suspected, Jeffrey Bowman.

"Because it makes too much sense," he said.

"That's not your job now, Jack ..." Harken said.

"But it's my letter, my name. He's going out of his way to *make it* my job."

"That's all the more reason to stay out," Harken said. "The farther he has to go to draw you back in, the more he risks exposing himself. It was Simon Smith's letter that nailed us Jason Smith ... Bowman will fuck up.

"He'll drag himself down going after you."

Jack thought of the words in the letter; *I do hope the ball-and-chain lets you play again.*

"What's to keep him from going after Mary and Paul?"

"We'll put a detail on them, Jack, I promise. Twenty-four-seven."

"We don't have the people-"

"I'll *make* the people if I have to!" Harken snapped. "You jump back into this investigation and he wins. He wants to ruin your life, Jack! Jesus! There's another way to lose Mary and Paul, you know ... you just narrowly avoided doing that."

"At least they'd be alive," Jack muttered.

Jack got a strange call shortly before his shift ended. It was Walter.

"Hey Jack," Walt said, "Got a second?"

"Yeah, sure, Walt. What's going on?"

Silence on the other end for a moment. Then he heard Walt clear his throat.

"I, umm ... had a couple of guys from the task force come over and ask questions about Bowman ..."

"Oh yeah, that's natural, Walt," Jack said. "We put your ... *encounter* ... with him into the database. They were probably just following up."

"Oh, I know that ..." Walter said, "that's not it. It's just that ..." Again, silence. Jack could hear Walter take a deep breath.

"I don't want to say anything over the phone," he said. "Is there any way you can stop by sometime?"

Jack thought of what he had to do after shift, and that it was the first day back with Mary and Paul.

"Can I stop by your house tomorrow morning?" Jack asked. "I just got Mary back home. I mean, if you need me to come over now, I will."

"No, it can wait," Walter said. "You're not working with that FBI agent anymore?"

"Nope," Jack said, "I'm back on homicide. The only way Mary would come back home."

"That's good, Jack," Walter said. "I'm happy to hear that ..." Walter paused, as if he wanted to say something but the words caught in his throat.

"You okay, Walt?" Jack asked.

"Yeah," Walter said. "I'll be okay ... but come to my house tomorrow morning. I just don't want to talk over the phone, that's all ..."

"Okay, Walt," Jack said. "I'll be there early."

"Take care of yourself, kid," Walter said, and he hung up.

"What was going on with Walt?" Gamble asked.

"I don't know," Jack said. "Wanna meet me at his house to-morrow morning?"

Jack pulled up to 169 Turner Street after his shift ended.

He would've driven past the State Police cruisers, but he saw Teague outside, talking to one of the troopers. He got out qui-etly, scanned the street.

He imagined Bowman was probably watching the whole scene from a sewer grate somewhere. There was a bodega on the corner; it gave him an excuse to stop.

Teague nodded as Jack walked over.

"Hey, Willie," Jack said, "I just need smokes." He pointed to the bodega. "You need anything?"

"Not really," Teague said, "but I know why you're really here, so you might as well grab me a coffee."

"Got it," Jack said, and he went to the bodega. Smokes were a staple at every bodega, but the coffee was always hit or miss.

Crack was the stimulant of choice in that once upper-middle-class neighborhood.

The pot of burnt coffee was for the sleep-deprived nine-to-fivers. He filled a Styrofoam cup, grabbed the creamer cups swimming in the dew of melting blue ice packs, and a couple of packets of sugar.

The store had more cameras than a check-cashing place. Jack paid for the smokes with his debit card and fished for his wallet for the coffee, but the clerk must've seen his badge, waved him off.

"Thanks," Teague said as Jack returned. "I shouldn't have you anywhere near here, but ..."

"Bowman was squatting here, wasn't he?" Jack said.

"Yeah, but there's more than that ..." Teague said. "It's a mess in there ..."

"Tell me this isn't where he-"

"Basement," Teague said. "And yeah, there's another tunnel under the house. We're waiting for a structural engineer this time."

"I don't get it," Jack said. "The second victim was burned alive, and we found the skin from the third victims in the other tunnel ... What could be *down there*?"

"More victims?" Teague said, "It's a horror show. Victims he never claimed credit for – prostitutes, by the clothes we found.

"Look, I can't take you in there, Jack, without getting my ass chewed off ... Some of it's ... *personal* to you. But what are you doing tomorrow night?"

"Nothing that I know of," Jack said.

"Meet me at the Post, then … say, eight-thirty," Teague said. "I'll get a copy of the crime scene pics. We might need you to … interpret … some of what's in there."

Jack left, bewildered. *Interpret?* What exactly was in his old house? Teague didn't have to bring him in on it; Harken may have his ass the next day, but he didn't care. Something in there had to do with him. He was a subject matter expert on himself … so he hoped.

He got home to the sound of the vacuum. He'd cleaned up his little fit, but it didn't go unnoticed. He hadn't thought to vacuum. Paul was in the living room, oblivious, playing a video game. He snuck up behind Mary and kissed the back of her neck. She nearly jumped out of her skin, then shut off the vacuum.

"Scared the hell out of me, you!" She smiled, kissed him back. "Mind telling me about the unmarked sitting outside?"

"I got a letter today," Jack said. "From Bowman."

"But you're not on the task force anymore. Why would he send you a letter?"

"It's been about me this whole time, Mary," Jack said. "He's gonna keep trying to draw me into this."

"But you can't let him," Mary said. "Don't you see that if you do that he wins?"

"I know, I know … I keep hearing it, and I know it, but he seems to have an ear to every wall I pass by," Jack said. "He knew I'd gone back to homicide, knew that you were the reason, even."

"He mentioned me?" Mary stiffened up a bit.

"In a manner of speaking …"

"What did he say?"

"Something about how he hopes 'the ball-and-chain' lets me play again."

"Ball-and-chain!?"

"His words …" Jack said.

Mary leaned up against the wall, arms folded. Jack brushed her cheek with the back of his fingers.

"Mary, I know you don't want me on this case …"

"He wants to ruin you," she said. "I don't want to see him succeed."

"I don't either, and I'm not asking to be back on the case," Jack said, "but I need to be in the loop. It's personal, and if he wants to make it *more* personal, I need to know when to get you guys out of here; hell, to Hawaii if I have to. The closer we get to him, the more dangerous he'll be."

"I just want this to be over, Jack," Mary said. Jack took her into his arms.

"It will be," Jack said, "one way or another."

Mary's dinner was delicious. It was meat loaf, Jack's favorite, but just having a normal dinner with his family made it exquisite. Tony showed up before his shift for coffee.

Tony had the ten-to-two shift, and it promised to be boring. It was Monday, after all. It would just be the usual smattering of drunken brawls and domestic disturbances.

No alcohol-powered weekend warriors laying down slurred gauntlets in the downtown. Jack briefed him on the letter and the mess at his childhood home.

"Do you want me to ride by there? See if he's lingering around?"

"Nah." Jack said. "He put that house in his rear-view by now. I'm sure of it.

"But watch yourself. If he's after me, he's after us all."

Jack's phone went off at three in the morning. Wiping the crust from his eyes, he cracked out a "Taggart."

It was Harken.

"We got a problem," Harken said. "Two of them." Something about his tone was off. "Get dressed."

"What's the address?" Jack asked.

"It's Emerald's," Harken said. "Just hurry."

Jack pulled up to the scene just as Gamble did. The evidence techs were already inside, and the entrance had been cordoned off with tape. Tony was standing in front of the bar.

"Tony, I thought your shift ended at two?"

"The call came in at one thirty-eight," Tony said. "I was the closest. It's Walt, Jack ... and Ralphie."

"What the hell happened!?"

"Looks like an armed robbery; the door was kicked in and the drawer was empty," Tony replied.

Gamble walked over.

"We got a witness," he said. "He says he saw an older man, camouflage jacket, jeans ... sounds like-"

"Bowman," Jack said. "Son-of-a-bitch!"

"Can we go in?"

"They processed a walkway for us," Gamble said. "We just gotta stay on it."

They walked into Emerald's. Jack didn't see Walt, but the techs had a spotlight behind the bar.

Ralphie was on the floor; blood spatter on the frosted glass privacy plate that surrounded a table with blood pooled on it.

The M.E. was there; he must've moved him. The bottom edge of the mirror behind the bar was shattered to a point, the spider fracture pattern peppered with blood.

Freddie came out from the back. He had his print brush in his hand.

"Freddie," Jack said, "Anything so far?"

Freddie set the brush on one of the tables. "This looks like a double homicide, maybe a robbery gone wrong. The bartender-"

"Walt," Jack said. "His name was Walt."

"Sorry ... *Walt* had a gun under the bar. He must not have had the chance to use it."

"So you think it was a robbery?"

"Looks like it," Freddie said, "the drawer was smashed, nothing in it ... You knew him?"

"Yeah, he was a retired cop... and a friend."

"Sorry, Jack." Freddie said.

Jack looked at Gamble. "Does that sound weird to you?"

"Yeah ... it's a Monday night. That drawer would've been near empty anyway."

"Let's go outside," Jack said. "Nothing we can get from here, and I don't feel like seeing Walt and Ralphie put in bags."

Jack and Gamble walked to the side of the building.

"This is Bowman," Jack said, "has to be. He damn near admitted as much in that letter!"

"But we can't prove it," Gamble said. "Circumstantial."

"The witness said he went down this way, right?" Jack said. Gamble nodded.

"Let's see if there's anything. We'll circle the building."

They walked down the side of the building, Jack shining his flashlight to and fro, catching garbage – bags, the shiny silver plastic of candy bar wrappers, cigarette butts and beer cans, crumpled in feats of petty strength. They kept on until the light caught a glint of steel in a patch of tall grass.

"Got a pen?" Jack said. Gamble fished one out of his pocket. Jack looped the pen through the trigger guard.

"A thirty-eight," Jack said. Jack smelled the barrel. "Recently fired. Can you grab Freddie?"

Freddie came out and unloaded it, careful not to smudge any prints.

"This fits the M.E.'s description of the gunshot wounds." He smelled it as well. "Yep. I think you got the murder weapon here. Let's just hope there are prints on it."

"Why empty the drawer?" Jack asked Gamble as they walked around the scene. They saw Harken's car pull up. He got out and leaned slightly against the car door to steady himself.

"Walt…"

"Yeah, Captain … He's in there. Ralphie too."

"Oh, Jesus," Harken said. "I'm gonna kill that freak with my bare hands!"

"He made it look like a robbery," Jack said. "Maybe it was in part, but …"

"No," Harken said, "he knew what he was doing. He's jamming us up."

"How do you figure?" Gamble asked.

Harken took out a cigarette, motioned to Jack for a light.

"We don't have proof that it was Bowman right yet," Harken said. "And since it looks like a robbery-homicide, we can't link it to the task force cases."

"So we gotta work it like a regular homicide," Jack said.

"Right," Harken said, "unless we can match prints. We don't even know if his prints are on file."

"Walt wanted to tell me something," Jack said as they stood at the edge of the crime-scene tape.

"What was it?" Harken asked.

"He wouldn't say ... He sounded spooked. He didn't want to talk over the phone. Like someone was listening in."

"So he didn't tell you anything earlier?"

"Just that they did a follow-up interview with him," Jack said.

"Who?" Harken asked.

"He didn't say."

"I'll find out tomorrow," Harken said. He flung his cigarette outside the tape. "Was that what spooked him?"

"I don't know ... maybe?" Jack said. He pulled out a cigarette of his own.

"This never should have happened," Jack said. "He needed to talk, and I more or less made him wait until tomorrow morning. If I'd just gone over ..."

"You can't think like that," Harken said. "Maybe it would've changed things, or maybe there'd be three bodies coming out of there."

Harken's words were encouraging in that morbid way of his, but Jack couldn't stop thinking about the trip to his old house on Turner Street. He didn't have to go there, try to pump Teague for intel, but he had. If he had gone to talk to Walt, it might not have stopped what happened. But he might have a clue as to *why*.

Harken slapped Jack on the back.

"Go home and get some sleep," he said. "Both of you. Until and unless the task force links Walt to Bowman, his case is ours to work.

"Tomorrow, we go after this prick on our own."

CHAPTER NINE

Jack slept like shit for three hours, waking up to gunfire. Paul's video game didn't have a snooze button. Mary was sleeping through the Battle of the Bulge. He got up without disturbing the bed. *Let her sleep,* he thought, *I'd rather she not know what our game plan is.* Jack told Mary everything; one of the joys of her being from a cop family was that she didn't care if he brought his work home with him. But they were set to track Bowman, and she didn't need to hear that. He didn't need to be alone again.

Dan came over last night when he heard about the letter. He had bagels and cream cheese out in the kitchen, with a pot of coffee on. Jack was slipping; he didn't smell it when he woke up.

He pulled up a chair, Dan poured him a cup, dressed in a bathrobe Jack had brought back for him from a fancy hotel in New York that he and Mary stayed at during an awards ceremony.

"I don't know what to say to you, Jack," Dan said. "Wish I did."

"It was him," Jack said as he hushed his voice. "Bowman; It was Bowman."

"So the task force ...?"

"Not theirs ... yet," Jack said.

"You gonna pursue it 'til then?" Dan asked.

Jack sighed. "Don't know if I should tell you or leave that blank."

Dan slid the cup across the table, "I never told Mary to leave. She's grown up around the fear that I wasn't gonna come home one night, or her brothers, but you almost didn't. She was inconsolable when you were in surgery."

"But you have that job. It's a homicide, and unless you're retiring early, you gotta' work Walt's case." he continued,

"I had the job myself back in the day. So as long as you watch your ass out there, Mary won't hear a thing from me."

"Thanks, Dan," Jack said. He chugged his coffee and grabbed a bagel as he got dressed. He made sure to leave a light kiss on Mary's forehead, not enough to wake her. Then he took off for the station.

Jack was greeted in the squad-room with a folder thrown at him. He barely caught it.

"What's this, Captain?"

"Open it, dumbass ..." Harken said, "*Detect...*"

Jack sat down at his desk and opened the folder; eight-by-ten glossies of rooms vaguely familiar; his old house. The walls were grimy, with pictures, newspaper clippings and larger sheets of paper affixed with push-pins.

He went through each picture, looking at everything that wasn't too small to see. *New Rhodes Police Bust a Major Meth Ring* was one title of a newspaper clipping. Jack remembered the article; he was the lead detective on that bust.

Jonathan Myers, the headline of another article read, *The Designer of the "New" New Rhodes.* Old; Jack could barely make out the words. There were many other articles; most were too small to see in the pictures.

"Is this all we're getting?" Jack asked.

Harken gave Jack the keys to the unmarked. "Nope."

"Where's Eddie?"

"He's out *showing a presence,*" Harken said.

"So he's not really doing shit."

"Pretty much."

"But he's in homicide. Why's he doing task force stuff?"

"Some newspaper shot a clip of Marion and Jackson joking around in uniform; they did a story on *police inaction* – a hatchet job, but they're desperate. So the task force grabbed a bunch of cops and made them do foot patrols."

"You mean Gamble's walking the beat?"

"In his old patrol uniform, yes."

Harken and Jack laughed.

"Does the media realize that putting a cop on every corner keeps 'em off the actual case?"

"They don't care." Harken said. "It was an Albany paper. C'mon, we gotta' drag ass."

They left the station in the unmarked and endured the squeal of break dust every time they stopped.

"I'm only letting you drive because I'm probably still drunk from last night."

"Really?" Jack said. "Last night? Really?"

"I had to get Teague liquored up enough to let us go," Harken said. "Now let's hurry the fuck up before he realizes what he agreed to."

They drove north up Continental Avenue, a quiet, sleepy street a few blocks away from the bustle of downtown traffic. It was still morning rush, and the house was three miles from the station. Harken donned his shades, folded his arms in full *tough guy* pose; Jack laughed.

"Ya folding your arms to look tough or to hold back a puke?"

"Both?"

"They get anything off of the crime scene, do you know?"

"I think they got pretty much everything; prints, hairs, blood – who knows whose blood – but ..."

"But what, Cap'?"

"Well, that's pretty fucking scary if you ask me," Harken said.

"What's scary?"

"It's a man-hunt now ... He's leaving evidence and he's getting desperate. He no longer cares. On the other hand, it could get him caught."

"Nah, I don't think so," Jack said. "He's going down with the ship. He's old, Cap'..."

"He's my age," Harken said.

"No offense."

"Hope to hell not!"

"He's not gonna stop until the grand finale," Jack said. "Until he's dead."

"Ya been talkin' to him in your dreams?"

"I just have a hunch," Jack said. "He likes the spotlight. He's *off-the-chain*, he's got nothing to lose.

"He can't fade into obscurity; every law enforcement agency in the country has his name and the last picture the Brooklyn M.E.'s office took of him. If he runs, he'll just get caught."

Jack let the wheel glide through his hands as he swerved to dodge a double-parked car.

"All I'm saying is, he's been putting ten grand on the table every hand so far, and with absolutely no offense to Walter, he ends it with a hundred dollar bet?"

"So you're saying he's gonna go *all-in*?"

"Count on it," Jack said. "And I'm willing to make my own bet … that he'll have me at the card game."

"Can't say I'd take your bet," Harken said. "Probably lose."

"Ya gonna tell Mary about our field trip here?"

"Not at all," Jack said. "He's gonna come after me and everyone I'm close to, no matter what I do to avoid it. We're investigating Walter's homicide, and that's what I tell her."

They got to 169 Turner Street, opened the trunk and pulled out two Maglites. Teague told Harken that he'd keep the walls the way they were until the next day at noon, so Jack and Harken had about two hours to look at it the way it was found.

The task force still had custody of the scene, of course; the tunnel underneath hadn't been explored, and State Police techs were still there, hovering like bees around a spring hive.

They saw Teague, sipping coffee on the porch, talking to two sheriff's deputies.

"Teague," Harken said.

"Harken … Jack …" Teague said. "I'm glad you guys are here. You won't need those." Teague pointed to the Maglites. "We had the power company restore power until we fully process the scene."

"So we can just go in?" Jack asked.

"Yes. They recovered as much of the trace evidence as they could yesterday. They're focused on the basement today."

"Jack," Teague said, "Prepare yourself. All I'm saying."

Jack had a knot in his gut as they walked into the house once soaked in his parents' blood.

The door creaked, the wooden floors beneath them groaned in protest, as they made their way into the foyer. Cobwebs hung in every corner, Jack's nose was assaulted with the smell of abandonment. He could smell must, mildew, piss and shit, and the faint note of decomposition. It was slight; Jack knew there were no bodies in the house. It was probably coming up from the basement; the tunnel.

They walked past the doorway to the sitting room, which was empty, and continued through the archway into the living room. That's where the morbid tapestry of Bowman's life was on display.

There was a sleeping bag and a wooden wire-spool in the center of the room. Empty cans of tuna fish littered the corner, and the place was strewn with broken beer bottles. One of them, the bottom half, was a *de facto* ashtray on the wire spool. There was a bucket in one corner, and Jack didn't have to go near it to know what Bowman was using it for.

Amid the grime and torn plaster was a riddle for Jack to try to solve. On the back wall were newspaper clippings about the murders, both past and current. In the center was an article about his parents' murder. The eyes were cut out of their picture, four hollow sockets staring blankly from their embrace.

Jack could've lost it; right then, he could've just broken down.

Harken would've understood; Teague might even have expected it. But they *were* empty pages to him. He didn't know them any more than a six-year-old knows anything.

There were clippings from murders in New York City, with *possible copycat* in every one.

"These are important," Jack said. "I'd be willing to bet he worked on all of these murders in the M.E.'s office; probably worked the original killers' victims for the inspiration."

He went on to the next wall. There were articles about Jonathan Myers, Jack's drug bust when he was working narcotics, and a recent article about his getting shot was pinned in the center of the wall by the door. But what intrigued him was the large map in the center of the opposite wall.

"Is that what I think it is?" Jack asked.

"Tunnels, by the look of it," Teague said. "The South End tunnel's on there."

Jack looked at the picture as a whole. The South End tunnel ran parallel to Fourth Street much further than he was told.

The "T" where the tunnel went up to St. Michael's Cemetery wasn't a "T" on the map; it was an intersection. Yet they found an east-west split there.

The South End tunnel seemed to travel north, all the way to a stopping point. In fact, all the tunnels on the map, in one way or another, stopped at the same rough point.

"Jesus ..." Jack said."

"What?"

"It's the Agora." Jack pointed to where it would be on the map. "All of the tunnels have terminal points under the Agora. But the tunnels are older, so ..."

"That site used to be the central business district in New Rhodes before the Agora was built," Harken said. "They must have gone into the basements of the shops."

"Whoever was digging up the foundation for the Agora would have found them," Jack said.

"We have to find out who was working the demo, and the foundation of the Agora, and anyone that had access to the basement, assuming the tunnels weren't covered over."

"I don't think they were," Jack said. "These tunnels don't physically connect. If he has free rein over the underground, they'd have to connect, or have a," Jack searched for the word, "...*relay*. The Agora has to be the relay."

"We need a search warrant to get into the basement, then," Harken said. "Flush the son-of-a-bitch out."

Jack scratched his chin.

"Why did so many houses have hatches?" he asked. "Mansfield told me they built the tunnels to transport goods down to the river from the mills on top of the hill. Why would people need basement delivery of textiles?"

"That's easy," Harken said, "he lied to you. Criminals do that. It was coal."

"Coal?"

"Yeah ... there's an old abandoned coal-mine about twenty miles east of here in Millfield. We used to go party there when I was a kid."

"When was it in operation?" Jack asked.

"Some time in the eighteen-hundreds," said Harken. "You'll have to look it up; I'm not a history buff."

"Webb & Mansfield was a mining company." Jack commented. "Makes sense now."

Jack moved on to the wall shared by the sitting room and the living room. Business cards had been fixed to it with push pins and then connected by a spider's web of strings. He saw Harken's card, Teague's, Melfly's ...

Jack stepped back to take them all in and realized that the display represented the task force. Every card was there except for his, and one other ... he had little time to think about it, as a file tacked to the center of the web gave the answer.

It was Agent Haskell's profile, marked *Confidential*.

"Haskell ..." Harken said.

"My card isn't there either," Jack said. "That profile was the one done before Haskell and I were working in the other office."

"If not Haskell, why would he have this?"

"It's wrong," Jack said. "Even I know that he doesn't fit that profile. It said that he was in his thirties, nothing about military service... and that profile was done when the Marcusen murder was linked to the others.

"Now we know it was Smith who did that one. It also said that he would be submissive to a dominant, older man; we know now that Smith was submissive to *him*.

"We worked on a better profile before I left to come back to Homicide," Jack said. "If Haskell's leaking to him, Bowman would've had the new one. But we do have a leak.

"We have to run a background search on everyone who had access to this profile; everyone who's been on the task force since it was published."

"Haskell too, Jack."

"Yeah," Jack said, "but that's not going to be easy, also Decker. We'll be background-checking FBI agents. Gotta expect some ruffled feathers."

"We can rule out Teague and Melfly," Harken said. "Just trust me on that. We'll need their help, and I've known Melfly a long time. He cheats at poker, but other than that, he's a straight arrow. Teague hates the fuckin' guy-"

"Melfly?"

"No; Bowman," Harken said. "He ... well, he just wants to put a spike in the guy's arm, that's all ..."

"Tell me why later?" Jack whispered.

"Yeah," Harken whispered back. "Later."

Teague promised Jack he'd fax him all of the documents in the house, but told them both that Walter's and Ralphie's murders were going to fold into the Bowman case. He asked them if they could make it to the Post that night, but Harken declined due to a tired liver. Jack agreed, calling Mary soon after to let her know he was pulling an all-nighter.

"It's Walt, Mary ..." And he needed to say no more. He felt awful using Walt as an excuse, even though he was technically telling the truth.

Harken commandeered the radio on the ride back. Stevie Ray Vaughn's guitar cried out as they passed by the pizza joints and bars on River Street, talking and taking their sweet time getting back to the station.

"Tell me why Teague wants to give Bowman the needle? I mean, aside from the fact that we all do ..."

Harken put his shades back on. "He lost his cousin in the bombing."

"No shit ..." Jack said. "They were close, I take it?"

"Willie came up here back in ninety-five from North Carolina ... Big family; brothers, sisters, aunts, uncles, cousins ... they're tight knit. One of his cousins is a trooper, another one's an Albany cop. They wouldn't let his trooper cousin work the case with him, though; obvious reasons."

"Why didn't he say anything?" Jack asked. "I would have understood ..."

"How has being in the middle of a personal case worked out for you?"

Jack got the point. "Well, he could've just told *me*."

"Look, we were drunk, and the only two people in the Post last night," Harken said. "Now tonight, don't, you know,"

"Don't worry," Jack said, "if he wants to tell me, he will. I won't let it slip."

"It's personal for a lot of us now, with Walt and all," Harken said. "His wake is Saturday."

"Yeah, I know,"

"Going?"

"Of course," Jack said. "I don't want to, but Joanie will want me there."

"I don't wanna see him like that either," Harken said.

"Walt had to know something," Jack said. "About Bowman, and Vietnam … Probably didn't even know he knew it. But Bowman killed him for a reason."

"So what are you saying?" Harken said.

"I say we pull Walt's military record. They have Bowman's record; I'll ask Teague if he can get us a copy. Somewhere they intersect."

"Why not Haskell?"

"I don't know," Jack said. "He says he's on that stuff, but I'm not really getting the results from him. Plus, he might still have hard feelings about me leaving."

"But, supposing we do get his records, how does any of that help us catch Bowman?"

"It doesn't," Jack said. "But there's a third person, someone who's connected to Bowman. And whatever Walt knew, Bowman wanted to shut him up."

"What if Walt just wronged him somehow? Like that time Bowman confronted him outside the bar?"

"Look at the rage Bowman's capable of," Jack said. "Walt and Ralphie were just executions."

"What if he did it to get at you?"

"Well, there's that … but I still say we go through Walt's Vietnam history."

"Fine, we'll do it," Harken said, "but Jack, you know where this is heading …"

"What do ya mean?"

"Walt's not our case anymore," Harken said. "Now I'm all for chasin' this lead; hell, I wouldn't mind another spin behind the wheel of the task force now. But you came back off it for a good reason … You willin' to roll the dice with Mary?"

Jack sighed. "I don't know, Cap," he said. "I get it, with Mary, ya know … but you wanna guess what my biggest fear going into Turner Street was?"

"What was that?"

"Seeing stills of her and Paul, shopping, at the school, anywhere, doing anything …"

"Yeah, but you didn't see that," Harken said. "He seems to be just after you."

"Until he's dead or behind bars," Jack said, "I'm considering it open season on anyone close to me."

Jack drove up to the Post to meet Teague at six. The place was packed, but not with people in the task force. With Emerald's closed, its refugees had been offered a safe drinking haven at the Post.

Teague was at a table in the back, staring blankly at the window. Jack got a soda "on-the-arm" from Larry Markes, the day-shift cop running the bar, and went over. He just sat down; didn't say "hi" or ask; they were beyond that.

"I heard Harken had to ply you with liquor last night," Jack said. He pointed at Teague's drink. "Hair of the dog?"

"Nah ... just tonic," he said with a laugh. "I'm not drinking for at least a week."

"Yeah, I hear ya," Jack said. "Hey, Willie, thanks for letting us go in today. I know you didn't have to ..."

"I kinda *did*, Jack,"

"I guess you did," Jack took a sip of his soda. "I might have a couple of leads."

"Good," Teague said. "I was hoping ..."

Jack took the straw out of his soda, took a sip.

"The Agora," Jack said. "It's the key."

"I saw that all the tunnels intersect there."

"I'm willing to bet he's been using it as an exchange between the tunnels or something," Jack said. "I think it's too neat to have been Bowman's discovery. He must have known about it from someone else, maybe Smith or Mansfield."

"But how was he getting in there? The place got bought up last year. It's being remodeled."

"Do we know anything about the developer that bought it?"

"Graham Developers," Teague said. "I just know that because I drive by it to get to the task force every day."

"We should go through their records," Jack said. "It may be relevant."

"You think it'll help us track down Bowman?"

"Maybe," Jack said. "Maybe not. But we need to get in there. And I have blueprints and other papers about the Agora from my father's estate. I can check them out and see if I can find the substructure layout, any variances or permits.

"I can also have Gamble pull up any records on the contractors who worked the demo of the area, the foundation pouring; anyone who worked there who might have discovered the tunnels. We can cross-link names with Smith, Bowman or Mansfield; look for any connections."

"So, I take it you're asking back in?" Teague smiled.

Jack leaned over. "I think we should keep this small; you, me, Melfly, Harken and Gamble," he said.

"Someone's been working with Bowman from inside; we don't know who right now, but we have to run background checks, you know, look for possible connections to Bowman." He paused. "I think that *third guy* Smith started talking about before he lawyered up is one of us."

Teague stirred his tonic; bubbles flowed around the rim of the glass.

"Not gonna be easy, Jack," he said. "I mean, everybody on the task force passed a background check. How do we do *another* one, in secret? What are we even looking for?"

"Well, it might be easier. Smith mentioned a war buddy. So we only need to check people who are old enough to have served in Nam. That limits the search."

"Hell, that limits it to only three people I can think of," Teague said. "I got an investigator: Carl Mendoza; he's old enough. Then there's Agents Decker and Haskell. Everyone else is too young, except Harken and Melfly, but …"

"We're not looking at them," Jack said.

"Didn't think so," Teague said. "But how in the hell are we going to check the military records of two FBI agents? I mean, that's something we'd give *them* to handle!"

"Can't you guys?" Jack said.

"Not without making an official request," Teague said. "And that means showing our hand."

Jack slugged down the rest of his soda. "How about this; if you can get me a copy of everything you have cataloged from Turner Street, and I'll work with Gamble to see what we can do."

"Deal," Teague said.

"Man, I hate this shit."

"You and me both." Teague kept stirring his tonic.

"If my wife finds out I'm back in on this, she'll probably divorce me. "I wouldn't blame her either."

"So why do it, Jack?" asked Teague.

"I don't know," Jack said, "I've been treating the Bowman case like any other case, or at least I've tried to.

"But I look in the mirror and I know that's a sack of shit. As soon as I knew he was targeting me, I should have been off this case. You can't work a personal case and say it isn't personal. I know how everybody looked at me when I was in the task force ..."

Teague rubbed his eyes, popping them open. Jack realized he probably hadn't slept much.

"I lost my cousin Ritchie in the bombing," Teague admitted. "We were close. And ever since, the case hasn't been the same. Now, please; this goes no further ... but I can imagine what it must be like for you, 'cause I'm feeling some of it too."

"That sucks, man. I'm sorry to hear it. How's the rest of your family handling it?"

"My other cousin is a trooper too, out of Troop K in Dutchess County. He's chompin' at the bit to get on the task force, but our boss isn't having it. And my brother works robbery in Albany. He's pretty much the same way.

"Plus, there's everyone else. I'm getting calls non-stop, getting pumped for information and I can't give it. I just want to snap sometimes."

"Yeah, it sucks when it's personal. You get stretched from both ends. I'll keep mum on it, don't worry." Jack said. "And Willie... we'll get him. We'll make him pay."

He went through Walt's wake and funeral in a daze. Mary and Paul were by his side, and Harken, Melfly, Teague and Gamble were there throughout. There was a sea of cops and fireman. Everyone knew Walt.

With the exception of the people working the task force those days, the rest came by, paid their respects and grunted condolences to Joanie. Jack was deep in his mind, could barely bring himself to look upon Walt, asleep in embalmed bliss in the open casket.

Walt got the best burial he could have, short of not needing one. The bagpipes played, the priest offered those congregated the promise of Walt's eternal peace as Jack stared at the flag draped over his casket. The honor guard fired three rifles, seven times, as one of their rank handed the tri-folded flag to Joanie.

Jack couldn't bring himself to face any of it, forced by every homage to Walt to remember his call, to talk, something wrong about his interview, "*I don't know who's listening*" on the phone.

All Jack had to do was be there for a man who had been there for him throughout his life on the force. Jack should've stopped by the bar right away; instead, he was in a sea of black suits and blue uniforms.

"Ya alright, Jack?" Gamble said as they walked away from the grave site.

"Yeah, Eddie ..." Jack said. "Just thinking..."

"What about?"

Jack took a long breath. "Walt calling me the day he died," he said. "He asked me to come over, and I was gonna put it off until I had time…"

"You can't see this as your fault–"

"Apparently I can," Jack said. "He said he was re-interviewed, something wasn't right about it."

"Who interviewed him?" Gamble asked. "Do you know?"

"No," Jack said, "and that makes me even more useless. Hell, we were *working* the case … that should've been the first *lead!*"

Gamble leaned on the roof of the car. "Jack, if you wanna call it quits right now, wallow in guilt, go ahead," he said. "But you just said it; we have our first lead. Maybe we can just let the past be for a minute and follow it?"

Jack wasn't used to Gamble talking like that; he sounded a bit like Harken.

"You're right," Jack said. "We gotta find out who went to interview him that day and what was said."

Jack sat in the study, Scotch sloshing in a glass in his shaky grip. Mary opened the door and, without making a sound, sat in the armchair beside him.

"A penny for your thoughts?"

Jack shrugged. "I got a million bucks worth, Mar.'"

"I won't pretend to imagine how you feel right now."

"I failed him," Jack said. "He's dead because of me."

"You can't think that," she said. "You said that Bowman killed him, right?"

"I could have prevented it."

"Could you have? How?"

"He called me," Jack said, "He'd been re-interviewed by the task force, and he wanted me to come over that day ... but I didn't; figured it could wait until the next day."

"So, wait ... Was he spooked by it or something?"

"Yeah, I guess ... That's what it sounded like."

"And he didn't ask you to get over right away, did he?"

"Mary, C'mon ..."

"He was a detective. Don't you think he would've foreseen it if his life was in immediate danger? Closed early? Went to the task force himself?"

"Mary, what are you getting at?"

"Walt was smart enough to know, and tell you, if he thought it couldn't wait." She said. "Jack, you're a detective. Put this together."

Jack washed his mouth with single malt. "Mary ... I know what you're saying. I just ..."

"Just what?"

"I just felt like Walt being interviewed by the task force was a thing I needed to shy from; I hesitated."

Jack wiped beads of sweat from his brow. "I almost lost you and Paul last time. I'm not risking that again."

Mary sunk into her chair, her face in her hands. Jack reached for her.

"Jack," Mary said. "I'm scared."

"I know, Mar'... I can't say I'm not, but he's coming after me whether I'm on his case or not. I wish I could say we were safe because I'm back on homicide, but it's not looking that way."

"I don't want you getting killed," Mary said, "but you can't hide from this monster ... I see it now."

"So what are you saying?"

Mary took a breath, grabbed a swig of Jack's Scotch, something she never did. She put a hand to her chest as it kicked.

"Go get the son-of-a-bitch." She said. "I know how to shoot."

Harken gave Jack more shit about getting back on the task force than Mary did. Not that he didn't want Jack on it, but the bureaucracy was a brick wall.

"Jack, they're circling the wagons on this," he said. "I don't know if I can even *get* you back on."

"How can they object?" asked Jack. "He's after me; how does having me off the task force help anyone?"

"They think that … well …" Harken hesitated. "They think Bowman will escalate if you're back on,"

Jack was furious. "Just what the fuck was Walter!?" he shouted. "The letter? Then Walter?! I go off the case, he escalates; I get *on* the case, he escalates … until he, or anyone working with him, is dead or in jail, he's gonna escalate!"

"Jack, calm down, I get it; I know," Harken said. "But there's other things too."

"Like what?"

"When we catch him, we gotta convict him … they don't want the defense to say you tampered with evidence to get arrests."

"You know I wouldn't do that," Jack said.

"Yeah, I do," Harken replied, "but the defense can spin any story they want."

Jack walked over to his desk and grabbed his coffee. Not the best thing for nerves, but it was all he had.

"So who's against this?" Jack asked. "I know it's not Teague or Melfly …"

"It's not," Harken said. "They want you on. It's your old buddy, Haskell."

"Why on earth would *Haskell* not want me on? He brought me back in once!"

"Oh, I don't know … but he requested that Teague not release copies of anything in Turner Street to anyone outside of the task force, and you were the only one that would've gotten copies. What does that tell you?"

"Do we know yet if Haskell served in Vietnam?"

"Teague hasn't told me anything."

"I need to know who interviewed Walt the day he died. Can we get that?"

"They took Walt's case, so, I don't know … If you can find Teague, he can tell you."

Jack sat down at his desk. He was seething. Haskell wanted him off the case? No matter the reason, Jack had to see it as personal. Haskell blew an interrogation, Jack wound up leaving and Haskell didn't want him back. He wanted to throttle the guy, but he knew if he had any chance of getting back on the task force, he needed to get on Haskell's good side. He just didn't know how.

"Cap', who ultimately makes the call on me getting back in?" Jack said. "The Chief, right?"

"Yeah, but he's gonna ask Haskell his thoughts on the matter."

Jack leaned back as the wood creaked in his chair. "Here's how I'd present it;" Jack said,

"If Bowman hits again and I'm on homicide, I'll get the call. If I'm on the task force, I'll also be involved in that case. Either way, the defense can say I was involved."

"Chief's gonna want more …" Harken said.

"Tell him I'll see Haskell for another psych eval," Jack said.

Harken laughed. "Puttin' yer head in the lion's mouth, eh?"

"There's something he's not telling us," Jack said. "Don't know what, yet, but I gotta see if I can pick it up."

"Okay," Harken said. "I'll talk to the Chief later today."

"Thanks, Cap."

"Don't thank me yet," Harken said, "you go south with Haskell, I'll see ya back here quick enough."

CHAPTER TEN

Jack stood outside of the task force the next day. The Chief had given him the go-ahead. He dragged on his cigarette slowly, packing everything he wasn't supposed to know into the same compartment he had in his mind for his undercover work. Turner Street, the living room, the map, the cards and the old profile.

The place seemed eerily quiet when he walked in. There were only a couple of New Rhodes detectives, two each from the State Police and the Sheriff's Department and, of course, Teague, and Melfly. Jack walked over to them; he was early.

"Hey Jack," Teague said, "can't stay in one place, can ya?"

"As soon as Bowman figures out where he wants to light, I'll stay there."

"Sorry about Walt," Melfly put his beefy hand on Jack's shoulder. "I know you guys were close."

"Yeah, thanks. We all were. You spent your share of nights at Emerald's."

"True. I can't believe I'll never get another beer from him…"

Teague approached Jack. "I have a buddy in the DOD; record-keeping," he said under his breath.

"Haskell was in Nam the same time Bowman was. It's a big file. I'm not looking to stir the nest here, but how about I bring it to the precinct at lunchtime. You just give me the Cliff's Notes, okay?"

"I can do that. Thanks." Jack said. "Can your buddy do the same for Walter's record? It could help a lot."

"Yeah; that should be easy. You want his whole file?"

"If you can, yeah. I'll owe ya big."

He fiddled with the pocket-watch Mary gave him for Christmas, opening and shutting it, staring at their beaming nuptial faces. He shoved it in his pocket to avoid breaking the clasp.

"Gotta go, guys." Jack said. "Gotta go face the music."

Jack knocked on Haskell's door and was invited in by name. The place looked much different than the first time he'd been in. Haskell had his own web; notes, crime-scene pictures, all connected with twine and push-pins. It was messier, but the couch was clear. Jack sat down. There was a mirror behind Haskell's seat.

Nice trick; make the person sitting on the couch face themselves. It worked just as good in the box as the observation room did when it came to confessions. He also noted the business card he gave Haskell on the desk, looked like it had been placed there in an attempt at subtlety.

Haskell looked weary, bags and wrinkles from squinting in the sunlight. His mug of coffee still had steam coming off it.

"Thanks for coming in, Jack," Haskell said.

"I know you don't want me back on the task force," Jack said, skipping the pleasantries, "and you know I want back on. So, how do we get through this?"

Haskell wiped his brow. "So much for the *how are you feeling?*"

"I figured we're both tired," Jack said.

Haskell let out a breath. "Yeah," he said. "Look, down to brass tacks; your continued involvement could be a conflict of interest if, and when, we do catch Bowman."

He paused. "But I suspect Bowman's going to involve you no matter what we do, so I need to know a few things from you, if you want my recommendation."

"Shoot."

"That's funny ... *shoot,*" Haskell said. "Kind of what I need to know. What if you found Bowman? What would you do?"

"Try to make an arrest," Jack said.

"And if you couldn't?"

"Look, if you're asking me if I'd kill him, I'd follow policy."

"That's easy to say..."

"If he pointed a gun at me, I'd shoot. If he had a hostage, and I had a clean shot? I'd shoot. But if I just got to him, I'd call for back-up and go for the arrest."

"He's had a target on your back, Jack. He killed Walter. He probably killed your parents. You wouldn't want to just see him dead?"

"He probably did kill my parents," Jack said, "and he definitely killed Walt. But he killed far more people, and if he's dead, their family members never get closure."

"Do you think he'll reveal his victims' identities if he's on Death Row?"

"Maybe; maybe not," Jack said. "But ... maybe."

Haskell propped his elbows on the desk.

"Have you ever killed anyone, J.R.?" asked Jack.

"No," Haskell said. "I'm a profiler – it doesn't come up much."

"Ever in the military?"

"I served in Nam, but I was in an office in Saigon. I had a master's in psychology back then, working on my doctorate."

"Really? What did you do?"

Haskell scratched his brow. "It wasn't psych-ops or anything; just counseling vets before they came home." He paused. "But back to you," Haskell continued. "Why did you ask if I'd ever killed anyone?"

"Because, if you had, even in the line of duty, you'd know how hard that is to deal with," Jack said. "First, you give IAB your badge and gun, then comes the investigation, then the psych eval ... but then come the dreams."

Jack slumped back in his chair. "I had an armed robbery in progress years ago, before I made detective." He said. "Meth-head; he held up a bodega in lower North Central, river-side. He was tweaked; maybe freakin' for more. He had a snub-nose, and he had the barrel on a twelve-year-old kid.

"I tried to talk him out of it, but he was talking crazy, tightening his grip, and then the kid bit down on his forearm. So he lets the kid go, pulls the gun forward."

Jack paused.

"I put one in his chest; he dropped like a sack. And that's what I saw in the dreams, the guy, dropping like a sack."

"I'm sorry to hear that," Haskell said. "But even more so, I have to know ... if you had to kill Bowman, could you pull the trigger?"

"Yeah, I could if I had to," Jack replied.

Haskell shuffled papers, but Jack knew he was just trying to make Jack nervous.

"Okay, then," Haskell said. "I'll be sure to give my recommendation to the Chief."

"Just like that?"

"Just like that." Haskell replied.

Jack thanked him and made for the door.

"One last thing, Jack..."

"What's that?"

"Do you think Bowman's gonna go gently into that good night?"

Jack shrugged.

"You're the profiler," Jack said, "you tell me."

Jack and Eddie sat at a folding table in the Cold Case room, a library of absent justice in the basement of the New Rhodes Main Station. They used to work down there before all the madness with Bowman. It was quiet, and the cold case squad came down only occasionally for the boxes to take another swing.

Eddie had his laptop plugged in, but it was closed, a stack of sheets draped over it as he tried to read one of the files. Teague had dropped off Haskell's military service record, but the pile was big. He told Jack he'd had it overnighted; otherwise, his buddy would've caught shit for accessing the file without anyone asking for it. Plus, the papers weren't digitized. They were all marked *Sensitive*.

"Some of this I can't make out," Eddie said.

"Yeah, I know. It's old as dirt." Jack held up a yellowed page. "You getting anything?"

"Well," Eddie said, "I think he was telling the truth about what he did in Vietnam. Some of this looks like transcripts from ... therapy sessions, maybe?"

"I'm seeing the word 'kill' a lot," Jack said, "but it was Vietnam, so ..."

Eddie handed Jack one of his sheets. "Look at this one," he said. "This is weird."

Jack looked at the sheet. It was different. It appeared not to be from Saigon, but from Washington, DC.

The text shocked Jack.

> *Haskell: How do you feel being back?*
>
> *JB237: I don't know what to do with myself. I just see everyday life, people happy, smiling, strolling down the street; people in love, people without a care in the world, and I just look at the sewer grates like Charlie's under there, just playing some big fucking joke on me.*
>
> *Haskell: Do you still feel the "itch" you talked about over there?*
>
> *JB237: Oh yeah ... I saw a woman today. She works in the coffee shop near my apartment. She's got a college boy for a boyfriend – I just thought of what it would be like to skin her alive.*
>
> *Haskell: Did you feel remorse for thinking that?*
>
> *JB237: Not really. I just knew I'd get caught.*
>
> *Haskell: Is that the only thing that stopped you?*
>
> *JB237: I don't know ...*
>
> *Haskell: If you knew you could get away with it; if this was Vietnam, would you have done it?*
>
> *JB237: Maybe? I mean, I got the itch ...*

The last line dropped Jack's jaw.

> *Haskell: Tonight, I'll give you free rein to scratch that itch.*

"Eddie, I need you to do something for me."

"As long as it doesn't kill me before dinner," Eddie said.

"No, just ... search Haskell. Anything he ever wrote before he joined the FBI; a dissertation, a school paper, anything. Something's not right here."

Jack flipped through the papers. He'd seen JB237 somewhere. Right up near the top of the pile, he found it.

JB237: Specialized in infiltrating underground fortifications in North Vietnam. Separated from his unit in 1971. Found in 1972 in DMZ. Detained by MPs for desertion. Reinstated; record amended.

"Son of a bitch!" Jack said.

"What?"

"JB237 ..." Jack said. "This is Bowman!"

"No ..."

"Read it! It's gotta be!"

Eddie read the brief description. He rubbed his chin.

"That sounds like Bowman," Eddie said, "but we can't be sure ..."

"But he was detained by the MPs... that could be how he tied into Walt!"

"You said Teague can get us Walt's file too, right?"

"Yeah." Jack said. "But that might take some time. His buddy took a risk getting this one."

"Be worth getting, just to make sure." Eddie said.

He placed the paper back on Jack's side. Jack kept reading the file, mouthing the words of what he was reading, when his brow lifted, his pupils opened up wide.

Haskell: Did you … "scratch the itch?"

JB237: I don't know if I wanna say …

Haskell: I'm your therapist, XXXX; I can't tell anyone.

JB237: Cops can lie.

Haskell: I'm not a cop.

JB237: Okay, so I scratched it.

Haskell: I know you did.

JB237: Then why'd ya ask?

Haskell: I wanted to make sure you were being honest with me.

Haskell: Do you feel remorse for what you've done?

JB237: No.

Haskell: Did you have any regrets?

JB237: I didn't have as much time with her as I wanted.

Haskell: You stabbed her repeatedly in the belly, and you cut her breasts off. Why did you do that?

JB237: I don't know … She reminded me of someone.

Haskell: Who?

JB237: I don't wanna say. Don't push.

Haskell: Very well, then. Her name was Julia; did you know that?

JB237: Yes.

Haskell: She grew up poor, and was the first person in her family to attend college. Did you know that?

JB237: No.

Haskell: She was an only daughter. Her parents loved her very much. Does that make you feel any differently?

JB237: Not really.

Haskell: Have you ever loved someone?

JB237: Love is a sucker's game. Put yer heart out and watch it get stomped by the popular guy from a good family with the car and the looks ... "Love" is a made up thing.

Haskell: Did you ever fall for the "sucker's game"?

JB237: I don't want to talk anymore.

Haskell: We can back off from that topic.

JB237: I'm shutting my mouth now. I'm done.

Haskell: Very well, then. We'll meet in two weeks. Please make an appointment with my receptionist.

"Holy shit!" Jack said. "I think we have something here!"

"What is it?" Eddie asked.

Jack handed him the transcript, pointing to the details of Julia's murder.

"Run that through NCIC," Jack said. "See if they got any hits."

Eddie opened up his laptop and pulled up the NCIC database. He typed in the details they had. He tapped the screen with his middle finger while the database was working. Then he got something.

"Julia Vitrenka," He said. "Found August fourteenth, 1973. Washington, DC. Multiple stab wounds to the stomach, mutilation of the breasts."

"They catch the perp'?"

"Nope," Eddie said. "Cold case. But they still have the murder weapon. We can have it tested for latent prints, assuming it's not too degraded."

"The FBI could," Jack said; "therein lies the rub."

"Fuck." Eddie hung his head in his hands.

"Waitaminit!" Eddie said. "Remember Special Agent Benning from the Lattimer case?"

"Yeah, we tossed him the case, right?"

"We did … and he told us if we ever needed to cash in a favor …"

Jack looked at Eddie. "We're cashing in," he said. "And we're gonna need a rush on that."

Eddie's laptop let out a beep. He swept his hand across the keyboard, deftly typing in whatever search terms he was using to work his magic. This time *his* eyes got wide.

"I think I found our missing link," Eddie said. "Haskell's dissertation, scanned in an archive from Northwestern University, 1975." He spun the laptop around to face Jack. Jack only had to see the title to unlock Haskell's inner world:

"The Reversal of Sociopathy: Can a Sociopath Be Cured?"

Jack took his work home that night. He didn't want to; he'd have much preferred dinner and a horror flick with Mary and Paul. But he didn't know if he'd be back on the task force by the weekend.

He needed to study Haskell, bring something to Harken, Teague and Melfly. But he knew they needed more.

Decker was in charge of the FBI contingent. He was a bit "by-the-book," his suit neatly pressed, shoes shined just so, his thinning hair combed back so that not a single one was out of place.

Jack knew that, ultimately, they would need Decker on their side against Haskell. And Decker wasn't exactly stuck up Haskell's ass. But Jack had to wonder; would Decker cut the dead weight, or circle the wagons?

He sat in the study, surrounded by papers. He'd had Eddie print out Haskell's dissertation and before he left the precinct, and called Benning.

Benning was more than happy to accommodate and told him he could get the results back in three days, a record for the workload at Quantico. Jack asked him to send the file to an email he had set up when he was undercover.

Tony knocked and poked his head in. "Ya want coffee, Jack?"

"Yeah, Tony … Can you grab me a cup?"

Tony came back in with Jack's plastic NRPD mug, light and sweet.

"You're here early," Jack said. "You goin' on at ten?"

"Nah, I'm here all night," Tony said. "They're cutting down the detail on Mary and Paul. I volunteered to do nights."

"Oh, okay…" Jack said. "Would've been nice if they'd told me …"

"Bowman's been quiet since Walt," Tony said.

Jack swirled his coffee with his finger. He stared at the pile of papers, rubbed his brow with the flat of his hand.

"You alright there, Jack?"

"Yeah… just tired of this shit, that's all. Scared, man."

Tony laughed. "You? Scared? Never thought I'd hear that!"

Jack leaned forward in his chair. "A cop without fear has a shelf life. You know that," he said.

"Yeah," Tony said. "Got a point. But what can you do?"

"Aside from catch the fucker?" Jack said. "*Kill* the fucker if I gotta?"

Jack motioned to Tony to come closer.

"I'm thinking of sending Mary and Paul to Hawaii for a little while."

"Paul's in school-"

"I know, I know ..." Jack said, "but Bowman's running out of ways to fuck with me.

So look; this is between us. No Mary, no Paul ... not even Dan. I'm booking the trip tomorrow, having them leave tomorrow night."

"When are you going to tell Mary?"

"In a little while," Jack said. "And I'm not taking 'no' for an answer."

"She's gonna be sore at you for such short notice."

"As long as she's alive and well, she can forgive me," Jack said. "I want you to make the arrangements with Paul's school, Mary's job. Just don't tell 'em where."

Tony sighed. "All right, man ... I'll back you."

As was expected, Mary wasn't keen on being shuffled around, even to Hawaii.

"Jack, you're going too far," she said.

Jack walked through the kitchen after her as she looked for God-knew-what in the cabinets.

"Mary, he's desperate," Jack said. "He killed Walt, and he's already mentioned you ... sort of ... in a letter. It means he recognizes how important you and Paul are to me."

"I got a lead on him now," he continued, "we're gonna tighten the noose, but that will make him *more* desperate. You and Paul are, to him, his last cards. And I don't want you two to be in his hand."

"Jack, I can't just ship out when your job puts me in danger!" Mary said. "Paul has school! I have work! If that bastard comes near me, you won't have to worry about me ... you might have to bail me out, but he'll be on the floor with a bullet in his chest."

"It's Hawaii, Mar', and just for a month."

"A month!?"

Jack nodded. "Or until we end him, one way or another."

"What if he doesn't get caught in a month, Jack?"

"If I have to go in the tunnels with a shotgun and blow away every living thing to find him, I will. In under a month." He paused.

"Mary," he said, "you can divorce me in a month, get full custody of Paul. At least I'd know you were safe. At least you'd be alive to divorce me. But if he grabs you - and he got the jump on Walt, remember - he'll use you against me, and in the end, all three of us might be dead."

Mary was quiet, her chin in her fist, rolling her bottom lip with her index finger. Jack went over to embrace her, but she put a hand to his chest.

"I'll do it," Mary said. "*We'll* do it. But if you don't catch this son-of-a-bitch in a month, then we're *all* moving, and you'll have to be a cop somewhere else."

"Where?"

Mary sighed. "Any city without tunnels," she said.

Jack was getting ready to turn in when his phone went off. He looked at the call ID; didn't recognize the number, but he had to answer it anyway.

"Taggart," he said.

"Hey Jack," said a gruff voice, breath ragged, scarred by what could have been smoking. Jack listened for background noises, but all he heard was the muffled sounds of a TV in the background.

"Bowman ..." Jack said blankly.

"Wondering how I got your number?"

"Not particularly," Jack said, though he was. He didn't know if this call was a one-shot deal or the first of a dialogue.

"Not even a little bit?"

"Well, a little ..." Jack said, "but I'm guessing you called me for other reasons than revealing your tricks."

"Sorry about Walt," Bowman said. "I know he was your friend."

"Couldn't be too sorry," Jack said. "You did kill him, after all."

"I know it looks that way," Bowman said. "I'm sure it'll get pinned on me one way or another, but I didn't actually do that one."

'Now he's just fucking with me', Jack thought.

"Okay, so who did?"

Bowman chuckled. "Now what good would I be if I told you that?"

"So what do you want to talk about, Jeffrey?"

"You, of course," Bowman said. "So how ya holdin' up?"

"You shot me! Why in the fuck do you care!?" *Calm down, Jack ...*

"Because you lived."

Jack shook his head, thumb and forefinger pressed to his temples.

"So if I'd died, you would've just turned yourself in?"

"Hell, no."

Jack could hear the sizzle of a cigarette, the hesitation in Bowman's voice as he exhaled.

"I would've moved on from here, though ..."

"You're a twisted bird, Bowman," Jack said. "You kill my parents, kill God knows how many people down in New York ... then you come up here, just to fuck with me?"

"I'm retired, Jack," Bowman said. "I'm doing what I love."

"I don't get your obsession with me," Jack said, "or my parents. So Mom went out with you once. And she and Dad embarrassed you at the prom. You never asked her to go with you, so whose fault is that?"

"Listen here, you little shit!"

Bowman was pissed; maybe Jack had pushed a little *too* hard. He cleared his throat, and spoke in a hushed voice, his control regained.

"You had it lucky, Jack," Bowman said. "You had two sets of parents, both of whom loved you."

"I only needed one set," Jack said, "but you couldn't let me have that, could you?"

"No," Bowman said. "You think you know me, know what kind of life I had back then, but you're clueless. You want to find out how you became parent-less?"

"Yeah, I do."

Bowman breathed deeply. "Then find out how *I* did." He hung up.

Jack and Eddie had breakfast at Ginny's before going in. They'd each had a long night, both been doing research. Jack told Eddie about the call, but there wasn't much to say about it.

"He said he didn't shoot Walt?" Eddie asked.

"Yeah."

"We found his gun with his prints."

"I think he was just full of shit about that," Jack said.

"He just wants to bait you, Jack," Eddie said. "So what did you find out?"

Jack sipped his coffee. "Haskell's dissertation was filled with all kinds of studies and statistics – and a bit of mumbo-jumbo I couldn't quite catch – but basically he was arguing that sociopaths don't always hurt or kill people, so that means the ones that do can be ...'cured' ... so that they're just regular, everyday sociopaths."

"So, do you think he got Bowman as a 'case-study' in Vietnam and kept track of him here?" asked Eddie.

"It's possible, man," Jack said. "I mean, you saw the file. The sessions started in Saigon, but they ended around the time he got to New Rhodes ... the first time around."

"Why would Haskell start tracking him ... or doing whatever he's been doing ... now, instead of the first time?" Eddie asked.

"And what about Bowman's time in New York?"

"We gotta somehow get Haskell in the box," Jack said. "No way around it."

Eddie popped a mini sausage link in his mouth.

"Oh, while you were looking over those files, I started going through the deep web for all things Bowman. I came up with some interesting leads. Shit I'm surprised we haven't already figured out."

Jack sliced into his pancakes. "Spill."

"Well, first, we missed something in his financials." Eddie paused. "Twenty million dollars-worth of 'missed.' He's fucking loaded."

"How could we have missed *that*!?"

"Clerical error," Eddie said. "Jeffrey Bowman is his adopted name. He was issued a new Social Security ID by mistake; he must have still had his old one."

"He was adopted?"

"Yeah, his parents died in a fire at the family business – Smith & Sons; it was a watch repair business on Second Street."

"Where on Second?"

"Between Independence and Colonial."

Wait; what side?" Jack asked.

"They bulldozed it on the Agora side."

"Shit. That's a piece of the puzzle."

"A corner piece."

"But wait," Jack said. "Smith? Not a relation to Jason Smith, right?"

"Cousin, apparently," Eddie said. "Jason Smith's parents were younger than Bowman's by a few years. They also died in the fire. He went to Mansfield, and Jeffrey … 'Smith' … was adopted by the Bowman family."

"So, wait … what about the twenty million?" Jack asked.

"Jeffrey *Smith*'s mother was from a family in Astoria, Queens. The Fremont family. About twenty years ago, Bowman received an inheritance from his grandmother. By then he had two separate identities. One for Jeffrey Bowman, one for Jeffrey Smith, which was the identity that his grandmother knew him by. So he received the twenty million, but he couldn't spend it without blowing both identities."

"So he's sitting on it?"

"Not quite. And this is where it crosses our path." Eddie leaned forward. "He created shell companies, just certificates on paper… and other shells and subsidiaries, so much so that he's completely insulated from a single company."

"Okay, don't keep me in suspense …"

"Graham Developers," Eddie said. "The new owner of the Agora."

The taste of syrup lingered, mingling with cigarette smoke as Jack stood by the back bench in the precinct pavilion. He and Eddie shared what they knew with Harken, including the phone call; he absorbed it all before telling them they weren't actually on the task force.

"Cap', they might let me back on," Jack said. "But I got a really short list of who I trust with the stuff about Haskell."

"Sounds like the stuff about Bowman alone could break the case," Harken said.

"But with Haskell, who knows if Bowman won't be tipped off?" Jack said. "We have to get Decker to consider Haskell as a person of interest and at least get him off the task force."

"I'll talk to the Chief about it," Harken said. "He's ultimately in charge. But you need to have a trace run on your phone."

"Over there?" Jack asked.

"Nah ..." Harken said. "We'll do it here and send the results. They'll want to question you about it."

Harken called Jack back in. Jack butted the cigarette and walked through the precinct. Despite the overwhelming odor of cigarette smoke hanging around him, his nose picked up the smell of sweat, paper, printing ink and burnt coffee. Harken hung out of his office and waved Jack in.

"I found out who went to talk to Walt," Harken said.

"Who was it?"

"Haskell and Decker."

"I gotta' know what he said to spook Walt."

"I'm assuming you mean Haskell."

Jack nodded.

"Listen, Jack, I talked to the Chief," he said. "I didn't tell him everything you guys told me, but it was enough to get you reassigned to the task force."

"What about Haskell?"

"Your problem, but the Chief is aware of the issue. Haskell can't touch you."

"So when do I report?"

Harken handed him his transfer papers. "As soon as Eddie gets out of the shitter," he said. "You're being assigned as a team."

Jack and Eddie got to the headquarters after lunch. Walking in, Jack realized why there wasn't much objection to him being back.

There were five detectives combined working it, aside from Teague and Melfly. Decker told them that Haskell was on a three-day break, cause unknown.

Jack and Eddie asked Decker about the interview with Walt. Decker said it was a basic interview, that Haskell had requested it. He did admit that he spent most of the time checking the back alley where Bowman had been. He didn't know what Haskell and Walt talked about.

"You can ask him when he gets back." He said.

Decker was the only one from the FBI there. He was briefed by Jack and Eddie about what they had learned. And he wasn't pleased to hear what they had discovered.

"Why didn't you come to me with your concerns about Haskell?"

"Special Agent Decker," Jack said, "I wanted to make sure my gut had some supporting evidence before I brought this to you. For all I knew, you wouldn't have taken a gut hunch from a local LEO seriously. I'm sorry I went behind your back, but I have the files right here." Jack handed him the folders he was holding. He didn't tell Decker he had copied them all.

"I need to review this," Decker said.

"I would expect nothing less," Jack said, "and I can be discreet, but I'd recommend keeping him out of the loop until you can definitively clear him as the leak, or worse, an accessory."

"You know, I could have you two kicked off the task force for investigating him on your own," Decker said. "But ... I am very interested to see what you've found." He leaned forward in his seat. "I have a gut, too, Detective Taggart."

"Can I ask a favor, if I haven't overstretched myself at this point?"

"What's that?"

Jack braced for rejection. "If you ... *when* you question him, can I do it?"

"One thing at a time." Decker said.

"In the meantime, I'll leave this out of the database until I can determine its merit. But you'll be the first to know if I find any merit.

"Because what you're telling me is disgusting, and if he's been doing that as an agent, he'll spend the rest of his life in prison. Hence my hesitancy ... and my discretion."

They finished up the details. As Jack got up to leave, Decker said, "By the way, if the FBI needs anything of you, you answer to me. Not him."

"Got it, Special Agent Decker."

"Just call me Decker," he said. "You know, unofficially. It's close quarters here."

"Okay."

Jack got home around five o'clock, expecting to see the lights on and to walk in on Mary and Paul raising holy hell about the impromptu vacation. But the house was dark and silent. Jack walked in, and it looked like nothing was happening.

Maybe they're shopping for sunblock or something, Jack thought, until he noticed a camcorder in the kitchen. It wasn't theirs. It was a beat-up, cheap piece of shit, with a sticky note attached. Jack picked up the camcorder with a tightening in his stomach.

Play Me! The note read.

Jack flipped out the camcorder screen. He hit the *play* button, and he nearly dropped it when he saw what was on it.

Mary and Paul were in a darkened place, terrified looks in their eyes and he could hear their shouts muffled by rags tied around their mouths.

Their hands were up, bound. Jack couldn't see much except for the dim circle of light and a square edge – like Mary and Paul were *in* something.

Then the camera shifted, and Jack could see Bowman's face. His hair was dirty, in clumps, his beard the same, streaks of white in the grey, down to his tattered shirt-collar. His eyes were wild – giddy, almost – and his smile showed jagged, rotting teeth.

"Welcome back, Jack!" he said. "I figured I'd take the family out to celebrate an important anniversary. I hope you can come down and celebrate it with us. It's gonna be a real BLAST!"

The camera went dead. A panic-fueled rage overtook Jack. A thousand thoughts a minute rolled through his head; most involved killing Bowman, but a few were useful.

They must be in the tunnels, but how? How did he get in here? How did he subdue both Mary and Paul?

Jack moved through the house, gun drawn. He saw a shattered hurricane glass by the basement door. *The basement!* Jack thought, *Fuck!*

He ran down the basement stairs, cursing himself for not finding the hatch in his own dirt-floor basement; he checked everywhere, or so he thought. When he got down there, he saw it; the square patch of disturbed dirt.

Jack got on the phone. He called Harken.

"Ray, It's Jack! Bowman took Mary and Paul! He left a video! He's in the tunnels and I'm going after him."

"Now Jack, hold on a sec-"

click

CHAPTER ELEVEN

Jack trudged through the muck, the darkness barely penetrated by the sweep of his Maglite. He had the presence of mind to change the batteries and grab the map of the tunnels before he dove in, but he didn't have the presence of mind to come up with a plan: what to do if he got lost, what to do if he caught up with Bowman. All he had was the map crumpled in his back pocket, a Glock in his hand and murder turning his vision red.

He didn't even need the map. He had it memorized, like so many set-ups on a chessboard. George had taught him to memorize boards. Jack knew where he was going, though he didn't know why: *The Agora*. All paths led to the Agora.

He'd probably get fired. He didn't care. Right then, he didn't care if he was found with Bowman's skin on as a box-back suit, so long as Mary and Paul were okay. But he was tired. He'd been sloshing through the dregs of the city above for two miles, by his guess. Ahead, he could see the light bounce back from a seal in the tunnel. He picked up his pace until he was right up on it.

He scanned the seal, shining light on its edges. There was a handle, and a chain with a padlock, but it wasn't locked. Bowman must have been acting alone; no one to lock it from the other side.

Jack grabbed the handle, and the whole partition creaked open. Heavy as hell; Bowman was definitely strong. Dim light poured out from the inside; a room of some sort. *Must be the sub-basement of the Agora*, Jack thought.

He walked in and smelled death. Lumps were on the ground; twelve of them, he counted. There wasn't enough light for him to make anything out, so he swept over them with his own light. He saw what he expected to see; bodies. There was a powdery substance on them.

Jack figured it was lye, as the smell wasn't overpowering. He saw one female, in full decomp', but he recognized her by her clothing and accessories.

It was Mallory Lamont, a crack whore who'd act as a CI when she got busted for either of her illicit activities.

Jack realized something: these were Bowman's other victims, the ones he didn't brag about ... the ones that no one would miss. This was his *itch*.

"Like what you see?" from the shadows, a gruff voice burned into Jack's mind. *Bowman*.

Jack swung his light and his gun onto Bowman. Bowman winced at the light; covered his eyes.

"If you wanna see 'em again, I'd say you lower the piece and get that light outta my eyes," he said.

Jack aimed the light off to one side, so that he could still see Bowman's face. He lowered the gun, but kept his grip.

"Where are they?" Jack said.

"They're safe," Bowman said. "For now ... as long as you play by the rules."

"Or I could shoot you now and get a few hundred of my cop buddies to comb through the tunnels ..."

"You're assuming they're still *in* the tunnels, Jack," Bowman said. "A person can last three days without water. Where they are right now, they have no water. You want to take the chance that your 'cop buddies' can search the entire city for them, and find them in three days? C'mon, Jack ... run the numbers ..."

Jack was quiet. He actually found himself running the numbers.

"Okay, fine," he said. He holstered his gun, probably the dumbest thing he could do, but he needed to establish trust.

Jack pointed to the ground. "So what's all this?" he said. "No taking credit?"

"Nah," Bowman said. "Ya gotta practice and all..."

"Ya know, I've been wondering ... what's with the 'Welcome Back, Jack'? I don't get it..."

Bowman chuckled, an awful sound. "Back in Nam," he said, "I was a tunnel rat. But you know that. Anyhoo, the tunnels, ya know ... The VC would build these crazy tunnels, I mean everything from shitty squirrel-holes to underground bunkers, hospitals, command posts, you name it. But, after so long, the tunnels get to have a life of their own ... they beckon you ... in my mind when I went in, it's like I could hear the tunnels saying 'Welcome Back, Jack!' ... Your name's Jack ... it just kind of fit."

"Last night you told me to find out how you lost your parents, and I did," Jack said. "They died in a fire at their watch company. But I don't see how that affects *me*."

"Did you know it was an electrical fire?" Bowman asked.

"No, I didn't get that far."

"That whole block, above us here, was getting squeezed out by a property management company," Bowman said. "They wanted everyone out, but couldn't force us out."

He rubbed his chin. "So they let the properties go to shit. We couldn't afford to pay their rent *and* update our electrical system ... and then the fire happened ..." Bowman was quiet for a while.

"So how is that my parents' fault? Jonathan Myers just designed the Agora. He wasn't the developer or the property manager."

"Did you ever bother to look up who the property manager was, and then the developer?"

"No."

"Then you have a little bit of homework to do before the anniversary."

"Wait! What anniversary?"

Bowman laughed. "I gave you the two clues on the tape. Here's a third clue; look around. Just ... look around."

"And that's it?"

"Yup," Bowman said. "You figure out the clues, you show up on time, and you'll see Mary and Paul again."

"So I just let you go?" Jack said.

"For now," Bowman replied. "You go back the way you came, and you lock that door, and you walk back as far as your legs will carry you. If your buddies find you, you never made it here. If you tell them, and they bust in here, your lovelies are dead."

Harken, Eddie and a small contingent of cops found Jack crumpled against the side of the tunnel, about a half-mile from the entrance in his basement, shaking and sobbing uncontrollably in the flickering glow of his Maglite.

Jack tapped his fingers along the armrest in Teague's office at the task force.

Harken and Teague were there, Harken on a folding chair, Teague at the desk. They were all staring at the video.

"I saw him," Jack said.

Harken straightened up. "Bowman?"

"Yeah ... about a mile past where you found me; I reached the sub-basement of the Agora. He was in there ... with about twelve corpses."

"You didn't arrest him!?" Teague cried.

"Shhh ..." Jack motioned with a finger to his lips. "No, I couldn't. He took ..." Jack felt his gut quiver, "... Mary and Paul hostage, and he's hidden them somewhere in the city."

"We could've broke him, Jack!" Teague said.

"Cut him slack, Willie," Harken said. "We weren't there; we don't know what we would've done."

"You're right, you're right ..." Teague waved his hand up. "So what did he say?"

"He wants me to find out who the property manager of his parents' shop was, and the developer who hired them.

And the anniversary he's talking about ..." Jack waved his arm around. "He did that in the sub-basement. That was my 'third clue,' so he assumed he'd given me the other two in the video."

"He said 'anniversary,'" Harken said.

"... and 'blast,'" Teague added.

"And the Agora," Jack said, "the anniversary has to be connected to the Agora, or to the fire that killed Bowman's parents."

"It has to be something easy to figure out, don't ya think?" Harken asked.

"Whatever it is," Jack replied, "he's gonna blow something up. My money is on the Agora; it's the only thing that makes sense."

"The Agora opened up on the bicentennial, July fourth of seventy-six," Harken said. I remember that."

"Maybe the fire, then," Jack said. "Whenever it is, it's coming soon."

"Not to go off-topic, but we can get a search warrant for the Agora right now," Teague said.

"No!" Jack said. "We do that, and Mary and Paul are dead."

"Jack, what do you want us to do? *Bury this*?"

"No, not … *bury* it …" Jack said, "just give me and Eddie a chance to dig up all we can, based on what Bowman told me. Just a couple of days. If you go in that sub-basement, he'll know … that's his world."

"Jack, we'll give you a little rope on this," Teague said, "but if you can't figure out a game plan soon, we have to do something."

"Jack's our best chance," Harken said to Teague. Then he looked at Jack.

"But you're not doing *anything* alone again. I'll have your badge, got me?"

"Yeah, Captain. I'll stick with Eddie if you let me."

"Not a problem," Harken said.

They heard a rap on the door. Decker popped in.

"Hey, Jack," he said. "How are you holding up?"

"I'm not on the floor," Jack replied, "guess I'm good."

"I was gonna talk to you," Decker said, "but I might as well tell everybody."

Decker leaned up against the wall, his arms folded, a paper, legal-sized, in his hand.

"I read everything you gave me," Decker said. "And I did some digging you couldn't do. I get now why you couldn't come to us ... Haskell is a fucking nightmare, and we would've circled the wagons." He brushed his shoulder. "Probably still will."

"So what are you proposing?" Teague asked.

Decker handed Teague the paper. Teague scanned it.

"FISA Court?"

"It's a secret court, used for foreign intelligence, but it can also be used in a case where you need to search a location or wiretap someone without their knowledge. That warrant is for everything, including wiretap. Jack," Decker continued, "Teague, Harken ..." He paused, "I'm handing this off to you guys. I'll support, but I'm not calling in the Bureau until I'm sure we've gotten everything we can from him."

"I have the knife Bowman, maybe, used to kill a woman in DC at the crime lab at Quantico ... cashed in an old favor, sorry ... but it could corroborate JB237's confession in those files."

"I'll keep a check on it. It's in NCIC, right?"

"Yup."

"Haskell's staying at a house in New Rhodes we're renting for him," Decker said. "The address is on the warrant."

"I'll need a wire if he's there," Jack said, "I can always say I'm there to talk. Hell, maybe even confront him and see if he slips."

"Just be careful, Jack," Harken said. "Don't tip your hand."

"I gotta meet up with Eddie this afternoon," Jack said. "If that 'anniversary' is tomorrow, then I need a plan. I can search his house tomorrow on that warrant, right?"

Decker nodded. "Seventy-two hours, and it was just granted."

"Ya know, we might not want to do anything to Haskell."

"What do you mean, Jack?" Harken asked.

"What if Bowman's blackmailing him?" Jack asked. "What if Bowman's expecting him to play his sick game? If Haskell gets pulled, maybe we'll tighten the noose around Bowman, but Mary and Paul's necks are in that same noose right now."

"He's gotta pay for what he's been doing," Decker said.

"Yeah, I'm not saying he gets a pass, but it's weird; when I had to get a psych eval before joining the group, he wasn't asking me if I could *keep* from shooting Bowman, which I'd expect," Jack said. "He kept asking me if I *could* shoot him if I needed to."

"So what's his game, ya think?" Harken asked.

"Maybe he realizes he failed," Jack said. "Maybe he's finally got it, grown a conscience, but Bowman's got him trapped. Maybe, in some way, he *needs* me to kill him."

"Maybe *I* should ask you if you can capture Bowman *without* killing him, assuming you had the chance?" Harken asked.

"I just want Mary and Paul back, Bowman locked up … killed if need be, but as long as he can't hurt anybody I'll be happy. If I wanted him killed, I'd have done it last night."

Decker's ears pricked up.

"Last night?"

"I think I found the anniversary Bowman was talking about," Eddie said, looking up from his laptop.

"Give."

"The fire at Smith & Sons," Eddie said. "January twenty-ninth, nineteen sixty-two."

"The twenty-ninth…that's Saturday," Jack said.

"Three days from now." Eddie flipped the laptop closed. "And I looked up the stuff Bowman told you to find out… You're not gonna like it."

"Tell me anyway."

"The property owner, and developer for the whole block was Myers Realty Group."

Jack wasn't even shocked.

"Figures."

"Your grandfather owned it."

"Fat lot of good it did him." Jack said. "When I got the inheritance, it was at the end of a noose. He killed himself two years after my parents were killed."

"Yeah, it said it closed down in eighty-three."

"Jonathan was their only kid." Jack said. "I met my grandmother when I was sixteen, but she was a hermit. She died before I graduated high school."

"Sorry, man." Eddie said.

Jack swiped his arm. "It's history." He said. "I didn't know them."

They shared a moment of silence.

"Jack, if he blows the Agora, it's gonna go all over the place. A lot of people are gonna get hurt, or killed. We gotta evacuate, section off the block that day."

"If he knows there are cops, he'll kill Mary and Paul!"

Eddie rubbed his eyes.

"You're my partner. I trust you with my life, but you have to trust me. If you can't stop him from killing Mary and Paul outright, he'll kill them anyway.

"But going it alone … even if you're over a barrel like this … fuck; even listening to him and doing what he says, he'll kill a lot more folks, including you."

"I know," Jack replied. "I have to see Mary and Paul as civilian hostages, but that's not so easy …"

"Jack, how far would you go to save the life of a mother and her son, if they were hostages?"

"I'd do everything possible."

"But you wouldn't let the kidnapper tell you what to do, would you?"

"No …"

"You gotta remember … you're a cop. *A detective.* You worked undercover in narcotics; use those skills to beat him at his own game. And I'm here right along with you. If he's got eyes in there, any part of there, I'll hack into them. His eyes will be *our* eyes."

"Thanks, Eddie," Jack said.

"Have you talked to Tony yet?"

"Nah, I gotta go home and do that. Tony was there last night; he went in the tunnel to find me, but I was a mess. I imagine he'll be there today; he has a key." Jack had a knot in his stomach. "Dan too, I'll bet."

"Jack, you know this wasn't your fault."

Jack looked out the window, a thousand yard stare at a crumbling brick wall. "I could've stayed home. I should've, just helped them pack, drove them to the airport … Why didn't I?"

"Who knew?" Eddie said. "Me? Tony? Hell; you didn't even tell Dan!"

"Maybe he has a tap on my phone," Jack said, "or he hacked into my computer. Wouldn't put it past him."

"He didn't hack your computer," Eddie said. "I designed your security software, remember?"

"Okay, so, phone …?"

"Look, we'll check, but Jack, it could have been just chance. It could've been a crime of opportunity – a random chance kidnapping by a desperate man. How many cases tie up nice in a bow?"

"I don't follow …"

"Remember the Forner case?"

"Yeah," Jack said. "Guy got a Bunsen burner shoved in his chest."

"You know how we tried to figure out how it fit, what it meant?"

"It didn't mean anything," Jack said. "Just an object in the room."

"Right," Eddie said. "And there were scalpels and glass beakers, and we wondered why he'd used the Bunsen burner. When we caught him, it turned out it was just closest to him."

"So Mary and Paul were what … a flip of Bowman's coin?"

"No, I'm just saying that maybe he didn't do it to keep them from evacuating; maybe he didn't even know about that."

"I think you're giving him too little credit," Jack said.

"And maybe you're giving him too much," Eddie replied. "When he had the Smiths and Mansfield to help him, he looked unstoppable, but now they're dead. He guns down Walter, and what's he been doing? You said he had twelve corpses, one was a crack whore, right?"

"Yeah."

"He's basically been reduced to shooting people and picking working girls off the street," Eddie said. "He's dangerous, not omnipotent."

"I just can't believe I didn't check my basement," Jack said. "They'd be safe if I'd just checked it and poured a few feet of concrete over it."

"Stop blaming yourself, Jack. This is exactly what he wants you to do; be guilty, unsure of yourself, make stupid moves … If you wanna catch this fuck, you gotta be better than that. You gotta be the best you can be right now, and be better than *that*, even."

"I don't know how I do that."

"You're the chess-master," Eddie said. "Put the pieces on the board and play."

Jack did just that. He and Eddie found out that there was indeed, a set of security cameras in the Agora, and Eddie was able to hack into them.

They found out that the feeds went to a security station in the basement. The cameras were high quality, but none were present in the sub-basement. Of course, Bowman wouldn't have wanted that.

"I'll see what I can do with the cameras," Eddie said. "Maybe I can make a loop … but it only works if he's watching the screens. It's dicey, but we'll keep it as an option."

"Nothing for the sub-basement then?"

"Well, not cameras. I can also patch into the building's electrical system and play with the lights, HVAC, stuff like that."

"I thought it just had emergency lights?"

Eddie tapped on the keyboard. "The Agora has full lights, even in the sub-basement. High wattage too, from the look … they're all rated at a thousand watts, except the sub-basement, which is still four hundred watts. That's street-light bright."

"But Bowman had just a couple of dim lights," Jack said.

"According to this, they are connected to a master dimmer in the sub-basement," Eddie said. "They're set at five."

"Out of …?"

"A hundred."

"Can you change that?"

Eddie looked at the screen. "Yeah, but these are old bulbs. Some of them might pop."

Jack leaned forward in his seat. "But how bright would it be?"

"It would look like heaven …" Eddie said, "ya know, apart from the corpses. But that would be cranked at a hundred, so it might only last for a couple of seconds."

"Would it hurt my eyes?"

"Yeah, but it wouldn't blind you. You'd have to be light-sensitive for that to happen."

Jack and Eddie looked at each other.

"Hold on to that," Jack said. He rubbed his eyes. "Thanks, Eddie. Really, for everything. It's just been rough …"

"On me, too, Jack. You guys are like family to us. Mary helped Sarah out a lot with the pregnancy, and even after that. We'll get this scumbag, and we'll bring them home."

The ride home was greyscale, people moving about in a mindless shuffle, blurs swept across Jack's windshield as the wipers cut through the rain.

He wasn't going *home*. Granted, he was going to the house, but it may well have had a gaping hole in the center going all the way down to the tunnel beneath.

As he turned down the drive, he saw Tony's squad car parked outside. Dan's SUV was parked next to it. The lights were dim, but the TV was on. As he walked to the door, he didn't hear any sound coming from the TV. He fumbled for the key, but the door swung open.

Tony looked like hell. Jack was sure he looked like hell himself. They exchanged nods.

"How's Dan?" Jack asked.

"I don't know, man …" Tony said. "Not good. I've been keeping an eye on him."

"I'll take over, Tony, you should get some rest."

"Not till this fucker's dead," Tony said. His eyes were hollow.

"Seriously," Jack said. "Get rest. Be sharp. I'm gonna need you for the next three days. I'll ask Teague for the transfer to the task force."

Tony just stood there. He was barely on his feet.

"Look," Jack said, "just grab the couch. You and Dan can stay here with me."

"Alright." Tony walked over to the couch and slumped over onto it.

Jack went into the basement. He'd already looked everywhere else. As he got down there he saw Dan sitting by the entrance to the tunnel, a half-kicked bottle of bourbon next to him.

"Dan," Jack said. Dan looked up, and got up, staggering. He stretched out his arms, and Jack spread out his.

He wasn't expecting Dan to punch him in the face. Jack saw white as the blow landed, glancing as it was.

Jack braced for another punch, but he just felt Dan's hands gripping his lapel, dragging him closer, his weight dragging him and Jack both to the floor. He had tears in his eyes, a choke in his voice. Jack hugged him tighter than he'd ever hugged a man.

"My baby, Jack … He took *my baby!*"

"We'll get her back, Dan," Jack said. "*All of us* will."

"I coulda' had him… all those years ago. With your parents, Jack… I fucked up and now he's got my babies!"

"Don't think like that," Jack said. "It's here and now, and we have to get them back. I need you to be strong, 'cause we're gonna get 'em." Jack felt tears well up in his own eyes.

They just sat there, Dan lamenting, Jack trying his hardest not to lament, reassuring Dan that it wasn't his fault, that they would find Mary and Paul.

After a while, Dan settled down and they talked.

"I'm sorry I slugged ya, Jack," he said. "Don't even know why I did it."

"No worries," Jack replied.

"When Mary was a little girl, I tried to teach her everything," Dan said. "I knew the job; the dangers, what could happen. Did you know Mary was a yellow-belt in Karate?"

Jack laughed weakly. "She never mentioned it."

"I taught her Morse code, how to get out of handcuffs, took her to the firing range every Saturday, for as long as I could re-member; as soon as she was old enough. She won sharp-shooter competitions," he added.

"Wow," Jack said. "I'm surprised she never told me any of this. We've been married for fifteen years and I'm just finding out she can out-shoot *me*."

"She probably didn't want you to feel bad," Dan said.

Dan grabbed the bottle with both hands, spun it between his fingers.

They spent most of the night reminiscing, each with his own cherished memories, each holding back the feeling that they were eulogizing. They were alive; Jack knew it.

Bowman wanted a grand finale; he wanted Jack to suffer, and he could only make Jack suffer more by killing Mary and Paul in front of him. Not that Jack was going to let that happen.

He'd search Haskell's place tomorrow, and later he and Eddie were set to meet to run plans. Maybe Jack would have him come over to the house. Eddie had a bug sweeper, and he wanted to make sure Bowman couldn't listen in.

Jack fell asleep in the study, thinking about the chess game he'd thrown.

Jack, Eddie and Tony arrived at Haskell's temporary residence at 79 West Street at eight the next morning. His car was in the driveway, and Jack prepped himself to be calm if they had to interview him. He wanted to choke Haskell, but if he did, he wouldn't get any answers.

"You got the warrant, Jack?"

Jack pulled it out of his coat pocket and waved it. They got up to the door and knocked. Jack didn't want to just knock; he favored the ram-rod. They waited; no answer.

Jack motioned to Tony.

"Police!" Tony said as he pounded on the door. "Search warrant!"

Jack drew his gun, Tony and Eddie followed suit, and Jack kicked the door in. He almost fell, as he realized the doorframe was already cracked. They rushed in.

After clearing the rest of the rooms, they found Haskell in the kitchen. In pieces.

His left hand was holding a pot of coffee, arm attached, but nothing else. His other limbs were arranged around the kitchen, his bloody mess of a torso they found stuffed in the oven. His head was suspended from the ceiling fan, held by a piece of thick twine around his disembodied neck.

They all walked out of the kitchen, some of them dry heaving. Jack called it in, and they secured the house and waited for the evidence techs.

"Well, if he was in it, he ain't now," Eddie said.

"Yeah," Jack replied, "but everything we could've got out of him died with him."

"I'm sure he kept notes somewhere," Eddie said.

Jack scratched his head. "We got what, two days left?"

"If we got the right anniversary," Eddie said.

"I'm sure Bowman will wait till the last minute to call, so we'll have no lead time."

Eddie patted him on the back. "We'll find what we can here today, and play war games tonight. It's not like we've never had to go into something blind."

"Wish I could get you in a sniper's nest somewhere and just pick him off."

"I don't think he'll make it that easy for us," Eddie said.

The evidence techs allowed Jack and Eddie in to search the place early. Freddie was there, oddly, and Jack let him in on the time crunch.

"Just wear these," Freddie said as he fished out two pairs of gloves.

They first searched his office, but all the reports were procedural, nothing about Bowman they didn't already know. They avoided the kitchen, and quickly searched the rest of the rooms before hitting the bedroom.

"That dresser has a false bottom in the top drawer, a 'safe-keeping' compartment," Jack said.

"How do you know that!?" Eddie looked at him.

"He has the same exact one at the house," Tony said, looking on. Eddie started rifling through the top drawer.

"Don't get your hopes up," Jack said, "Haskell probably doesn't know about it. Mary and I found out by acc-"

"Pay dirt!" Eddie said. He pulled out a manila envelope. It looked like it had a few pages in it.

"It's addressed to you, Jack," Eddie said. "Just your name; no address …"

Jack walked over to look at it. It was Haskell's handwriting; he'd seen it often enough to know.

Eddie handed it to him. "Open it."

It was unsealed, just folded in. Jack opened it, and there were five pages, handwriting filling every page. He got to the first page and started to read aloud.

"Dear Jack," he said, "if you're reading this, Jeff Bowman has either killed me, or I've gone so far over the edge that I'm never coming back.

"I've spent my life's work on sociopaths. Some go about their normal business every day and harm no one; some become … Bowman. I met Bowman in Vietnam. Walter, your Walter, caught him returning to his unit adorned with human body parts.

The Army asked me, with my specialty, to see if he could readjust to civilian life. And, misguided as I was, he became my case study, a relationship that has lasted until now.

I thought I could cure him if I tried the right techniques, or if new drugs came out, but I now realize that Bowman has been playing me for a fool, for an enabler, which I have most certainly been.

"After Jason Smith nearly revealed me, I tried to cut ties with Bowman … but he drew me back in under threat of blackmail.

"I know what he has planned; what he will do and when he will do it. Jack, I never meant for your family to get dragged into it. But they will. And if I tell you right now, he'll only do it sooner."

"I don't find him anymore; he finds me. But what I know of him; his defects, his flaws, errors – most importantly, his *plans* …

"I will not let that information go to my grave with me. This is my confession … and my *true* profile of Jeffrey Bowman."

Jack scanned the remaining pages. "Eddie," he said. "This is *everything*."

"Can we use it?"

"... *he's totally deaf in his left ear* ..." Jack said. "It's all stuff like that... stuff we can use!"

Jack's eyes got wide as he read the last page of Haskell's profile.

"What is it?" Eddie asked as he looked over Jack's shoulder.

"He has a weakness," Jack said, "And not a bum ear..."

Jack pointed to a set of lines. A name and an address.

"Who's that?" Eddie asked.

"Bowman's illegitimate daughter." Jack said. "Diane Severino. She lives in New Rhodes. Works in the county dispatch. He's been following her around... and she doesn't know about him."

Eddie said what Jack was thinking.

"Holy shit!" He said. "The 9-1-1 calls!"

"He must've been stalking her at work," Jack said.

Jack, Eddie awwnight.

They talked about possible strategies, tactics, and eventually the part where Bowman was set to blow up the Agora.

"Jack, there's a lot of people we need to evacuate!" Eddie said.

"I know," Jack said, "but Bowman can't know we're doing it, or that could be it for Mary and Paul."

"Look," Tony said, "she's my sister and he's my nephew. We're family, you and me, and we both care about them as much as anyone can. But at what point do we need to bring the task force in on this? Haskell's dead; there's no leak anymore."

"You're right. We need to bring them in, but not until we have our plans set, 'cause this can go sideways a million times over if the 'fog of war' sets in."

They sat at the table with the plans of the Agora, blueprints old and new, and ran scenarios; Bowman with Mary and Paul, combinations of where they might be, where Bowman would place the explosives, blast radii, etc.

"Okay, guys," Jack said, "if he keeps us in the sub-basement, we got our plan for that. And if he brings us into the Agora," he looked at Eddie, "we got a plan for that too. If he does anything else, we're scrambling …"

Jack stared at the sheet they had laid out on the table, their plans of attack labeled with sticky notes and pushpins, notes and lines in black marker.

"I'm okay to bring in the task force," he said, "but they *have* to play by the rules. If Bowman still has eyes, he'll be watching."

"I just got one visit to make first," Jack said.

Jack stared at his parents' graves in the utter silence of four-thirty a.m. He wasn't contemplating life, or his moves … he was making one.

It was a gamble, and no one knew anything about it, but he knew Bowman liked playing with his meat. Jack set himself up as bait … but after reading Bowman's profile, he had his own hook.

"Thinking about joining them soon?" Bowman's voice came from his right, back about five yards.

Jack spun around to see Bowman in a ratty tan overcoat. He hadn't washed from the time Jack last saw him; Jack wondered if he bathed, period. He didn't have a gun in his hand. Jack's was free of the holster guard, ready to be drawn.

"Are you?" Jack asked.

"Have you figured out the clues?"

"Yeah," Jack said. "Where and what time?"

"We'll get to that," Bowman said. He tossed a piece of paper on the ground.

"Go ahead," he said. "Pick it up. It's *proof of life.*"

Jack walked over and picked up the paper. It was a picture of Mary and Paul, alive, but beaten up, holding a copy of the day's paper.

"I see that," Jack said. He fished in his pocket for a printout of a photo he'd snapped just hours earlier with his telephoto lens. He tossed it to the ground.

"What's that?" Bowman asked.

"*Proof of life,*" Jack said. "It's time-stamped. Diane hasn't been touched ... yet."

"Diane?!"

"Were you *ever* going to tell her that you're her father?" Jack said. "I mean, from D.C. to New Rhodes to New York, back to New Rhodes ... You've been watching over her your whole life and she doesn't even know ... that's crazy, Jeff."

"If you touch her ..." Bowman growled.

"What? You'll kill Mary and Paul? Judging by that photo, the way you beat 'em up, you may already *have* killed them. I'll just keep my informants; you know, those junkies, drug dealers and pimps I picked up along the way when I was undercover ... and we'll just, ya know ... *keep watch on her.*"

"You're a good cop!" Bowman had panic in his voice. "You c-can't do that!"

"What I am is a desperate man who had his wife and son kidnapped, probably killed, one of my best friends killed, my parents *killed* by the guy standing right in front of me. You know what I am, Jeff!? What you've turned me into!?"

Bowman shook his head, puzzled.

"You," Jack said. "I'm you now, Jeff … with a badge and a gun."

Bowman turned about in place and started pacing in a tight circle, scratching his head and mumbling.

"What do you want?" He said, finally.

"My wife and son come home today, in one piece, and I pull my meth-dealing informant off of watching Diane's morning shower."

Bowman looked like a dog trapped in the center divider of a busy street.

"I'm going to kill you," Bowman said, "you and this whole fucking town!" He turned around and rushed off. Jack wanted to chase him, but Jack was in awe over what had just happened. Jack could've just killed Mary and Paul …

… or saved them.

CHAPTER TWELVE

Jack was a wreck as he stood in the bathroom, shaving. He had a bottomless pit in his stomach that was feeding on the guilt he felt over what he'd done just hours ago. Dan was staying at the house. He said he could leave, but Jack wouldn't have it. If Bowman did kill Mary and Paul, they'd have to lean on each other. Dan hung by the door.

"So Haskell was telling the truth about Bowman's daughter?"

"I'd say so," Jack said. "He freaked out when I said I had Diane in my sights. I just hope it was wise."

"Ya had to do something, Jack," Dan said. "How'd he take it?"

"He was stunned that I had a meth-head snitch watching over her, or that I'd *do anything* to her because I was a *desperate man* now."

"Are you really using a meth-head?"

"No, of course not," Jack said, "I cashed in a favor with Rimona. You remember Rimona? He was at the picnic last year, ya know, the Yankees fan you spent all day talking to."

"From narcotics?" Dan asked. Jack nodded. "Yeah, he was a nice guy. He has a few kids, right?"

Jack laughed. "Five kids," he said.

"Wow," Dan said. He sipped his coffee. "She doesn't know anything, right?"

"Clueless," Jack said. "She never knew her father. Haskell wrote that he thought Bowman raped her mom and she kept Diane…"

"What if it doesn't work?" Dan said. "Hell, what if it *does* work?"

"It was a Hail Mary," Jack said, "no pun intended. But if something happens to Mary and Paul, I'll make sure he never sees his daughter again."

"Oh, Jack … You're not saying …"

"No," Jack replied. "But I will tell her who he is, scare the shit out of her, and do everything I can to get her into witness protection. I'll pay for it myself if I have to."

When they were eating breakfast, Jack told Dan all about the morning's events.

"It was weird," Jack said. "I felt like control had passed. He wasn't calling all the shots, holding the cards … It was like he was looking at a mirror image of himself, and it jarred him.

It took everything to play like I assumed Mary and Paul were dead, but I figured my hope would've fueled him. Now he thinks I have nothing to lose, and I'm thinking less like a cop and more like a man who's snapped, staring at the source of his rage … I don't think he's ever been in that place."

"Just remember who you *really* are, Jack."

"Of course … but in his proof of life picture, they were bruised up. I did feel that rage."

"Do you still have it?"

"It's on my dresser," Jack said, "but Dan, they look like shit; fair warning."

Jack's phone rang. It was Harken's ringtone. He wasn't due in for an hour. His heart leapt in his throat and his skin got clammy.

"Taggart," he said when he answered.

"Jack, it's Ray. I got some news. It's about Mary and Paul."

Jack's breath stopped.

"Oh Jesus ..."

"They're here, Jack. At the task force. They're beat up some, but they're alright."

"Meet me at Saint Joseph's; we're taking them there to check 'em out." Jack was in tears.

"Yes, Captain," he said, "right away."

"And Jack," Harken said, "he told them something."

"What did he say?"

Harken sighed.

"He said you've forced him to pick a new target."

Jack and Dan rushed to room 307 at St. Joseph's hospital. Dan was barely dressed, his hair uncombed, a thirty-six hour shadow on his face. Jack left his gun at home, just grabbed his coat as they ran out the door. As they passed the corner of the nurses' station, he saw Teague and Decker in front of the door. They were a pair: Teague, big, black and tall with a State Police uniform on, versus Decker's slight build and meticulous suit.

"Are they in there?" Jack asked. "This is Dan. He's a retired cop, and my father-in-law."

"Yeah, go on in, guys," Teague said, stepping aside to let Jack and Dan pass.

Mary had bruises all over her face, Paul too, and judging by the hospital gowns, the bruises weren't just centered on their faces.

"Mary! Paul!" Jack went to hug Mary, but she pushed him back.

"No hugs, Jack," Mary said. "How about a kiss instead?"

Jack and Mary kissed like they were at the hotel after the prom in high school. Dan had to clear his throat.

"Sorry," Jack said. He walked over to Paul as Dan gave Mary a peck on the forehead.

Harken was sitting in the chair, reading the paper.

"Hey, Captain," Jack said, "can you take Paul down to the cafeteria to get a soda?"

"Sure thing." Harken turned to Paul. "C'mon, kiddo," he said, and they walked out.

"Mary, what do you remember?" Jack said. "How did he get you guys?"

"Wait, Jack, let me ask *you* something," Mary said. "What did you *do*?"

"What do you mean?"

Mary sat up on her pillow, winced. "The past two days, he was beating the crap out of us ... and this morning, he was just ... *different*. He looked scared, even, but he was rambling on about you being just like him."

"I, uh, kinda' told him that I had a meth-dealer informant watching his daughter's house."

"He has a daughter?" Mary asked.

"Yeah, just found out yesterday," Jack said. "I led him to think that I assumed you and Paul were dead already, so I had nothing to lose."

"He could've killed us, Jack!"

"Mary, for all we knew, he could have killed you yesterday. I had to take the gamble."

Mary shrugged. "Thank you, Jack," she said. "You probably did save us, but if you hadn't ... I would've haunted the fuck out of you."

Jack laughed. "At least I'd still see ya," he said.

"Did he ..." Jack started, "... do anything ... to you, you know ..."

"He didn't rape me, Jack, if that's what you're getting at," Mary said.

"Thank God," Jack said.

They talked for a while, undisturbed. "Harken must've bought Paul a breakfast down there," Jack said.

"He had a message for you, Jack," Mary said, "but I don't know if I want to tell you."

"Mary, I need to know. I might be the only one he fears – the only one that can stop him. You know how dangerous he is now."

"That's what scares me." She took a deep breath, then continued. "He said he's going to blow up six *high-value targets*, his words, unless you meet him in the Agora, alone, tonight at eight o'clock, not a second earlier. He said if he sees a cop, he'll 'ring the bombs' right away."

"Ring the bombs?"

"His words," Mary said, "and he said he would be picking up another hostage. One *you* created."

Jack let Dan talk to his daughter as he walked out of the room. He rubbed his face, turned to face Teague and Decker.

"She tell you guys what she just told me?" he asked in a hushed tone.

"Yeah, probably," Teague said. "Jack, I gotta talk to you about something ..."

"I'm listening."

"You've made more progress on your own against Bowman than the whole task force," He said. "And at every turn, you've been ... marginalized at the headquarters. You're a victim, or a liability, but truth be told ... you're the one getting things done."

"So what do you mean?" Jack said. "Am I off the task force again?"

"No," Teague said, "the opposite. We took a vote this morning, and we decided to transfer leadership to you. It's your task force; you have the keys."

Jack sent Dan home with Mary and Paul, telling him the combination to his gun safe with the instructions to "shoot on sight". He met Eddie outside of the headquarters to find a sea of cars; government, marked, and unmarked vehicles from the sheriff's department and the State Police. They watched as an ATF van pulled in and stopped, its back doors opening to let out twelve agents in full gear.

"The cavalry's arrived," Eddie said. "You up to this?"

"I'll know when we get in there," Jack said. "We got our original plan; we'll just have to modify it. Hopefully the kids in there can play nice together."

The main room of the headquarters was packed. As Jack expected, everyone was segregating themselves by affiliation. He saw Teague and Melfly near the whiteboard, waving him over.

"Everybody, listen up!" Teague boomed. "This is Detective Jack Taggart, New Rhodes PD. As long as we've had this task force, Jack has made the most progress. Now some of you are new; some of you have been here before. But Jack's got the lead now." He looked over at Jack. "You ready?"

"Yeah, Willie," Jack said. All eyes were on him. He grabbed a picture of Bowman, blown up big and tacked to the whiteboard.

"This is Jeffrey Bowman," Jack said. He passed it to one of the FBI agents. "I want that passed around to everybody."

"Jeffrey Bowman has decided to pick six high value targets and blow them up, and we believe he's got enough RDX to pull it off. This will happen sometime after eight p.m. tonight. He also plans on blowing up the Agora, a vacant mall in downtown New Rhodes. He will seek collateral damage.

"He has taken a hostage," Jack continued, "and he wants me to meet him in the Agora at eight p.m. exactly." Jack paused.

"I will be doing this. If we fail to find the bombs, it will be on me and my team to stop him from setting them off. That said, nobody touches the Agora.

"I know we come from different jurisdictions and we may not trust each other fully, but let me assure you that Bowman will light this city up tonight if we can't stop him.

"I want collaboration, so I know we have the FBI, ATF, State Police, the Sheriff's Department, and the New Rhodes Police here.

"We're going to compose teams, one member from each. Captain Harken."

"Yeah, Jack?"

"I want you to run point. If anybody finds anything, learns anything, any evidence or intel, it comes into here, and you will make sure it goes to all teams on an encrypted channel. Can you do that?"

"Sure can," Harken said.

"Eddie," he said, "I need you, Agent Decker, Commander Teague, Sheriff Melfly, and … the agent in charge from the ATF, who are you?"

"Special Agent Morrison," a voice came from the crowd, "I'm the agent in charge."

"Special Agent Morrison, welcome, and … I need the city emergency manager … I thought I saw him in here. Are you in here, Mark?"

"Yeah I am, Jack."

"Good, I need you, too. Everybody I just mentioned, follow me. Captain, we're gonna call out teams we need. Can you help put them together?"

"I can."

Jack led everyone into Haskell's old office. It was cramped, but Haskell had a big desk. With a swipe of his arm, Jack knocked the contents to the floor.

He spread out a map of the city, and a map of the tunnels on a large sheet of tracing paper. The tunnels were marked where they had found access points. Jack's house was marked.

"He's picking six high value targets," Jack said. "There are twenty-two miles of tunnels in total.

"But, subtracting tunnels that have nothing significant over them, we're looking at ten miles in the city proper." Jack drew a line from his house to the Agora. "This is how I'm getting to the Agora, so I'll be able to check this line out myself. This covers two-and-a-half miles, including side-tunnels. That leaves seven-and-a-half miles.

"Special agent Morrison," Jack said. "How many men do you have?"

"I have twelve."

"Trained in Explosive Ordnance Disposal?"

"Yeah."

"Now, Bowman said he's gonna 'ring the bombs;' I'm thinking cell phone. I know there's no reception in the tunnels, but I want to cover bases. How many teams would you assign the tunnels, given that we have twelve hours to find anything and we can only put one of your men on each team?"

Morrison scratched his head. "If he's setting them off with a cell phone, I'd concentrate more on the targets themselves. He won't get a signal in the tunnels. To be safe, there's four access points, is that what these are?"

"Yeah," Jack said.

"So four teams, but save our people. We can assign two to travel if a search team finds bombs in the actual tunnels. This would give us an extra four agents top-side.

"The tunnels; they all terminate here," he pointed to the Agora. "That's the Agora?"

"It is," Jack said, "and we know that's wired. So, just to there and back.

"Eddie, can you call out four teams to Harken, tell him where they're going?"

"Sure, Jack." Eddie hopped out of the room.

"Now for the targets," Jack said. "He's gonna set them off at night and he's looking for high casualties. Mark, where would you put them if you were him?"

Mark took a breath.

"St. Joseph's and New Rhodes General, to start," he said. "They're twenty-four hour, and hitting the hospitals would be a force multiplier. As for the offices, there won't be many casualties at night, but housing complexes, like Fitzgerald Tower and the Armas Senior Center … those are tall buildings that will have vulnerable populations. Plus all of the bars on lower Canal."

"We'll never be able to cover the bars, but we can make calls asking them to keep their eyes open. So that leaves the hospitals and senior apartments." Jack said. "We'll need the ten remaining ATF agents on those; they're big."

"Some of our guys have explosives experience," Teague said.

"Good," Jack said, "Because we're going to have more teams than ATF agents. Also, we have a signal jammer. Can anyone get us a better one, preferably more than one?"

"I can," Decker said. "I can run to the Homeland Security Office and get you four, high quality."

"Okay, do that," Jack said, "'cause if we can't find these, maybe we can make detonating them a moot point."

They spent the rest of the day strategizing. Jack and Eddie shared their plans for eight o'clock. They talked about evacuating the buildings, and how it might be done quietly.

They talked about many things, but ultimately, Jack had a date with a madman at eight o'clock. He left at five; if he could've left earlier he would've. But he had to head across the river before he jumped back down into that tunnel.

Though he knew he wouldn't want to do it, he had to say goodbye.

His Maglite was giving out. He only had a little way to go, and his phone said *7:45*. He thought about seeing Mary and Paul earlier.

Their bruised and battered faces strengthened his resolve, making turning back impossible. But Mary had begged him to.

"Please, Jack," she'd said, "let the team do this; you don't have to!"

Mary had tears in her eyes, puffing them out. It only added to her beat-up look.

WELCOME BACK, JACK **287**

"He'll just keep ruling our lives," Jack said, "and he has another hostage. This time it *is* my fault. I'm not going to be stupid about this, Mary. I have back-up."

"I think you've done enough ..." Mary said.

"He doesn't think so," Jack said. "Tonight, it will be over."

"Yeah, one way or the other."

Jack rubbed his forehead.

"I have to do this, Mary," Jack said. "No one else can."

Mary paused. "I know you do. I don't want it, but I know you have to."

"I'll come back, Mary."

"Will you kill him?"

Jack was taken aback. "If he doesn't come quietly, I'll have to."

"I want you to kill him anyway," she said.

"Mary, I'm a cop. You know-"

"I know he won't come quietly," she said. "I just want to know you won't hesitate."

"I won't, Mary. I've got no love for that animal. But if he gives up, I can't just blow him away."

"No one will blame you if you do. You won't even lose your job."

Jack laughed at that.

"Mary, I love you."

"I love you too, Jack." She hugged him and they kissed like they were never going to see each other again ... which might have been true.

"I know you have to go. Paul's resting; go give him a hug and a kiss too, okay?"

Jack walked into Paul's room. He was playing a first-person shooter.

"Paul."

"You're going, aren't you?"

"Yeah, bud … You gonna talk me out of it?"

"No, Dad," he said. "Blow his brains out."

Jack sighed. "Can I get a hug and a kiss?" he asked.

"Nope," Paul said. "I'll give you a hug and a kiss tomorrow."

Jack laughed. "Okay," he said, "I gotcha …"

"Better be here." Paul didn't look at him, just stared at the screen. But his right eye was welling up. Jack patted him on the shoulder and walked out.

The Maglite gave out just as Jack reached the entrance to the sub-basement of the Agora. It was unlocked, of course.

He opened the door with his leg and swept his gun around.

It was the same as before; dim, with the same corpses on the floor. He scanned the room and found the security station. The door was cracked open. He crept up to it, flinging it open in an attempt to surprise Bowman, but the station was empty.

He looked at the phone. It read 7:55. Jack found the stairs up, and, gun in hand, heart in throat, he quietly opened the door to enter the main floor.

The Agora had been a beautiful place once. Surrounded by glass and ornate stonework, it was a bustle for the residents of New Rhodes, once the old-timers accepted its presence. Malls were the big thing for a while, and New Rhodes wanted one right in the heart of the city.

It was an architectural marvel in those times. The exterior was reflective glass framed in chrome coated steel. The walls, where there were walls, were polished granite.

Inside, the center had a marble floor, drawing visitors to a marble stairwell that wound up from the ground floor to the top level and outer deck, interlaced with flowing fountains arranged around the stairwell and the circular landings between each floor, the back-lit green, blue and yellow water cascading into the fountains below.

There were slim chrome poles at the base interspersed throughout the ground floor; later Jack would realize that they had outlets at the bases for kiosks, but as a kid, before the kiosks, he would wrap his tiny hands around the poles and swing himself dizzy, looking up as the poles split into four branches, arching to interconnect at the glass ceiling. As a kid, Jack thought the whole building was held up by those tiny poles.

After his parents' murder, he'd still gone there. Everyone did. Of course, he never knew his father had designed it. Later he would have other memories.

He could remember seeing movies at the theater every Saturday, because it was only five dollars for the matinee; hanging around the gift shop with Mary when he was too shy to tell her he liked her; him and Mary stealing kisses on the upper deck after he finally fessed up his crush.

By the time he joined the force, the Agora was in decline. The theater left, as did the gift center, the arcade and most everything else. The whole second floor was taken by the Department of Motor Vehicles, but then even they moved out. When Jack saw the Graham Developers sign, he felt sort of hopeful.

Now it was dark as he cleared the steps from the sub-basement. The plastic over the windows obscured most of the light, but enough street light came through the opaque layer for Jack's eyes to adjust.

"*Jack, don't talk, it's me.*" Eddie's voice came through in his earpiece. "*We have the cell-jammer in place. It won't jam the frequency I'm using to talk to you.*

"*We have four of them. We also have half of the tunnels cleared, and units on standby at the eight places we identified. They're searching with dogs, and no hits yet.*"

Jack got into position by the stairwell. He could smell the rust of the metal basins lining the empty fountain beds. He saw bricks around the support columns with wires and electronics connecting them. Bowman's RDX; Jack figured there wouldn't be anything left of the Agora. Eddie's jamming teams were back on the roofs of the adjoining buildings, close enough to cover the building, but far enough away so as not to get killed if the bombs went off. People had been quietly evacuated from within the projected blast range. Jack just hoped their predictions were right.

Jack heard the muffled whimper of a woman coming from the back hall of the Agora. There was an escalator there; now defunct. That's where Bowman must've been keeping her.

The silhouette of Bowman grasping a struggling woman in a headlock emerged from the shadows.

"Come out, Jack!" Bowman said. Jack watched him get closer. Bowman's peripheral vision was shit from what Haskell had said, plus he was deaf in his left ear. Jack picked up a chunk of crumbling masonry from the stairwell, and chucked it off to his left. It cracked against the window facing Continental Avenue, and Bowman spun around, gun in hand, something else in the hand around the woman's neck.

Jack stepped up to his blind side, his own gun drawn. He closed the distance to a few yards. Bowman turned to see the steel of Jack's Glock. He backed up only inches in surprise, but not more. Jack knew he wouldn't back up any more than that.

"Glad you could make it. Welcome Back, Jack!" Bowman said. "Recognize her?" He held up her head, removed the cloth from her mouth. As Jack suspected, it was Diane.

"That's your big revenge?" Jack said. "Her? You're gonna take out the only good thing to come from you?"

"You made her a target, Jack!"

"You made *her*, Jeff."

"Help me, please!" Diane shrieked.

"I'll get you out of this, Diane," Jack said. "Just be calm."

"No one's getting out of this, Jack!" Bowman said.

"Kind of eerie, huh, Jeff? We're probably standing on the very spot Smith & Sons used to be."

"So? What of it?"

"You blame me, blame my family for what you've become… but who lit the rag by the electrical box?"

"I don't know what you're talking about!"

"Who locked the front door?"

"If you're stalling, it's your funeral…"

"Haskell spent forty years following you… You don't think he'd have figured out your childhood?"

"Haskell didn't know shit."

"No? The beatings, the molestation… We could never figure out why your cousin would follow you like he did. But he was getting it too… Only he was getting it from *you*."

Bowman thrashed Diane around.

"I have the phone that kills us all, Jack!" He said. "Do you really want to piss me off right now?"

"So me and her are your last victims?" Jack asked.

Bowman held up the phone, waved it around. "Oh, I got a whole *slew* of last victims!" Bowman said.

"Hundreds! Maybe a thousand! All because of your selfishness.

"I was just going to take out you, your family and what your fortune was built upon. I was just going to take back what should've been mine!"

"Let's be honest, Jeff," Jack said. "You've followed Diane around her whole life. You've killed everywhere you went, but you were always going where she went. Coming back here? *She* came back here.

"It's not some grand plan you've been preparing your whole life. You're just killing time, and, well, people ... and you're getting old. No retirement package for serial killers, after all ..."

"I'd rather take her out myself than let *you* do it with your meth-head snitches!"

"It was an undercover cop, Jeff," Jack said. "I actually *am* a good cop. I wouldn't willingly put a civilian in danger. *You're* the one who kidnapped her, brought her here."

Bowman hesitated. Jack realized that as much value as the task force put on his skill, without Jason Smith, without Haskell, he was just a desperate guy; a dangerous guy, but not a mastermind - just a killer.

"I still have all those bombs floating out there," Bowman said. "You'll never find them all."

"Ya know, I heard it's impossible to get bars in here," Jack said. "Is that true? Let me see ..." He grabbed his phone with his free hand and flipped it open. As he well knew, he had no bars.

"Yeah, I got nothin'," Jack said.

Bowman checked his cell phone, looking for bars.

As he eased his grip on Diane, she elbowed him in the ribs hard. He doubled over, and she ran for the doors.

"Lights!" Jack whispered.

"Blink hard, Jack," Eddie said. Jack blinked hard as the lights went into overdrive. He opened his eyes to see Bowman covering his eyes with the cell phone, shrieking, trying to aim blindly at Diane with the other.

Jack opened fire, putting one round through his shoulder and one into his gut. Bowman hit the ground, the gun flew from his grip. Jack ran over and kicked it away. He stood over Bowman's bleeding form and aimed.

"I thought you were a good cop, but you're just gonna kill me."

"I'm debating it," Jack said.

"You got about three minutes," Bowman said. "The bombs in here are on timers. It's almost go-time. So go ahead and kill me."

Jack yanked Bowman up by his wounded shoulder and dragged him to the nearest pole. He reached in his back pocket and pulled out the cuffs, swiftly cuffing Bowman to the pole.

He ran over and yanked Diane's arm, moving quickly.

"Jeff Bowman," Jack said as they ran for the basement, "you're under arrest for the murder of Walter Brinbey, Ralph Williams, Ritchie Teague, Don, Sheila and Kyla Mason and you know all the rest…"

He turned to Diane. "We gotta go through the basement," he said. "Just hold my hand."

"Aren't you gonna read me my rights!?" Bowman screamed.

"Nope!" Jack screamed back, "I have no plans to question you, asshole."

Jack and Diane ran down the stairs to the basement, then the next flight to the sub-basement. Diane threw up on herself as they passed the corpses.

Jack glimpsed bricks of RDX in the corners; he hadn't noticed it before. Even the sub-basement was wired.

Jack kept tugging at her, getting her through the tunnel entrance. He pulled the door shut, and locked the padlock, as if it would help. Seconds were ticking away, and a thousand feet separated them from the side-tunnel that Jack could only hope would shield them from the blast.

Diane was out of breath; she tried to ask questions, but only came out with the five "W"s: *who, what, when, where* and *why* before she had to stop to keep up the pace.

Jack had his phone in front of him, the light providing the barest of guidance. He only saw the shadow of the side tunnel as they were coming up on it, and he felt the thunder, heard the groan coming from the Agora. He flung Diane through the side entrance and made the jump himself, as he felt the pressure wave and the flames lick his shoes.

EPILOGUE

The backhoe dug through the rubble as Jack blew on his decaf, having had to quit caffeine as he quit smoking. He lived, and he wanted to stay alive. He couldn't believe it was three months since the Agora had been blown up and Jeffrey Bowman met his end. He regretted having to tell Diane that Bowman was her biological father, but they were trapped in the tunnel for hours. Eventually Eddie found them, and a team got the rubble out of the way.

Fortunately, the Agora took the real hit. Morrison had no explanation, except that the Agora was over-designed. It didn't stand, but it fell on its own terms. The buildings around the Agora got minor, cosmetic damage. The Agora, in its death, defeated Jeffrey Bowman.

They eventually recovered bombs from the two hospitals, and they diffused them without incident. Bowman's "six high value targets" was a stretch.

Mary and Paul had healed well, not a trace of what Bowman put them through remained. Paul did in fact kiss and hug Jack the next day, as did Mary and Dan and Tony … hugs only from the last two.

Tony still came over after his shift now. He'd passed the Detective's exam long before the Bowman case, but there hadn't been an opening. He got his gold in March, and Jack was training him. Paul still had his eyes locked onto a video game most of the time.

Mary was talking about having another baby. Jack thought of Eddie's kid, just about to turn one, but he was kind of okay with it. He asked her if they could name it Walt if it was a boy, and Kyla if it was a girl. And she was okay with that.

Special Agent Decker agreed not to mention the fact that Bowman's charred body was found handcuffed to a twisted pole, and Jack agreed not to mention that an FBI agent helped a serial killer for forty years. It seemed like a fair trade.

Jack received all kinds of awards and accolades, and if he'd wanted to, he could've gone on the national circuit. He was even offered a book deal. But he declined. The past five months had been circus enough. He took the Sergeant's exam, and got promoted. Eddie followed suit, but the department split them up. Jack stayed on homicide, and they stuck Eddie on cyber-crimes. They met at Ginny's every morning for breakfast.

Jack dipped into his money to buy some real estate. He felt it was time to renew the city, even if in some small way.

His phone went off. *Harken.*

"Taggart," Jack said as he picked up.

"A couple of kids found a body in the alley between 6th and 5th, Eulen Avenue cross-street. Tony's en route. Going?"

"On my way," Jack said.

He tucked his phone in his coat and looked again at his purchase; 169 Turner Street. He hopped in his car and drove away to the sound of splintering wood and cracking brick.

ACKNOWLEDGMENTS

My mother and father, as always. Julie Lewthwaite, Leon Bristol, Drew Rentz, Chris Pimental, Kelly Thompson, Janet Stark, Paul Capobianco, Henry Lyman, Angelia Relyea, Stephanie Cardinale, Katie Biddle, Erin Hennessey, Michael Obrien, Caleb and Tonya Trawick, and all of the people unmentioned who I will kick myself in the ass over later...

ABOUT THE AUTHOR

Liam Sweeny was born and raised near Albany, NY. Growing up around a four hundred year-old city, he has had an appreciation for history and a passion his whole life. As an author, he began with Sci-Fi/Fantasy before turning to crime fiction and mysteries. When not writing, he is an active volunteer for the American Red Cross, in Disaster Services. He has worked in disaster areas of all sizes, from minor flooding to hurricanes.

Liam has three other novels published, as well as two novellas and a collection of short stories. He has been published in many online fiction journals, including *Spinetingler Magazine, Powderburn Flash*, the *Flash Fiction Offensive, Shotgun Honey, A Twist of Noir* and others.

Please be sure to stop by and check out his website **www.liamsweeny.com**, for book reviews, interviews, information on purchasing or ordering this book and/or any of this author's other titles.

MORE FROM THIS AUTHOR

ANNO LUCE

An enigmatic homeless man has two mysterious pasts, separated by two millennia. In an engaging, action packed and vibrant apocalyptic tale, follow Barney Sheehan and Yashua as they travel the world to save it from a ruthless billionaire and a serial killer antichrist.

ANNO LUCE - ANNA'S BOOK

A prelude to Anno Luce, Anna's Book is a tale of psychic prisoners and a diabolical plan to reshape the world in a matter of minutes.

THE SERPENT AND THE SUN

In a world decades beyond an asteroid impact, the money and power in the world is collected in the hands of shareholders of whom live in sealed sanctuaries, powered by generated weather phenomena. Their every need is taken care of...

This is the story of the resistance.

These titles and news can be found at the American Apocrypha Press website:

www.americanapocrypha.com

CPSIA information can be obtained at www.ICGtesting.com
Printed in the USA
BVOW08s1929071013

333118BV00002B/15/P